Doubled

BarbarianSpy

FOR LITERARY HEAT

www.barbarianspy.com

This book is copyright © habu 2013
habu asserts his right to be known as the author of this work.
Published by BarbarianSpy in 2013
Cover design © S Bush 2013
Cover image: Manipulated - symbol **Copyright:** Ola-Ola
ISBN: E-book 978-1-922187-58-1
ISBN: Print 978-1-922187-64-2
All rights reserved

BarbarianSpy
Jindalee St
Toronto 2283, NSW, AUSTRALIA

Doubled

A DP Anthology

by

habu

Table of Contents

Introduction

For a seeker of stories featuring one of the most extreme gay male fetishes, double anal penetration, the hunt is often a frustrating one that requires extensive research for sometimes only tertiary satisfaction. That hunt is over.

This anthology provides twenty-five stories by the prolific erotica author habu that each include at least one lesser or large scene of what you are looking for when you are in just "that" mood. These works run the gambit from being centered on men seeking that particular sexual coupling, like "Doubling Bets" and "The Exchange Students," to excerpts of scenes including that sexual act from habu's many previously published works. There is no need to search extensively for just a hint of a mention here and there—this anthology centers on this specific fetish, from the romantic to the exotic to the nonconsensual and dominated. So, if you are so inclined, get comfortable, open up *Doubled* and prepare to double your pleasure. There is nowhere else you are going to find a collection as extensive and as focused on this particular theme.

This is a BarbarianSpy relaunch of the 2010 eXcessica anthology by the same name. For habu double penetration stories written since 2010, see the follow-up anthology, *Doubled Again*, also available from BarbarianSpy in conjunction with this relaunch.

Back to the Coven

(Excerpt from the novella *Vortex)*

I wasn't all that surprised to find that I was being taken back to Donatien's mansion in the suburbs. The Jamaican hustled me into the stone-vaulted chamber and over to the corner where I'd seen a young man hanging from a hook in the ceiling during my initiation ceremony. This time I was the one who was hanging from the hook with the leather straps around my wrists. The Jamaican untied my legs and stripped off my sweat pants so that once more I was naked.

I looked into the center of the room, and there was Doug, strung up where I had been fastened during my initiation to male sex. He had been beaten even more after they had taken him from our home and had been lashed as well. Blood dribbled from welts across his torso and legs, and I assumed that his back had been lashed as well. But he stood there, glowering, defiant, not yielding to the coven.

As before, the room was full of studly men of all ripped body styles, dressed in their red leotards with bare crotches and butt cracks. The room was hushed, as Donatien stepped out of the smoke-enshrouded shadows. As before, he was naked except for the leather straps peeking out of the hair on his chest. But, upon reflection, I saw that he wasn't as naked as before. His cock now was encased in a thick leather-strapped sheath, with silver studs dotted around the leather. His smile was as devilish as ever.

Donatien strode up to in front of me and back-handed me from both sides across my face. My head snapped back, and I could feel blood in my mouth.

"You've been very naughty," he said to me with a malevolent smile. "Very inventive—and I admire you for that—but very naughty. Not only haven't you accepted my invitation to join the coven yet, but you also subverted one of my best men."

He leaned into me with his face, took my head between his hands, and gave me a deep kiss on the lips, making sure that he'd sucked my cut lip before he disengaged. I jerked my head out of his grasp, and arched back from him. This brought our pelvises into contact. Donatien reached down with one hand and encased our cocks together. I felt rough leather and cold studs on the tender flesh of my dick. His other hand went to the small of my back, and a long, elegant finger pushed down between my exposed butt cheeks. His mouth went to my nipples, and it was impossible for my cock not to respond by engorging. He was rubbing our cocks together and gently stroking them as one. His finger entered my ass and rotated around, causing me to gasp.

"Ah, I remember how sweet your body is," he whispered to me lovingly. "Thomas has reported that he took you many times earlier this evening, and that he found each position and fuck invigorating and highly pleasant. I feel you and he are going to be very good friends. So, tell me, are you melting at the prospect of being regularly serviced by our Thomas? Are you ready to join the coven now?"

"No, never," I hissed at him. Donatien's teeth bit down on the aureole of one of my nipples, and I let out a little scream. He lifted his head and gave me a look of deep disappointment.

"Never say never, my friend," his whispered in a throaty voice. "At least don't say it in haste. Perhaps you should get some sense of what is at stake."

He then moved behind me, his torso closely touching my back. His cock came between my thighs, the head pushing at the root of my dick and my ball sac. The rough leather and studs gently rocked back and forth along my perineum. He took my head in both of his hands again and turned it to where I could see the trussed up Doug directly.

As I watched, the giant Jamaican, Thomas, reappeared in the room. From another corner, an equally giant, but thinner, Asian man appeared. Both were completely naked except for a sheath encasing their cocks. Light glinted off these apparatuses.

"Rhinestones," Donatien hissed in my ear. "Very pretty, but also very sharp."

The two men circled Doug, like sharks. He gave them a defiant look.

"What . . .?" I started to ask.

"Shhhh," Donatien hissed at me. "You were quick to say no. Both for his own sin and for your flippant response to my repeated invitation, you'll see just how careful you need to be and how carefully you need to consider your words when it concerns the coven."

"No, please," I cried. "It's not Doug's fault. Not any of it. I tricked him."

"Regardless, he chose to stay with you."

Doug lurched in surprise, and his face showed a sudden grimace of pain, as Thomas approached him from the rear. The Jamaican had one hand on Doug's belly, and the other was hidden behind Doug's back, but I had little doubt that Thomas was positioning his massive cock at Doug's asshole. The Asian approached Doug from the front, and, upon a command from Thomas, the chains on Doug's wrists pulled his body up and those on his ankles pulled his legs up into the air. Both the Jamaican and the Asian had their pelvises under Doug's now, their massive dicks poised to strike, and were arching their backs away from him.

Tears came to Doug's eyes, as the first inch of the two cocks entered his ass. Thus far, most of what had entered him was exposed dick helmet, and he'd been doubled before. Nevertheless, rhinestones must already be cutting at the rim of his ass. He set his jaw, though, determined not to scream.

I screamed for him, however, as Donatien stood close behind me, his arms wrapped around me with one hand playing with a nipple and the other gently stroking my dick. I could still feel the roughness of his stud-covered cock running across my perineum, but I felt shame at Doug's and my respective predicaments.

"Give our Doug a little bit of the rhinestone razzle-dazzle," Donatien commanded in a booming voice. A bit more of the two cocks disappeared up Doug's ass, and now he involuntarily screamed. Rivulets of blood ran down his inner thigh.

"No!" I cried. "What do you want from me?"

"Tell me you accept the invitation to my coven," Donatien said in a hoarse voice.

"Yes, yes," I cried.

"Yes, what?" Donatien hissed.

"Yes, please let me in the coven," I said loud enough for all to hear. "Please, I accept your invitation."

"You realize that that would mean you could no longer have sex with Doug, don't you? Doug has forfeited his rights to be in the coven."

"Yes, yes, whatever you say," I answered. "Just let him go."

"But you want to tell me why you so easily give up a relationship with Doug, don't you?"

"What?" I moaned.

"You want to tell me that I give you a much better fuck than Doug does, don't you?"

"What? Oh, yes, yes."

"Yes, yes what? I want everyone here to hear it."

"You're a much better lover than Doug," I said. "You are and will always be the master."

"And so, what do you want me to do to you now?"

Silence.

Long, slender fingers went to my balls, and I could feel the pressure. Not pain yet, but the promise of pain.

"Fuck me! Fuck me now," I cried. "I can't wait for you to get inside me."

And then he was pushing into me from behind with an already-generous cock, further thickened now by leather straps and silver studs. He pulled my pelvis back, and I arched my torso, and my eyes went to the floor, as Donatien's cock plowed up my ass. I had been stretched so much so recently by a bigger Thomas that I could accommodate the assault, but the studs did a real job on my prostate and ass walls. I grunted and moaned without reservation, which pleased Donatien greatly. I was reverifying his position in the coven with his adherents.

I looked up at the sound of repeated screams from the center of the room. More inches of the rhinestoned cocks had disappeared into Doug.

"Let them rip!" Donatien commanded.

"No-o-o," I wailed.

"Halt!" Donatien rescinded his earlier command.

"Doug's life for your total willingness," Donatien hissed into my ear. "My men must see that you truly want me."

"Yes, yes," I moaned back. "I'll do anything if you don't kill Doug."

"Untie this one," Donatien ordered, and my hands were immediately unbound. Donatien pulled out of me and came to stand in front of me.

"Kiss me. Kiss me passionately," Donatien whispered to me, and I did as he directed. He led me over to the low-slung altar, sat on the edge, and told me to make love to him. I started with another kiss on the lips and worked my way down his hairy torso with my tongue and licked the insides of his thighs and the helmet of his cock that protruded from the leather casing and sucked his balls. After a few minutes, he rose from the edge of the altar and had me sit in his place. We kissed some more and played with each other's nipples, abs, and bellies.

"Look like you are enjoying it," Donatien whispered. I spread my legs wide then, arched my back, took his sheathed cock in my hands, and guided his cock back into my asshole. There was an intake of breath around the room at the demonstration of my submissiveness to the master. He pumped me for some time, eventually bringing my torso up to his lips and tonguing my nipples again. He guided my cheek to his; we were both facing Doug, still shallowly impaled on two rhinestone poles.

"Ruin him!" Donatien commanded the posed Jamaican and Asian. "Stretch him and cut him up so he will never be of use to anyone again. But don't finish him. Let him live."

"No, you promi—!" I screamed, but Donatien brutally took my mouth in his and stepped up the rhythm of his deep stud-encrusted fuck.

"Shut up!" he hissed in my ear when he took his lips off mine. "Protocol calls for death. You are saving him. I can still change the command."

"Show them you want it," Donatien whispered in my ear. "Change of position; you fuck yourself and show them you love it."

He pulled me off the altar, sat on the edge again, and I climbed into his lap, facing him, and descended on his cock. He pushed my torso toward the floor briefly to show to all that he was in to the root, and then, on his command, I rose up and down on his joy stick and rotated around it, until I felt him tense. With a powerful lift, he pulled me off him and into the air above him, and his cock shot off in a powerful arc that hit me in the belly. Then, he rose from the altar, laid me on its top and sucked my cock until I came.

Standing above me, his voice rang out. "Enough with the renegade. Take him and clean him up as best you can and then toss him out in the street." Then they released Doug and he slipped to the floor.

Brazilian Soccer Team Balling

Pete and I had just finished playing a couple of sets of tennis at the club and had sat down at a big courtside table for a beer before showering and leaving when five Latin hunks— all bulging muscles and steamy looks—descended on the court. We'd been told that members of a visiting Brazilian soccer team had signed up for the court after us, and I reasoned that these must be that lot. I could clearly see that they were all beautiful, with tanned hunky bodies and flashing pearly white teeth, as two of the Latin studs took to the court while the other three, after asking politely for permission in charming broken English, took the empty seats at the table Pete and I were sitting at. The three at the table introduced themselves as Filipe, Thieago, and Rafael. They told us the two on the court were the team offensive stars, Gustavo and Raimundo.

I quickly assessed all five and found them all to my liking—no, to my loving. I could already feel my cock stir. Gustavo was the only blond among the lot, and I wondered if he had some German blood in him. Whatever the case, he was just as heavily muscled and hunky as the rest of the lot.

Pete got a little peeved when he said he thought it was time for the two of us to hit the showers and I said I wanted to stay around and watch the Brazilians hit the ball for a while. Neither of the two on the court were all that good at tennis, but they were mighty fine-looking athletes and moved with the grace of dancers. I knew that most of Pete's peeve was because

I was warming fast to these Brazilians and I had promised him that he could fuck me after our tennis session. He saw the opportunity fading fast, and, in this, he was quite correct. Pete was a honey, but I literally melted at the thought of these five Brazilian hunks surrounding me.

After he saw he was in a losing battle with the Brazilians, at least for today, Pete stood and leaned down before he left and gave me a possessive kiss on the lips, no doubt in a last-ditch effort to mark his territory. I could tell by the hissing of released breath all around us at the table, however, that his gesture had had the opposite effect. It had sent a strong signal to the Brazilians that I could be approached by any of them who might be interested—and they all started showing their interest in taking such an approach as soon as Pete was gone.

Thieago and Filipe, who were sitting on either side of me, moved in closer, while Rafael, who wasn't in reach of me, sent me steamy looks and tried out his limited English in chatting me up. Between trying to watch the somewhat fumbling tennis match and responding to Rafael, I didn't notice for a bit that Filipe was running his fingers lightly along the hair of my forearm and Thieago had a hand gently placed high up on my thigh.

Rafael called out something in Portuguese to Gustavo and Raimundo on the tennis court, and all five Brazilians had a good laugh. For the few moments I was there after that, I noticed that Gustavo and Raimundo were investing more attention into looking over at the table now than they were in wherever the tennis ball was going. I was beginning to feel more and more like one serving of dessert being eyed by five hungry men.

Filipe had tightened his grip on my forearm and the fingers of his other hand were buried in the hair at the back of my head. Just as he brought my face to his and engaged me in a searching kiss, I felt Thieago's palm cup my basket. He said something like "Yiy, yiy, yiy," and then a run of Portuguese, and all five of the Brazilians were laughing again. Their laughs seemed more guttural now than before, however.

I probably should have felt threatened—or objectified—but after the subterfuge and oblique approaches I was used to from American men in general, and Pete, in particular, it was refreshing to be among guys who didn't try to hide their testosterone—and their humor about that—in public. There was something fresh about guys who made a straight line for what they wanted and did so with good humor.

I disengaged from Filipe's kiss and noticed as I turned to ask Rafael what had been said that Gustavo and Raimundo were no longer hitting the ball back and forth. Now they were plastered to the wire fence just beyond our table, smiling big and licking their lips.

"Oh, Thieago was just saying that it was really hot out here and he really needed to take a shower," Rafael answered me with a big grin. "And we all agreed with him. But we are new here. We don't know where the showers are. Perhaps you could show us?"

The expression on Rafael's face left no doubt why they all wanted to find the showers, and they had turned me on to the point where I was more than ready to take on a whole Brazilian soccer team.

"And of course you don't want to shower alone," I said.

"But of course not," Rafael agreed amiably.

We left Gustavo and Raimundo blowing kisses at us and muttering what had to be very suggestive encouragements as the other three Brazilians hustled me into the men's dressing room, not seemingly at any loss on where it was located.

In the showers, I found all three equally arousing, attentive, and delightful. Filipe and Rafael were nicely hung, but Thieago had a veritable monster cock on him. All got hard quite quickly, with Thieago mainly watching, as Rafael sucked my cock under streams of water and Filipe worked my ass, first with his tongue and then with his fingers, and finally with what seemed to be his whole fist. I was well used, so only Thieago's cock gave me pause or any form of trepidation. While Filipe and Rafael were working me over, Thieago stood a bit off, but well in my vision, and entertained me with showing that he

17

could make his cock get longer and longer and thicker and thicker.

When I had shot off, Filipe pushed my torso down with a strong hand, rubbed his cock up through my crack for a minute or so, entered me forcefully from behind, and started stroking me deep, while Rafael pushed his dick into my mouth and face fucked me in rhythm with Filipe's pumping. I thought this was mighty fine, taking it from both ends from two magnificent Brazilian studs. Filipe must have been overwhelmed at this opportunity, because he came quickly and removed his dick and went back to fingering my ass, now well lubed with his cum.

When Filipe had a good bit of his hand up my ass, he called out in Portuguese, and I heard a reply that sounded like surprise and delight from the dressing room. Apparently, Gustavo and Raimundo had decided to change their game from tennis to some kind of other balling. As I worked hard to swallow the semen Rafael was now sending spouting down my throat, the five had a short discussion and I found myself lifted by Filipe and Rafael and delivered to the dressing room.

There I found Gustavo and Raimundo, buck naked, facing each other, in close, and straddling a wooden changing bench. Raimundo had his fist around two docked dicks, which were already hard. They were both long, Gustavo's a little longer than Raimundo's, but both were a little thin.

Filipe and Rafael, one on each side of me, lifted me by a thigh and arm each, with Thieago cupping my butt cheeks, and literally carried me over to the bench. These Brazilians were pretty good at their teamwork.

I started objecting loudly and giving a nervous scream or two as I realized what was going to happen to me. And then Filipe and Rafael inserted me between the facing Gustavo and Raimundo, and lowered my ass onto their now bundled, upward thrusting cocks. I nearly fainted as the two ramrods were forced up inside me—together. Laughter, moans, groans and Portuguese chatter abounded as Filipe and Rafael raised and lowered my pelvis on double throbbing cocks. Gustavo, who I was facing, had his fingers working my pecs hard, while

Raimundo, behind me, had his hands wrapped around my waist and was helping to control the rhythm of the double fucking. I had my head thrust back on Raimundo's chest and was yelling in loud tones of protested pain and, yes, I admit it, pleasure at having taken two cocks working me in unison. More of that superb Brazilian teamwork.

So as not to raise alarm throughout the club premises, Thieago came up on the bench between Gustavo and me, hunched down a bit, grabbed the back of my head in his hands, and forced my mouth onto his gigantic cock. I did what I could to envelop his cock, but he was so long and thick that I could get less than half of it in my mouth. Some semblance of calm eventually came to the scene, which now was dominated by grunting, groaning, moaning, and sighing times six. Gustavo took my cock in his hand and treated it like the joy stick on his favorite sports car and was rewarded with three spurts of cum that were almost simultaneously coordinated with Gustavo's and Raimundo's ejaculations.

So, I had said I would take on the whole Brazilian soccer team, and this was what that was like. I must admit that it was more than a bit all right with me—certainly better than whatever Pete had planned for me this afternoon.

When most of us with cocks in play—Thieago still holding his shootoff—had cum with great shouts of abandon and release, the various hands and cocks that were handling me disappeared. I collapsed, belly down, on the bench, and I heard happy chattering decreasing in volume as the Brazilian soccer team hit the showers, another stunning victory under its collective belts. Well, most of the team that is. When I was able to lift my weary head and chest from the surface of the bench, I saw that the giant Thieago was still there, giving me the eye, waving that monster cock at me.

With a big grin, he turned me on the back of the bench, spread my legs with strong arms and worked that huge cock inside my now-gaping asshole. With just one cock, he was stretching me more than Gustavo's and Raimundo's two cocks had been able to manage. I stretched my arms down and back and held tightly onto the legs of the bench as Thieago rode me hard, long, and deep—and to our great mutual satisfaction. I had no questions as to who the captain of this soccer squad was.

Coach Hazard's Training School

(From the novel *Hard Knocks U*)

The training regime for the elite wrestlers in my university's wrestling team was known as Coach Hazard's Finishing School. I had worked hard for three years to make this squad team for two reasons: this was the best of the best in wrestling in our regional division and I had the hots for Coach Hazard, who was handsome in a rugged Marine way, was solid muscle, and had the biggest cock I'd ever seen. But I didn't think Coach was ever going to notice me. Although now twenty, I still was pretty small everywhere but where it counted and was lithe and young looking, not at all like the big hulking wrestlers Coach Hazard surrounded himself with. Still, I was solidly in the light-weight division and had maintained an admirable win record my first three years at the university.

As I was doing all I could to get the coach's attention and earn a shot at a place on this squad, the buzz that got back to me was that a superior wrestling performance wasn't the only thing a guy had to put out for the coach to make the squad, but that was quite all right with me. My friend Pete was on this team, and I had repeatedly told him I'd do anything to be on the team with him. This must have gotten back to the coach, because I'd finally been summoned to an evening session in the wrestling gym, where Pete said I'd get my shot.

When I got to the wrestling gym that evening, there were Coach, Pete, and several of the other wrestlers, waiting for me, with big grins on their faces—all naked, most with respectable hard-ons. I wasn't all that surprised, because I'd also heard that Coach Hazard trained this squad in the nude so that they would have no inhibitions during the actual matches. Many on the team thought this was precisely what gave our team an edge in regional competition.

"Strip and come over here," Coach said gruffly as I entered the room, and, when I was naked, he led me to a strange alcove off the gym, which was shaped like half a hexagon and was completely lined with mirrors—on the walls, on the ceiling, and even on the floor. A wooden bar went all the way around at about waist height.

"Like it?" Coach asked. "This is where the wrestlers and bodybuilders can come to get a good look at how various muscles are developing. We have other good uses for it too. This is going to be a sensory lesson for you. I want you and Pete to stand over there in the middle of the alcove, facing each other, hands at sides. Yes, but closer. But not too close yet." I looked into Pete's eyes. He had that "eat you up" expression on his face. It wasn't at all unpleasant.

"First, I want you to take note of yourself and Pete in all of the mirrors around you. Let your eyes see everything. Okay, now, as you are doing that, I want both you and Pete to reach out and gently explore each other with your hands. All the time, I want you to drink in what is happening by scanning your images in the mirror. See what various touches do both to what is being touched and to other areas of your body. There, that's good. Ah, I see that you're enjoying this." Pete was brushing his hands around my nipples and down to my belly, and my cock was rising in reaction.

I reflexively backed away from him, hesitating slightly. Coach Hazard was quick then to ask me if I really wanted to join the elite varsity squad, if I really was willing to do anything to be on the team.

"Yes, Coach. I do. It's just a little embarrassing and strange."

"Well, son," Coach said. "We win because we are a close-knit team—as close as a marriage. Each member is totally loyal to every other member and has an intimate relationship with each and every other member. Do you understand fully what I'm saying?"

"Yes, Coach," I answered with a big gulp.

"Are you sure, I wonder," Coach said. He moved over to me and ran his hands over my torso and down to my engorging cock. "I've been watching you for two years, son. And I like what I see. I even like your wrestling style. You look so small and vulnerable when you approach the mat, which tends to throw the competition off. Because underneath that boy's body of yours, you are all steel and grace and smart moves. And I like this cock of yours, too. Looks like a seven incher. Have my eyes measured well?"

"Yes, Coach, I think so," I squeaked and then gulped. I didn't really know how long my cock, just that it was really long for the size of my body, but if Coach wanted to think it was a seven incher, that was fine with me. And I couldn't believe it. The coach had his hands on my cock. I didn't know if I'd be able to control myself.

"Do you want to be on this team enough to give yourself totally to the team?" Coach continued. "Because if you do, before you leave here tonight, you are going to be intimately linked to each and every member of this team. For the hard of understanding, that means everyone here is going to have a chance to fuck you tonight, if they can master you on the mat and if you are going to be a member of this team. If you win, you don't fuck them—not tonight. But when you're a full-fledged member of the team, you'll get that privilege too. Do you want to leave now?"

"No," I answered almost in a whisper. "I want this."

"OK, then proceed, Pete." Pete drew me back to him and resumed running his hands around my torso and thighs.

"See, not just your cock is reacting," Coach was continued in a low, husky voice. "Look at your other muscles. Your body is coming alive to Pete's touch. See your butt muscles twitching. See your knees getting soft. And as he moves his hand to your cock, see yourself leaning into him. You want him. Your body wants him. Connect the touch sensations with the visual. See what you are doing to him with your touch. See his eyes take on a dreamy look, his mouth open and his tongue moistening his lips. Yes, see how your lips come together and open to each other, how you move into each other, nipples touching nipples, pelvis against pelvis, cock against cock. See how you both start to grind a bit. He's got his hands on your butt cheeks. Feel that, let your eyes see that, feel how the visual intensifies the pleasure of his hands squeezing your butt. Yes, you can put your hands on his butt, as well.

"Uh, I saw you flinch. Did you see yourself in the mirrors flinch as Pete did whatever he did? Draw apart a bit, Pete, and let us all see what caused that flinch. As yes, do you see, Sam, Pete has your cocks encased together and he's gently stroking them together. How does being able to see that in the mirrors enhance how it feels? Doesn't it double the pleasure?

"Now Pete is moving down your body, kissing and sucking your nipples, tonguing down your six pack, playing with your navel, kissing and tonguing down across your belly. Watch him do this from every angle, Sam. Feel his worshipping of your beautiful body. Those are your balls he's licking, Sam. Did you notice how you broadened your stance to give him access? Did you see that in the mirror? Do you realize that this means you want him? You want him to suck your balls and make love to your cock.

"There, he has the head of your cock in his mouth now. Did you see as well as feel you throw your head back at that? Did you hear your moan? Did you see you burying your hands in the hair on his head, holding him to you, loving what his mouth was doing to the head of your cock? There, did you see as well as feel your cock disappear, reappear, and then disappear? Look at the floor mirror, right under you. That's your big cock being swallowed, disappearing in Pete's mouth. Doesn't it give you pleasure to see what you are doing to Pete and how much he wants you in him? Do you see as well as feel his hands on your butt, the finger he has at your asshole? Do you see as well as feel your cock grow even longer and thicker as it disappears and then reappears; disappears and reappears in his mouth? Do you see yourself shuddering and your legs turning to jelly? Being able to both see and feel will double your pleasure, but it will also shorten your jackoff time. There, just as I said. Did you see how your body jerked and spasmed right before and you shot off all over Pete's welcoming lips and face? Do you see that if he wasn't supporting you with his hands on your butt, you would have just collapsed on the floor?

"Now, Pete wants attention too. Turn around, Pete, hands on the bar, chest parallel with your butt, legs well apart. Look in the mirror, Sam. What stands out? First, that big dick swinging between his legs, right? Look in the mirrors, Sam. Look at Pete's dick from every angle. He was so busy working on you that it let it go a little soft again. Help him with that, Sam. You can take that big rod in your hand. Yes, like that. Milk him, Sam, and watch yourself milking him from every angle of the mirrors. And watch him loving it."

I could see in the mirrors that all of the wrestlers standing around on the periphery were also milking themselves, or each other, and loving it.

"Now what's the other thing you notice calling to you, Sam? Yes, right, that puckered asshole. It's calling to you. Kiss it, lick it, tongue it, giving him a good rimming. And watch yourself in the mirror—and also watch how Pete is writhing from and loving your attention. Now, see, I'm going to get behind you and reach through your legs and work on your cock as well. See that in the mirror, Sam, and feel it doubly fine because you can see what I'm doing? We want you hard again, because in just a few minutes, you're going to be ramming that ole seven incher of yours up Pete's ass, and we're all going to be loving watching that in the mirrors."

I worked on Pete and Hazard worked on me for a few minutes, until Pete started to babble, "Now, now. I can't take this teasing any more. Fuck me now. Ram it up there."

"Well, do as he says," Hazard directed as he released my now-engorged cock.

"But you said I wouldn't—" I started to say.

"Do it. You have to learn I can change my mind if I want to. I want to see you fuck Pete."

25

I stood and approached Pete's rear. I positioned my cock head against his asshole with my hand and slowly worked my way in, watching, as Coach wanted me to, from every angle in the mirror my cock disappearing into Pete's ass. I had both of my hands on his hips now, and Pete was pumping his own cock. Hazard was standing behind me, working up his own rod. I had to admit it; being able to watch it was twice the pleasant sensation.

I was so concentrated in working Pete, which it came as quite a surprise when I felt hands on my butt cheeks and a mouth on my asshole. I looked around wildly to see Coach's face plastered to my ass. He was good enough, though, to lather me up with some ointment before he mounted me from the back. The mirror revealed me as a sandwich, the meat between two ecstatic pieces of white bread. I came quickly inside Pete, but then I just held on to him for dear life, as Coach plowed me hard and fast with that big nine incher of his. I threw my legs out wide, trying to open as wide as I could for all that the coach had to give me. Leaving my pelvis plastered to Pete's buttocks, Coach Hazard wrapped his arms around my chest and pulled my torso back to his hairy breast. He buried his lips and teeth into the hollow of my neck, while he stroked me hard and deep and fast from behind.

When he'd shot off in me, Coach let Pete and me just collapse to the floor and spent twenty minutes in telling me what the stringent rules and regulations were of his elite squad.

After this, he grabbed me by the head and pulled me up to his cock and made me suck him big again and then said that the rest of the evening would consist of me finding out the wrestling skills of every member on the squad, including him. I was to wrestle each man in turn, and whoever made the pin got to fuck his opponent in the position of the pin.

I thought I was an excellent wrestler already, but the squad quickly showed I had a long way to go to truly be in their league. Coach Hazard pulled me out into the center of the mat and had me on my belly in a full Nelson in no time flat. He then proceeded to keep me in that hold as he fucked me from behind again, rotating his cock around inside me both near the surface and deep by revolving his hips. I must admit I didn't half compete with him, because having his huge cock up me was part of my dream.

After Coach had fully taken me again and shot of hot jizzm inside me, each of the other members of the squad showed me their specialties—and that their specialties trumped mine—and I had cocks of all sizes and thicknesses working my ass for the rest of the evening.

* * * *

My next team punch event defeat wasn't too taxing. I was getting steeled to these attacks on my body. The winner was one of those lean, mean Marines, without an ounce of fat on a very efficient body and a shaved haircut.

Not much to brag about in the below-the-belt category, which probably is why I'd seen him hang out with one of the bantam-weight wrestlers, a willowy, but obviously strong, young man who didn't look a day older than eighteen, although he must have been at least that age to be going to this university.

The Marine-type had me pinned in no time flat. Then he sat down in a cross-legged lotus position and had me sit down in his lap, facing him, my legs stretched out in front of me with his torso between them. He told me to arch back and support myself from behind with the heel of my hands, and then he let his hands roam across my torso and stroked both my cock and his until his was large enough to work with. He told me to dig my heels in and lift my pelvis a bit, which I did, and then he inserted his engorged, but not all that long or thick cock into my ass, leaned back on his own hands to give himself leverage, and fucked me with short jabs upward, making up for any shortfall he had in length and girth by making me feel like a hundred fingers were flicking around inside me.

What he lacked in equipment, he also made up for in stamina, as he pumped me for a good long time, and I must say I probably was enjoying this as much as he was. My enjoyment showed in the condition of my own pecker, and a short time later, the Marine's little bantam-weight type, probably in an act of jealousy, came over and settled between the Marine's torso and mine.

My cock was running up the cleavage of his pert little butt, and he put a hand back there to simulate a channel for me to fuck, so I dry-fucked him. I figured he and the Marine were a matched set because of his size and the size of the Marine's penis, so I didn't press the point about trying to enter the tyke myself. The Marine and his lover went into a session of kissy-face and mutual nipple nibble, and I figured they had forgotten me altogether when I felt the Marine withdraw from me and start skewering the Bantam-weighter.

I slid right on out from underneath them after I'd shoot off up the Bantam's back, and they gave no evidence of noticing I'd gone.

In my next team punch match, I lost quickly to the university's star wrestling champ, the very athletic Greg. After winning, Greg accentuated his athletic prowess by making me swing both my arms and legs over the parallel bars set up at the side of the gym and then getting on a bench under me and fucking me first from the front, my ass tipped up and then from the back, my ass tipped back, and then back again. The trick for him was in making the transition, which he did several times, without dislodging his prick from my ass. The trick for me was to take the pressure and weight on my arms and biceps for the thirty-minute performance. The other weightlifters seemed to be quite entertained by this.

By all rights, I should have been exhausted by now, but, the gleam of surprise and respect in Coach's eyes being worth the effort, I didn't lose the next team punch match. I didn't win, either, but, hey, a draw was better than getting fucked. The guy was a surly Hispanic with an attitude—not that there was anything wrong with being a Hispanic, and a surly dude of any ethnicity was to be avoided at all costs. He was pumped up with steroids or something that made him look like a professional wrestler, and he had a whole display of one sprawling tattoo that covered one whole half of him. It came down from his skull—he had half of his head shaved and the hair on the other half drooped down into his eyes. The tattoo descended his neck, covered the left half of his torso and his left arm, and descended down his left leg after making a detour around the root of his cock. It was a rather intriguing design, but I wasn't all that interested in getting a better look at it. He had a ring in his eyebrow, in his lip, in his right nipple, in his navel, and, most shocking of all, in the foreskin of his penis, which was a pretty respectable size and uncut. He looked like he'd just stepped out of a gang-banger comic book, and I was mighty glad I didn't lose my match to him. I could tell, though, that he was going to demand rematch after rematch until he could get me in his power.

Coach could see that this disturbed me and, after explaining that a tie meant neither one of us would get to fuck the other, he said. "Remember what he wants, Sam. And if you set your mind to not giving it to him, you will continue to develop a winning form with this team."

I had assumed that achieving a draw would bring me relief for the evening, but Coach wouldn't have it. I was still panting from the effort of holding the Hispanic tattoo display off, when Coach called my next match. This last event I had to face was really unfair, but Coach Hazard seemed to be looking forward to something special, and the Pratt twins apparently didn't go anywhere or do anything separately.

I was faced with two identical, accomplished wrestlers. Of course it was no contest, and the gym roared with delight and everyone was cheering and groping each other as the twins, as their reward for winning such a one-sided battled, shared me. First one went down on the floor with his legs stretched out in front of him, and then the other one helped push me down into the first one's lap, facing him, my ass slowly opening up to his average-sized cock, not yet ready for the onslaught. This twin wanted to kiss me and lick and nibble at my nipples. The first one's rod was only an inch in when the second one scooted under me from the back. Now the twins were essentially sitting facing each other close, the legs of the first one stretched alongside the hips of the second one and the legs of the second one extending over the thighs of the first and wrapping around his butt. I was between them, my legs now on top of those of the second twin. And the second twin's cock had joined that of the first one at my asshole, and as I was stretching and opening up, I was descending on two cocks. Luckily they both were of average size. Both twins were frenzied at sharing me and running their cocks together up my ass canal, and I was a little excited too. As Twin Number One continued to kiss and nibble at me in front, Twin Number Two wrapped his arms around me, found my cock and balls, and gave them attention. He also kissed and nibbled at my shoulder blades and neck.

Upon almost imperceptible command after they were both rooted in me, Twin Number One lowered his back onto the floor, and, with his hands squeezing my butt cheeks got his feet up onto the ground, raising me with his thighs and tipping my butt into the air. The other twin then came up on one knee and got the foot of the other leg onto the ground and, with this new leverage, power fucked me with his cock, at the same time creating friction with his twin's cock that sent the three of us into exclamations of ecstasy, panting, and grunts and that sent the audience into cheers. The three of us came in near succession, although I'm happy to say that I outdistanced either of the twins in this category.

As I untangled myself and hobbled for the showers, Coach Hazard patted me on the butt, told me this had been my best performance yet, and welcomed me to the varsity wrestling team.

Coach Hazard's finishing school certainly had some nonstandard aspects to it, but the incentive to not be topped repeatedly at every session was enough to make me one of the best wrestlers in the region before the season was finished. I made it a point, however, to never put up much of a defense against Coach and his luscious ramrod.

Doubling Bets

     I should have known that the sneaky Dutchman had all the angles figured when he suckered us into betting against a myth in the Men Only back room at Cowboy's Bar in Bangkok's Patpong district. He waited until the third revolution of the happy hour clock—when we were all soused and sluggish—and then entered with a boy-built Thai. I recognized the Thai immediately as a champion bantam-weight kick boxer from the arena over by Lumpini Park. Knowing the Thai, I figured he probably was a lot closer to thirty than he was to twenty, but he wasn't much over five feet tall and was skinny as a rail. All corded sinew, though, and I'd seen him put opponents in the hospital over in the ring. He still had all of his facial features where they belonged and was quite well turned out in looks, so it was obvious he'd been able to defend himself successfully.

     Those of us holding up the bar couldn't isolate—even when we revisited the issue several days later—who exactly brought up the question of whether the myth that two guys could fuck another one in the ass simultaneously was fact or fiction. But it must have been the Dutchman. He must have had it all planned before he brought the Thai kick boxer into Cowboy's.

     It came down to the boys at the bar against the Dutchman. We all said it was a myth, and he asked us if we wanted to take up bets on that. Suckers that we were, we did.

We even thought we'd put one over on him, when one of us had the presence of mind to stipulate that we could pick the cocks that would be buried and, that stipulated, took the time and effort to do some comparing and measuring. The Dutchman even let us check out the Thai's hole on a surface inspection, and led us into doubling the stakes when we saw there was nothing especially slack about the Thai's backdoor.

I came up second longest and thickest, so I was picked as one of the house champions. Dennis, a news agency journalist, who was a good fuck buddy of mine, got highest honors, which pleased me; we'd taken turns with each other as top and bottom, and I enjoyed either position with him.

After Dennis and I had stripped down, I was pleased to see that the Thai was showing that he thought this was all a good idea. He was all smiles and winks and lustful looks. It should have been another signal for us when he didn't seem to mind what was going on—but for all we knew, he hadn't been clued in on the plan at that point yet—or, indeed, just didn't understand English very well. We cleared a space in the center of the room and someone found a cot mattress from somewhere in the depths of Cowboy's back establishment, and we had our arena.

Dennis, the Thai, and I engaged in a good half hour of three-way feeling and kissing, and stroking, cocksucking, and greasing ourselves up lavishly with lube to get us all in the mood and to get Dennis and me lengthened and thickened to the point where we assumed our bet was well covered. In time, though, I found myself on my back on the mattress and the Thai straddling my hips with his thighs. And then he was settling on my cock. Dennis had a hand under there, fingers wrapped around my cock and rotating my dick head in what felt like a tight ass opening. But then the Thai arched his back above me, settled his pelvis, and he was coming down on my cock, swallowing it with his ass, the muscles of his canal walls undulating along the sides of my cock as he settled down into my lap. He was driving me crazy down there, and I managed to tell Dennis between gasps what was happening. The boxer had magic ass muscles and was going to make me cum and start going flaccid before Dennis got his cock into position.

The Thai was grinning above me, going for my nipples with his strong fingers, trying to bring me past the brink. I figured his strategy was to make me go flaccid before Dennis started to join me with his engorged cock. That way the Thai wouldn't have to try two cocks at their fullest.

Forewarned, however, Dennis pushed the Thai's chest down toward mine, tipping his hips up, and I felt the giant mushroom head of Dennis's cock at the base of my dick where it was encased by the Thai's asshole. Dennis was grunting mightily from the effort to enter the Thai, and the Thai, his face very close to mine, was registering pain in his eyes and panting with exertion himself.

But slowly, ever so slowly, Dennis's cock was sliding in and I felt its warm, hard, yet pliable skin pushing in on the underside of my own cock. All three of us were straining now from the effort. But somehow the Thai took us both. He reached a point where we were both beyond the entry-level of muscles in his ass, and I could see the transition in his eyes from overriding pain and some sense of uncertainty to triumph and "ride me hard" lust.

We'd lost the bet to the Dutchman, who was showing no pain or exertion at all as he walked around the circle of oglers, pulling in cash. But, without the exchange of audible signals, Dennis and I managed to agree to get a good ride for the money. We started pumping the Thai in counterpistoning that produced arousing friction I've never felt in a corn-hole encounter since. And good sport and magnificently conditioned athlete that he was, the Thai went with us and we all bucked to near-simultaneous ejaculations.

So, now, whenever I hear anyone pooh, pooh the idea that double penetration can even be done, I just smile a little smile and remember how I got more value in losing a bet in the backroom of Cowboy's bar than I'd have gotten if I'd won.

Doubling the Client's Pleasure

(Excerpt from the novella *Deal Closer*)

Having royally fucked our prospective client on his desk, the wheels of CJ's mind were spinning for the ultimate deal closer. He turned to me and said, "Now for a change of pace. Here, help me turn him." And there, on the desk, we rotated Binggum around CJ's buried cock so that he was face down. He held Binggum down on the tabletop with one hand in the center of his back and held one leg out to the side, while I held the other. And then CJ began to rotate his hips in a revolving motion that stretched Binggum's ass even further and moved CJ's dick around the happy client's ass rim.

Binggum was moaning in pleasure, and he brought his hands back to spread his butt cheeks himself.

"Join me?" CJ asked after a series of varied-rhythm pumpings.

"I really shouldn't," I answered. "This was only supposed to be the appetizer. I'm supposed to be the main course, after the papers are signed."

"But you can't resist, can you?" CJ responded with a laugh. "I don't think we need to worry about spoiling the main course or about the papers needing to be signed, do we, love?" CJ lowered himself on Binggum and nuzzled his face into his neck.

"No," Binggum gasped. "Do it. You know you promised me a double the next time we did business, and I've never been this open before."

"Well, okay," I said, "but don't look. The strip is part of the main course." I walked over to where Binggum couldn't see me, no matter how he strained to do so and stripped off my chaps, my pants, and my net sock jock. The freedom it brought felt good. I'd had a hard-on for what seemed to be forever, and the net had been chafing me.

As I pulled the jock off, I could hear CJ take in a gulp of breath. "God, you're beautiful, he said. I didn't know you could get so big."

"What?" Binggum asked. "What's happening? What did you say?"

"Just that you're a very, very lucky piece of ass," CJ said, with a chuckle.

I went over to the coffee table, took a big glob of ointment, and rubbed my dick down with it. It felt cool, and I found it had a numbing agent of the skin but something that increased the sensitivity of the glans. This was going to be fun. I walked back over to the desk, approaching from the rear so that Binggum couldn't see me, my big, thick tool freely flopping in the air.

"This might be tricky," I said as I approached. "Got any ideas?"

"Piece of cake," CJ answered. "I can crouch forever. You can have top." With that, CJ crouched down, but his chest went back rather than forward and he had his weight balanced on the toes and balls of his massive feet. His dick went down to the bottom of Binggum's asshole and retracted several inches as he crouched, and I could see what looked like a good bit of room open on top. I came up between CJ and Binggum's butt. CJ pulled out of the hole until only his glans had purchase, and I threw my leg over the space between the two men. CJ was crouched down far enough that I could mount the desk top and crouch down on Binggum's butt so that I fit between them, my weight distributed on my feet and my hands clutching at Binggum's waist, my butt cheeks cuddled into CJ's stomach, and my dick running up Binggum's butt crack. I gave him a couple of strokes there for effect.

Binggum shuddered with pleasure and reached back and had both of his hands running down my dick from glans to root before I could do anything about it. His hands began to shake when he discovered I was still wearing the cock ring he'd seen in the men's room back at the office. But then he squeezed it in a sign of approval.

This show was for him, so I left him to it for a moment. Then I said, "You might want to get back to spreading those cheeks again, at least at first, if you know what's good for you."

Binggum complied, and I lifted myself up a bit and guided the tip of my dick down to where it rested on top of where CJ's dick was positioned just inside the entrance. CJ was pulled back so that when I came back down, my dick was laying along atop his. His was a bit longer, but neither of us had any reason to be ashamed. I moved both of my hands down and encased our cocks into one unit. I held them there for a moment, my cock still rising, CJ's ramrod straight and strong. Then I undid the studded leather cock ring that had been nestled at my root, flipped it open from where it had been doubled up, wrapped it around our combined cocks, and fastened it again. A tremor went through CJ's body, his cock hardened a bit further, and he gave a little sigh and buried his head into my neck and nibbled along the artery pumping blood up into my head. My blood began to boil. I turned my head, and we kissed. Binggum was giving little pants of anticipation. I removed one of my hands and pushed his free leg up and out again.

And then, with me snuggled into his stomach, CJ slowly started to move forward and upward. A little thrill of sensation flashed through my glans as I felt it moving into Binggum's tunnel, largely under CJ's power. I wondered if there could possibly be room, but then there we were, both in up to the rim of our glans. Binggum continued panting and giving little mewing sounds. CJ's and my kiss lingered and we opened our mouths to each other. CJ pushed us in a couple of more inches and then stopped and gently rocked back and forth, waiting for Binggum to open more. A couple of more inches and then it felt like we could go in for miles, and so CJ pushed us right in up to the hilt.

My free hand no longer had any dick to hold, so I lowered it and found Binggum's dick and balls. I played with the balls briefly and then began slowly milking Binggum's cock. Binggum, very happy with himself, was giving little moans of pleasure and informing the world that he had done it; he had taken in two of the world's largest and most luscious dicks.

I could feel the change in CJ. The master of holding it was not far from giving up his load. I could feel that Binggum was loading up for another shot as well. I willed myself to time my load and Binggum's shot to match CJ's. CJ helped by losing control. He began to pump, and I had no control over that myself. His dick was supporting mine and he was providing the thrust from the rear with his massive thighs and calves. In. Out by a third and dive. Out by half and plunge. Out nearly all of the way and a deep thrust that was extended by a flood of CJ's cum. Then another spurt. And then a third, accompanied by my first. And then another by all three of us, simultaneously, that caused us to yell with pleasure in harmony—one well-oiled extraordinary fucking machine. Having cum before, Binggum's effort was short-lived, but CJ and I bathed him all the way up to his eyeballs in our semen.

When I was sure that CJ's legs must be about to give out, I stood up full, unfastened the cock ring, withdrew from Binggum, gave him a little pat on the butt cheek, and moved off to the side.

"Take your pants into the other room and clean yourself up," CJ said, as he held Binggum in place with his buried rod. "There's a bathroom in there. Don't let him see you yet."

I picked up my clothes and headed for the room, but I turned at the door in time to see CJ gently pull an exhausted Binggum up off the table and fold him to his chest with his arms under Binggum's knees. He moved them to the sofa and slowly sank down into a double fetal position without losing the dog-in-the-bun position. Binggum was being very quiet.

Masque Macabre

(Excerpt from the novella *Visits of the Schlange*)

The black ship glided up the Italian coast and hove to in Laguna Venita. The Venetians were a strange and decadent lot; only they would sustain a tradition of a two-day annual festival "celebrating" the twelfth-century visitation of the Black Plague to their canal city with a series of public and private masked balls. During the initial decades of the celebration—before the White Furies had forced him into an underground tomb—the Schlange had been in attendance each year—and the Venetians had inexplicably suffered the disappearance of one or two of their most handsome and virile young male citizens during this event. A freed Schlange reveled in the knowledge that this year would mark a glorious return to that tradition. And the Schlange was more than ready for the harvesting. He had become too anxious and self-indulgent, and his supply of rejuvenating nectar had failed him two days shy of the Italian coast.

By the time the black ship was dropping anchor in the eleventh hour of the last day of the festival, most Venetians were satiated and had taken to their beds in a drunken and lust-drained stupor. At this same time, however, Vincenti, the young prince of the Lombardy House of the Lancias was just arriving for his annual visit to the Serraglio Masque at the city state's most exclusive male brothel.

As the prince's golden gondola swept up to the canal portal of the moldering palazzo on the Calle del Forno in the city's San Polo district, the prince's two burly bodyguards, blond Nordic musclemen both of magnificent, foreboding proportions, clamored out of the vessel. One tied off the boat to one of several posts lining the brothel's dock, while the other pounded heavily on the heavy bronze door to the old palace. Both were dressed as eunuchs, although the prince could readily attest that both were in full possession of masterfully working equipment. They were only bowing to the spirit of the celebrations, as this was a masked ball, traditionally calling for a harem motif at this particular venue.

When the door had been opened and the identity of the visitor, the scion of an ancient noble family turned profitable carriage coach makers, had been established, the prince emerged from the low cabin of the sedan gondola. He stood tall, beautiful, patrician in the gondola before being handed up onto the dock by one of his bodyguards.

He held his head high, giving the impression he was looking down on everyone around him, including his two Nordic bodyguards, each of whom towered nearly a foot above him. His straight, Roman nose flared at the distasteful smells of the Venetian canal, and his eyes flashed, pale blue, incongruous against the jet-black, curly hair haloing his handsome face, itself a stark contrast to the alabaster skin tautly stretched over an admirable musculature of a well-worked body in its prime.

In contrast to the convention at this brothel, and probably to flaunt it, Vincenti was dressed—or more precisely, undressed—as a Roman gladiator in short Roman skirt; gold sandals, with golden-roped lacing winding around his well-turned calves; and with gold snake armlets encircling his bulging biceps. At first appearance he also appeared to be wearing Roman chest armor, but these looks were deceiving. His chest hair, which flared down from under his nipples and met at the sternum to descend into the low-riding waistband of his Roman skirt, had been gilded and arranged in filigreed curls, augmented by body paint that simulated filigreed torso armor. His abs were cut so perfected that, painted as they were, he initially seemed to be armored. His simulated torso armor seemed also to have tassels at the nipples, which, in reality, were gold nipple rings with ruby inserts.

In keeping with the prince's exalted position, he was met at the door by the brothel's "madam," a tall, willowy Turk of yet-to-fade effeminate beauty, at one time the favorite of the house and now its administrator. The keeper of the brothel was dressed in diaphanous, transparent harem pants, a scarlet-red sash, and gold bangle jewelry in every conceivable place, from nose ring to toe rings. He had black straight hair that cascaded down to his waist. His face was painted to a point where he could be described more as beautiful than as handsome—or could be if his face could clearly be seen behind the veil he wore.

The madam and the prince conferred in low tones momentarily, and the madam snapped his fingers and two meaty men in harem garb who were standing beside double doors to the right of the entrance opened these portals wide and the prince and the madam stood on the threshold of a suddenly noisy chamber in full sexual celebration. A ball was going on to the tune of a small instrumental ensemble in which the mood was distinctly gay and a good many of the invited guests and "entertainers" were already well into balling. The music being played was a melody from a rarely played composition, Hunziger's *Siren Song Symphony*, that hallmarked this brothel, that was only played here, and that had some haunting effect on loosening whatever inhibitions to lovemaking the house's clients might otherwise have had.

The prince looked, scowled, raised his patrician nose toward the ceiling, and sniffed.

"No. None of these," he said. "Young, slight, but well-formed, black . . . and, most important, fresh."

The madam whispered to the prince, who snapped his fingers, and one of his bodyguards stepped forward with a purse.

Weighed down with a bit more gold, the madam smiled and turned the prince to the doors on the other side of the foyer, which he opened himself.

The prince's eyes lit up with more interest, and after a few moments, he pointed, and a small, but perfectly formed, nubile and Nubian, youth of eighteen or nineteen, thick-lashed eyes downcast, and dressed in filmy, billowy harem pants that revealed perfectly rounded buttocks and a small cock and pert little balls stepped forward into the foyer. Other than the harem pants, he was wearing only a blue velvet vest that barely closed over his nipples on either side and a gold necklace and gold anklets.

"And full equipment as usual," the prince commanded.

"Ah, yes. We must discuss that; that might be possible," the madam said in saucy, teasing tones.

The prince snapped his fingers again and the purse reappeared. The madam snapped his fingers then and a servant appeared, received instructions, left briefly, and reappeared with several lengths of scarlet roping, a black-leather hand whip, and two black-leather dildos, one quite thick, long, and with a decided curve.

The Nubian's eyes went large when he saw these, but he quickly looked down again and stifled a small sob.

The prince had taken this in and was well pleased. This indicated to him that the youth either was virginal as promised or was a very good actor, either of which would suit the prince's needs very well.

The prince having indicated his satisfaction, the madam turned and, with mincing and jangling steps, led the procession of prince, Nordic bodyguard one, Nubian youth, and Nordic bodyguard two up the grand staircase to a bedchamber two floors higher.

The bedchamber was opulently appointed in red and black silk and damask, with maroon-based oriental carpeting spread across the floor. A sturdy four-poster bed occupied the center of the room, and French windows were open to the canal side of the palazzo, beyond which there was just the hint of a lacy iron balcony.

The five men entered the room, and the prince stood languidly leaning against the frame of the window, watching the traffic on the canal below, an offshoot of the Grand Canal, while his Nordic bodyguards laid the Nubian on his back in the center of the bed and tied off his wrists and ankles at the four corner posts. The madam stood near the door, the Nubian's harem pants, vest, and sandals in his hands, watching one of his prime investments being prepared for downgrading in his stables. He sighed satisfactorily, though. The price had been very good, more than he had expected. He asked in soft tones if everything was satisfactory, if the prince needed anything else.

"What? Oh, no. That will be all. You may go. My men will stay at the door." The prince had almost missed hearing the madam. His attention had been arrested by a gondola, with six men wrapped tightly in black capes with hoods and a golden-haired gondolier, which had just turned into the canal from the Grand Canal. The gondolier looked inviting. The prince had considered ending the night with the young, comely red-headed gondolier who had poled them here—and had paid him to remain at the dock for the return journey. But the prince rather thought he preferred the blond in the gondola with the six hooded men.

But who knew where that gondola was going, he thought, with a little sigh of regret. He turned and waved his bodyguards in the hall. Soon they were standing straight on either side of the closed door into the chamber, trying to look like they weren't hearing and enjoying the sounds of whimpers and moans and groans and short cries from beyond the closed door.

In the canal below, the Schlange and his five assistants were arriving at the brothel's canal entrance. The Schlange looked up the facade of the old palazzo as they glided toward it, and his gaze was arrested by the figure of the prince leaning gracefully in the French window on the third floor. The Schlange instantly knew what he wanted this evening. And he knew that room. He had used it several times himself in earlier centuries.

The madam heard the knocking at the door and slid open the eyehole to see who was there. His eyes grew large and he staggered back toward the back of the foyer. It had been centuries since that monster had chosen this brothel during the annual celebration of the Masque Macabre, but the madam, when told who the visitor was, had remembered legends of earlier visits all too well—and lurid descriptions of the monster, all of which seemed to have been true. He turned to run but stumbled on the hem of his harem pants and fell beside the staircase.

Knocking was a mere formality. The Schlange had the key to the door.

The madam heard the key slide home in the door and it swung open. The six figures were swarming into the foyer and tossing aside their hooded clothes. Those five loathsome satyrs. Big, hairy, heavily muscled, swarthy, nasty looking, with cloven feet, pelted legs, horns, and snapping tails. But, worse than that, there was the Schlange. Almost human form, but not quite. A man's physique, of magnificent god-like proportions. But its skin was greenish and scaly. Its face was flat and handsome and ugly all at the same time—nostrils, but practically no nose. Uncloaked, the monster was naked, and between its heavily muscled legs was the thick rope of an appendage, an inhumanly long and thick cock, at the head of which a bulbous slitted mushroom cap. Out of the slit flicked a red, forked tongue.

As the madam struggled back up, gripping the posts in the staircase for leverage, he saw the monster's almost-lipless mouth open and a red, forked tongue darted out—toward him.

The madam started running to the back of the foyer again but slipped and disappeared around the side of a high, wooden cabinet against the wall opposite the side of the staircase.

The Schlange slowly moved through the foyer toward the back, as the five satyrs burst into the room where the Masque Macabre was under full steamy bacchanalia to the lust-laden strains of the *Siren Song Symphony*. The initial sounds from there were ones of conviviality and welcome of the new surprise, but these soon turned to gasps and groans and cries of mayhem and debauchery as the satyrs took their fill of forceful lust.

Meanwhile, the Schlange overshot the nook that the madam had snuggled into in its journey beyond the staircase, and the madam briefly had a notion that he might be able to break free and get out the front door before he was caught. But the Schlange had known where he was hiding all along. The monster turned and sent its unwinding cock appendage slithering into the nook.

The frightened madam was burbling and making little yipping sounds as the Nubian's harem pants, sandals, and vest got ripped from his grasp and tossed out into the foyer, followed by the scarlet sash. The sound of gasping and ripping fabric, and the madam was being dragged out of the nook, a long snake-like cock appendage wrapped around his waist, the end tendril already sinking itself in the madam's well-used hole. Long strands of black hair and the gleam of gold rings on dragging fingers were the last to be seen of the brothel's manager as he was being dragged into the shadows at the other end of the foyer.

The noise from the ballroom was subsiding. Cries of shock and fear turned into burbling and then soft moans. Soon all was quiet in the ballroom, as even the members of the musical ensemble grew silent, instrument by instrument, except for exhausted murmurs and spent sobbing.

The madam had been vocal for a while too, as the Schlange's cock appendage dug deep inside his slack insides, stretching and filling him as he never had experienced before, and he weakly objected when the mouth tongue latched onto his cock cap and started sending its flicking tongue down his urethra channel into his ball sac, but he was no match for the Schlange and was soon being sucked dry of his male juices and having the Schlange's numbing venom being pumped deep inside his intestines. The milking did not take long and there would be no repeat. The madam was not made of the stuff the Schlange had been seeking out for the ability to pleasure for a prolonged period.

When the Schlange mounted the staircase to the third floor, the five satyrs were already there. Four were occupied with the Nordic bodyguards, who had already been subdued and had fainted under the attentions of the satyrs. Two each were still double-fucking the bodyguards with their massive, curved cocks, one from the front and one from the rear, with the beefy prey collapsed between them, arms drooping at their sides and heads lolling off to one side.

At a signal from the Schlange, it and the fifth satyr burst into the bedchamber, where the prince had finished with his toys and had just mounted a semiconscious Nubian youth, who was gurgling and mumbling softly to himself at the cruel taking of a thick real man's cock in a virginal hole.

Despite the shock of the vision of both the Schlange and the satyr, not to mention the inability of his Nordic bodyguards either to protect him or voice any sort of warning of attack, the prince's quick reflexes were impressive. He slurped out of the Nubian and bounded for the open French window.

The Schlange was quicker. It turned and its cock appendage shot out across the room and wound its cock tentacle around the prince's waist. Vincenti had reached the window, though, and he was gripping the frame, keeping himself from being drawn to the monster.

The satyr had fallen on the bound and helpless Nubian, who was very much conscious again and crying out at and writhing as best he could against the even thicker, curved cock the satyr was thrusting inside his barely used channel. The satyr quickly jerked away the ropes binding the Nubian. He wanted to play; he wanted the Nubian to struggle against him. They tumbled off the far side of the bed, and the Nubian clawed himself up onto the bed on his belly, his little fists gripping the silk of the bed cover in big bunches. The face of a sneering satyr, long, pointed tongue gliding up the back of the Nubian appeared above him. Long strong arms flowed along the Nubian's arms and satyr fists closed over Nubian wrists. The Nubian's mouth opened in a silent, breathless scream, as the satyr's cock head found purchase at his channel opening again and thrust home. The Nubian shuddered and his little chest bounced up and down on the coverlet, as the satyr began the pumping rhythm of his stretching fuck.

The Schlange just walked toward the window, sending coils of its cock appendage around the waist of Vincenti. When Vincenti felt the chest of the monster pushing at his shoulder blades, he arched his back and lifted his feet, thrust them back, and dug them into the Schlange's thighs in one last effort to propel himself out of the window and into the canal three stories below. It was his one chance at escape.

But the Schlange's cock head had slithered up under the Roman skirt and found the prince's hole, and Vincenti's mind was now occupied with screaming in reaction to that long, thick cock working up inside him.

He was still struggling when the Schlange rested its chinless face against the prince's shoulder and sent its mouth tongue slithering down across Vincenti's gilt-painted torso. It ripped away the Roman skirt on its way into young patrician's pubic thatch.

Vincenti's last writhing struggles were in response to the flickering mouth tongue piercing into his urethra and digging down to his ball sac and summoning up all of the semen he had been building to pump into the Nubian virgin.

Soon the proud prince lost his grip on the window frame and let his arms daggle at his sides. His legs collapsed and he was suspending in air in the frame of the window and held against the massive chest of the Schlange. He whimpered and moaned quietly as the Schlange hummed its pleasure at milking—repeatedly—prime, virile flesh at one end and ejaculating—again, repeatedly—venom progressively deeper at the other end.

The Schlange had chosen well. The madam had been merely a convenient preliminary of tired old inferior fluid. It could tell the quality of its lovers in the effect of their rejuvenation power on it. This one was prime. It would take time with this one. Keeping him sedated with its venom but on the edge of his recovery powers. prime specimen could be brought into production and milked every couple of hours for quite a long time before drained dry beyond usefulness if farmed properly. Prime stock this one.

The Schlange felt decadently patrician already. It hadn't had such a tasty morsel since its last visit to Venice in the fifteenth century.

The gondola had extra passengers on its trip back to the black ship. The Schlange was in the low cabin in the middle of a third extraction from a panting and murmuring, but totally subdued prince of the House of Lancia while it watched a satyr toying with a last-gasping Nubian in the middle of the gondola, keeping the young man at the edge, continuing to plow him and working at timed, mutual ejaculations, but not letting him slip away.

At the front of the gondola, a satyr was on his back, the prince's gondolier stretched along his body, the satyr's thick cock curved up inside the red-haired gondolier's ass from behind, while another satyr was crouched over the gondolier's hips and stroking the Italian boatman's cock and the satyr was pushing his cock inside with that of the other satyr's. They had just started on this one, and he was still being very vocal and lively and letting them know they were having just the effect they wanted on him.

The pole man of the gondola that had brought the Schlange and the satyrs from the black ship, the blond the prince had fancied, was bent over the top of the cabin, his chest bouncing up and down on the cabin roof, as the fourth satyr fucked him from the rear. He seemed to be rather enjoying the servicing. The fifth satyr was poling the gondola out toward the black ship. Half way out, he would exchange positions with the satyr topping the blond.

The night was late. The celebration of the Masque Macabre was winding down. And the citizens of Venice had long ago taken to their beds to recover and heard and saw nothing of what happened at the Serraglio that night.

While the Schlange was happily humming and harvesting from Vincenti, running its hands and forked tongue all over the young prince's body, coaxing him to quicken production, its eyes fell on the Nubian. Perhaps a snack for later if there was anything left. And perhaps it was time to visit Alexandria. It had been centuries. It was sure there were

Egyptians there in their prime. The Schlange had heard of one who frequented that port—one who both was a prime nectar candidate and who might help the black ship escape the confining bounds of this sea and the clutches of the ever seeking White Furies.

Men in Tuxedos

"Man, don't you ever give up?" I asked in exasperation, removing Zane's hand from my basket and rising from the sofa and moving over to a stool by the bar. I was going to put out for Zane, but I didn't think he'd been told yet that he was going to be mentoring me for Rex Reeson's stable of male escorts, and I wanted him to work for it a bit more. Besides, there were a couple of things I wanted to ask him about while I had some hope of getting an honest answer.

"No, Brian, I never give up. Not when there's something I want like I want you."

"I should have known when you brought out the good scotch that you just wanted to get me drunk and have your way with me. True?" I'd already let Zane kiss me when I'd come back from my signup session pitch from Reeson, the guy who wanted to be my new employer in the high-class special-services male escort business, and his French sidekicks, so we both knew I was just playing with him now.

"Yes, that was the general idea," Zane said dryly, a smile of perseverance on his lips. "What's the problem? You don't find me attractive?"

"Yeah, you're plenty attractive all right, Zane," I said. Still, I tried to put a glint of defiance in my eyes—trying to work in some acting on him. "And well you know it too. I just don't open my legs for anyone who says he wants me."

"You sure open them for the customers down at Thunder Road," Zane retorted, the smile just as sparkly as before.

"That's different," I said. "And I don't do much of that there anyway."

"Right. They have money and position and are proper sugar daddies. You're so obviously on the make for connections to give you a start in movies. You know what that kind of arrangement is called, don't you?"

"Yeah, that's called good old American trade," I shot back. "Quality goods for quality services. And I see no reason for you or anyone else to look down your nose at it."

"Oh, I'm not," Zane answered calmly. "Believe me, I'm there myself."

"Excuse me?" I said. I gave him the surprised and intrigued act. "You of the Ivy League education and Porsche Boxster and expensive clothes?"

"Right," Zane responded, giving a glint of an opening here.

"So, what do you know of what a guy's got to do to make it in this town?" I challenged. I was going to make him tell me he was a male prostitute working for Reeson and opening his legs on demand, just like he said I was doing at Thunder Road.

"I didn't come from money, Brian," Zane shot back. "I know it looks like I did from car and clothes and from my education, but I earned my education on my back—just like you are doing at Thunder Road."

"What do you mean?" I wanted him to say it. To tell me something that would open him up to me emotionally before I opened my legs to him and let him fuck me.

"I put myself through school by working for a hard-core call boy service—one that put me out on the street advertising for tricks," Zane said. "I came to this lifestyle through hard work and sucking cock and lying on my back."

There, it had been said. Now to push him just a bit farther. I returned to the sofa and started pelting Zane with some of the questions I wanted answered before I signed up for Reeson's stable. I took a couple of swigs of scotch from the generous portion Zane had poured out for me and settled back in the sofa cushions. I purposely didn't pull away when Zane put a hand on my thigh and started working it up my leg.

"And what was your strangest assignment?" I asked Zane at the end of a flurry of other questions that Zane had dutifully responded to. "I mean, can you remember any? There must have been some." One of the real burning questions I had with this was just how kinky this arrangement might get— and might it be more than I thought I could handle.

Zane chewed on that one briefly—but only briefly. He had his hand on my bare belly now, under the hem of my shirt. His other arm was snaked around my shoulder. I acted like I didn't even know his hands were there, letting him play his little seduction game. I knew this would end with him fucking me just as much as he hoped that was where this was going.

"Hmmm, let's see. That might have been the night of the men in the tuxedos."

"The men in the tuxedos?" I said, showing him I was interested and also that talking to me like this would get him what he wanted. To drive that home, I put my hand on top of his and moved it below my waistband, on the warm skin of my lower belly, letting his fingers glide into my pubes. Then he started into his story.

＊ ＊ ＊ ＊

"Yes. As the night was starting out, I knew I was in for a workout, because the caller had specified he wanted someone experienced with men and had authorized for the full unlimited service for a four-hour period. That usually meant multiple ass work, although it's true that some out-of-town hicks just didn't realize what the various options were and had more money than brains when they set up a session. I knew there was big money involved, though, because the gig was in New York. I was flown across the country for it.

"The address I was given was for a large, but nondescript brownstone, up on 57th Street, near Central Park.

A polished brass plate by the doorbell simply stated that I was at some club, Hedgewood or Hedgeneck, or something like that. I later assumed that it was one of those old-world highly exclusive men's clubs that had existed for a couple of centuries without catching the public eye.

"I was met at the door by the epitome of a butler type who told me to follow him toward the back of the house. Outside a double oaken door set in a wide hallway of polished oaken paneling carpeted with an Oriental rug in vibrant colors, he told me to strip entirely and to leave my clothes folded on a Chippendale arm chair that was located next to the door. I did so, and then he knocked twice on the door, opened it, and ushered me into the room.

"I was in some sort of club room. Leather-upholstered armchairs sitting on a huge Oriental carpet in the middle of a wood-paneled room with glass-fronted shelves of books on three walls and on the third wall a fireplace flanked by French doors that apparently led to garden at the rear of the building. At the opposite end of the room from the fireplace was a large mahogany desk with a leather top. The armchairs were arranged in a circle in the center of the room, facing each other, with a clear space out in the center. There were six chairs, each with a little cigarette table beside it and a brass floor lamp behind it. All of the lamp shades were turned up so that they functioned as spotlights trained on the circle in front the chairs. Each of the chairs was occupied by a man in a tuxedo. All of the men were fairly young—none older than his mid forties—and all had the air of pampering to a high gloss and well-toned physiques and of highly successful positions. They had brandy snifters in their manicured and bejeweled hands, and each was smoking a cigar. The air was cloudy with the smell of premium Cuban cigar smoke.

"'Come to the center of the room, please, son,' a strong, willful voice commanded me from the depths of the cigar smoke cloud. I did as I was bade.

"'Turn, please. Turn completely around. Slowly please. Again please. Stand straight and tall, please. You have nothing to be ashamed of.' I slowly turned a few times, obviously letting them all see what they were paying for, for whatever purpose—which I had yet to discern.

"'Now masturbate for us, please. To completion. Do not worry about where it goes.' The same commanding voice. From the intensity of the light directed from the lamps and the thickness of the cigar smoke, I could not be sure which tuxedo had spoken.

"'Excuse me?' I asked. In shock more at the incongruity of the setting than at the request itself. I had known it would be a performance evening for me. They had paid dearly for it. This assignment would carry me nearly a month at school all by itself.

"'Masturbate, please. And do it slowly and don't hold back on your expression and response, please. Just be genuine with it; we aren't interested in cheap theatrics.'

"So, I did as they asked. I had been trained what to do with this sort of request, but I had always assumed it would be something involved in a one-on-one situation.

"I was progressing pretty well, when I sensed movement in the room behind me, and I heard the rustle of rich material close behind me and hot breath on my neck. I looked down, and saw an arm come around my waist from behind. It was clothed in luxurious black material. White starched cuffs showed at the wrist, with gold nugget cuff links. An elegant, manicured hand with a signet ring wrapped itself around my engorged cock after brushing my hand away.

"Another black-clad figure was now at the other side of me. I turned enough to see the brilliant white shirt front and the satiny lapel on the tuxedo. The hand of this figure also went to my cock, and the two tuxedos worked my cock in unison and rubbed their expensive evening suits against my bare arms.

"Another figure, a commanding figure, probably the source of the voice that had given me direction, appeared through the cloud of smoke before me. He was sucking on a long cigar and giving me a very intense look. He was perhaps the oldest of the men present. Very handsome, with strong facile features and intense black eyes. The light was reflecting off the diamond studs cascading down the front of his perfectly cut tuxedo. I remember thinking that one of those studs alone would be enough to get me out of the business and cover the rest of my college. He gave me a grin, almost a leer, and then he turned the cigar in his mouth, took it out, and pressed it between my lips. It was moist from his saliva. He rotated it in my mouth, adding my saliva to his, and then he grinned again and moved out of my line of vision.

"He obviously had moved to behind me, because I felt hands pulling my butt cheeks apart—in fact I found hands everywhere on my thighs and belly and nipples, in addition to the two that were stroking my cock—and I bowed my legs outward as I felt the moist end of the cigar working its way into my ass.

"The heel of a hand came up under my chin, the fingers covering my lower jaw and the thumb pushing its way into my mouth, obviously wanting me to give suck, which I did. Meanwhile, the two hands were still stroking my cock, the fingers of both of my hands were being taken into mouths and sucked, and that cigar was being rotated in my ass, being screwed in deeper and deeper and rotated around.

"I was panting heavily at the attention, the feeling of being shrouded in elegant black satin and silks and white starched shirts, flashing studs, and heavy cigar smoke. Aroused by the contrast of my being completely naked and vulnerable and being stroked and invaded everywhere by fully and elegantly clothed men.

"The cigar twisted out of my ass, and the commanding figure came back around to close in front of me. He gave me that leering, possessive smile, and then he put the cigar back in his mouth and twisted it. His eyes lit up with a mischievous gleam, and I felt a strong hand cupping my balls, coming in under the stroking hands of other tuxedos, and he squeezed hard. I threw my head up in a primeval scream of pain and surprise and release to the ceiling, jerking my mouth away from the thumb I was sucking, and shot a strong fountain of semen I know not where.

"The teeming mass of black silk and satin took my ejaculation as some sort of sign, because I was lifted and carried by a bevy of tuxedos over to the leather-topped mahogany desk. At first I was bent over that on my belly. Once again hands pulled my cheeks wide. Then fingers, slippery with lubrication, of different sizes, invaded me, pulling my well-used hole wide.

"The commanding, disembodied voice spoke, reminding me that whatever they were to do with me was agreed to and paid for. I grunted my agreement, steeling myself, because that told me the taking would intensify from here. But, still, it was comforting that they would take a check on my willingness at this point.

"The cigar again now, soggy with lubricant, entering between the fingers and twirling and screwing into me. I was panting and moaning now. The cigar twirled out, but the three fingers of different sizes remained, pulling me, stretching my hole wide. I arched my back, as a thicker, throbbing object, a cock, slid in between the fingers.

"This was it, I thought. The start of the serious business.

"The fingers pulled out as the cock plowed in, deeper, deeper, deeper. And then it started a furious rhythmic slapping back and forth into me as I counterthrusted my hips back to it until I heard a deep-throated cry and felt my insides being creamed. A second cock replaced the first and I was fucked vigorously and deeply from the rear by one cock while another tuxedoed figure on the other side of the desk pushed another cock into my mouth. At no time did I see man flesh during the whole ritual. Cocks were buried in my ass and mouth, but the tuxedos remained fully in place otherwise.

"All reserve aside now. This was the familiar frenzy of a gangbang.

"I was fully naked, being fully possessed by six elegant tuxedos, heavy, hard, virile cocks invading me from within the folds of the rich material, but never seen.

"When the first set of tuxedos had spent their seed in either end of me, I was turned on my back and fucked repeatedly in succession, each man obviously taking more than one turn at me, with two tuxedos holding my arms out and two more spread-eagling my legs.

"As something of a finale, I was lifted off the desk and a tuxedo came in under me and settled me on his black silk lap, his cock buried in my ass, and another tuxedo came in at me from the front and penetrated me with his member as well. I was being double fucked. This always came as a surprise and shock to me even though I was on the short list of escorts who would take two cocks at once. Of course it brought a premium price. The most athletic of the tuxedos was hunched on top of the desk, black silk pant legs against my naked chest and me deep-throating his cock, chaffing my chin and cheeks on the zipper of the only slightly parted fly. Other than him, though, I had the sensation that all of the other tuxedos had drawn back to observe, in awe and arousal, the two cocks working inside me.

"I found myself draped, naked and covered with repeated semen of six men over the top of the desk, moaning my elegant defilement, trying to concentrate on the fee I had earned for the evening. When I was able, I pulled myself up to a sitting position. The six chairs once more were occupied by six sedately and richly clad gentlemen sipping their brandy and puffing their cigars and looking very satiated and pleased with themselves.

"The commanding voice then thanked me for my time and told me I was to leave. I dragged myself out into the hall, dressed with my aching muscles feeling every move, and received a generous tip from the butler before I was shown to the door."

* * * *

When Zane had finished this story, the room was silent for the longest moment except for the heavy panting coming from me, and not just from the sensuous tale he had spun, but because, while telling the story, he had pulled me over close to him and leaned both of us down on the sofa, and his hand was completely below my waistband and was encircling my cock. I found myself fully aroused by his story, not put off at all by the kinkiness of it—drawn to it, somewhat frustrated that it had been his experience, not mine.

"Yes, I think that might have been my strangest assignment," Zane said finally, marking closure to his tale.

"Wow." That seemed to be all I could say at the moment. I was breathing too heavily to contribute much to sophisticated conversation.

Zane sensed he had me now, and that I was completely ready for him. He wasn't wrong. I unzipped my fly myself, and Zane correctly took that as a sign that he could bring my cock out into the open, which he did, and began to stroke it.

"So, what do you think?" He asked.

A few more moments of silence except for my soft moaning and sighing and the rustle of the cheap cotton material of my pants in its rhythmic countermovement to Zane's slow stroking motion.

"You wouldn't . . . You wouldn't happen to own a tuxedo?" I asked in a hoarse, struggled whisper.

"Why, yes. Yes I do. I think I can find a box of fine Cuban cigars too," Zane said just before I lifted my lips to his and sank into a deep, passionate, moaning kiss.

Zane didn't know it yet, but his indoctrination of me for Reeson's escort service had already been quite successfully launched. Within a few short weeks under his guidance, I was to become a full-fledged member of the Reeson team and would start collecting melting stories of assignments all my own.

Neighbor's Hot Tub

A foreshadowing that summer again would follow spring descended on my neighborhood in the form of a minor heat wave one early May evening. We'd had a particularly cold winter and early spring, and thus when the sun had brought us an unusually early warm day, we had opened the windows on the bedroom level, giving the house its first breath of fresh air in over three months. My home office was on the bedroom level in what had once been the house's second-largest bedroom, down a long hallway, over the garage and at the front side of the house. It had been light outside when I was called to dinner, but it was dark before I returned to my office to take up the editing of a book I was working on for a major publisher.

I entered my office and raised my hand to turn on the lights. But my movement was arrested by the sound of murmuring and what I distinctly recognized as moaning. I had two windows in my office, now both open. One was on the front of the house over the driveway that led into the double garage beneath me. The other window was at the side of the house, only about ten feet from the fence line to my neighbor's back yard.

It took me several seconds to realize that the moaning sounds were coming from the window on the side. I moved to the window in the darkness and looked out and down into my neighbor's yard.

I hadn't known he had put in a hot tub, but there it was, at the back corner of his house. It was fenced off, but my window looked almost straight down into it. There was decking and soft patio lights around the hot tub and even softer lights inside the tub, diffused by the gently roiling, gurgling water, which obviously was being moved by a pump. It was really a surprise to see. It hadn't been there before, back in the fall, the last time I actually had come to this window and looked out. He must have had it installed sometime during the winter.

A trim, well-muscled man of late middle age, undoubtedly my neighbor, was sitting on the side of the pool, facing me. He seemed to be the one doing the moaning. Another, younger and slighter man was crouched down in the water between his knees, facing him. I could not tell positively what was happening, but the expression I could see on my neighbor's face illuminated by the pool lighting and moaning he was doing left little doubt that he was receiving a blow job.

This sudden, totally unexpected view conjured from below my home office window on a warm night following a confining winter and early spring shocked me into inaction. I just stood at the window, staring at the scene audaciously being played out below my window. Even when my neighbor stood and changed positions with the young man who had been giving him suck and spread the man's legs around his thighs and began to fuck him, I remained there, a surprised voyeur. The moaning changed to a higher pitch. The young man was the one doing the moaning now down in the hot tub. I quickly realized the moaning had taken on a stereo tone, though— tenor and baritone after the initial bass. Now I was moaning as well.

I stood there, transfixed, all the way to the climax, which was punctuated by the young man writhing and groaning hard and my neighbor's bulbous buttocks undulating at an ever-quicker pace until he cried out and lurched with a final definitive, long-held thrust. And I remained there, watching, long after they both had sunk down into a close, sitting position inside the tub, their arms entwined and their mouths joined in a prolonged kiss.

I tried to force the images out of my mind, but when I went to bed that night, they started to flood into my consciousness, preventing me from sleeping, causing me to twist and turn in the bed. I found I could not keep my hand off of my cock, which was at full arousal. I could not masturbate myself into sleep, however. My wife would have felt the movement of the bed. I briefly considered rising and going out to the hall bath and shutting the door behind me and stroking myself to relief.

But my wife turned in the bed and reached for me and found my aroused cock. She murmured her surprise and delight. I rolled over on top of her, spread her thighs and settled my pelvis down between them, and we fucked languidly in the breeze coming in from the open windows. The rhythm of our familiar mating brought my cock relief. But her moans conjured up what I had seen from my home office window, and all of the time I was fucking her, images of what I had seen in my neighbor's hot tub raced through my mind.

* * * *

Three days later, with us still enjoying the warm spell, my wife was off to see her mother for a week. My neighbor, Marty, had come down to the bottom of his driveway when I was waving my wife off. I took the occasion to casually note that he seemed to have put in a new hot tub, and he congenially invited me over to try it out, making the remark that, since my wife was off for the week, we could have a boys' night of it. He didn't notice that my face flushed at that remark—or, if he did, he certainly didn't say anything.

Marty was divorced and probably was in his early fifties, judging from his graying hair, but he had kept himself quite fit. He was a businessman, and I could tell he was doing well at that because of all of the money he must be spending on fixing his house up. His fitness probably was a result of the many hours he spent at the gym. I knew that he had a good gym in his basement, but he still frequently went to a big fitness center in town. Marty said he went there for the people he met; he had already had a string of subtenants pass through in the two years he'd been here who he said he'd met at the gym. He said he could use the company and that it was always good to have someone at home to take care of his dog and the house when he traveled.

I hadn't given any of this much thought until the recent night when I discovered he had a hot tub—and saw what he did with it. I was now able to deduce for myself, of course, what the real reason for the string of young, buffed male tenants was. For this reason, I had contemplated and planned what I was going to say if he ever asked me to visit his hot tub.

The last couple days I had noticed him eyeing me when I was doing yard work with my shirt stripped off. I didn't usually garden without a shirt, and I told myself I was doing so because we had waited so long for the warm weather. But I really knew I'd done it because I'd already made a decision and hoped that my neighbor would notice me. I was the curious type and I was always ready to experiment. My wife and I were quite inventive in our lovemaking, and I hadn't exactly been celibate or strictly conventional in my sexual activity before I settled down with my wife. I'd never done it with a man before, though. Well, not full penetration. There had been some other experimentation.

I racked my brain whether this was new attention from Marty or whether he had shown interest in me before and I just had not caught the signals. The little performance I'd seen the other night had knocked me off my blocks. I was in heat—and confusion—in ways I'd never felt before.

When Marty did ask me over, I was prepared, although I wondered if the minimalist Speedo I had bought and not yet worn would give too obvious of a signal to him. I had always been curious about that lifestyle, and I couldn't get the images of the other night out of my mind.

It was dusk when I walked around my fence and into his yard, with both a T and some shorts on over my Speedo, so as not to arouse the other neighbors, and a big towel draped over my shoulder. I had called my wife at her mother's shortly before making the trip next door to assure myself she had arrived at a destination a good five-hour drive away—and, more important, that she was safely located that far away.

Marty was already in the tub, and his CD player was set on some music that had a real good steady beat to it and at a volume that would not impede discussion in the tub but would keep it to the near vicinity of the tub. The tub itself was quite large, more than eight feet in diameter—and a good thing too, because Marty wasn't the only one in the tub. Across from him was his most recent tenant, Seth, I think his name was, a big, black, handsome dude with Mulatto features. He had a massive chest that I could see above the waterline, and a blue, intricate tattoo following the curve of his left chest muscle and wrapping up around his left biceps and down his arm to just above his elbow. I must admit that his presence was a little intimidating, but I'd waited for several agonizing days in anticipation of the possibility of a new experience, so I gave him a friendly wave back in answer to the welcoming gestures from both of them.

"Come on in, neighbor," Marty invited. "The water's great and is bubbling up just fine. You've met Seth, haven't you, Glen?"

"Hi, Seth," I said. "We haven't actually met yet," I said, but I've seen you around."

"And I've seen you gardening too," Seth said with a big, friendly grin. "Strip down and come on in."

I pulled my T over my head, glad just now that I'd put so much work into my own physique, pulled my shorts down, taking my loafers with them, and stepped down into the tub. The water was warm and swirled around my legs with a pretty forceful pressure.

"Here, over by me," Marty said. "Here's a beer."

I pushed my way over near Marty and took the beer gratefully. I downed a swig to calm myself, hoping that neither Marty nor Seth could see my hand shaking, and settled down on the bench ringing the inside of the tub.

Marty spread his arms around the rim of the tub, and his left arm was draped loosely behind me. We chit chatted for a short while before I took the initiative that I had planned to take. We were talking about the placement of Marty's hot tub, and I said, "You know, Marty, that I can see your whole tub from my study window. I don't think it can be seen from anywhere else, but I can see it."

"Yes, I know," Marty said. "I've sensed that you were up there looking down here on occasion." There was a short silence, and Marty added, "And I'll bet you know I don't bring young men home from the gym because I need the rent money, don't you?"

"Yes," I said quietly and took another long swig of beer. "I guess I figured."

"And that doesn't bother you . . . as a neighbor?" Marty asked.

I turned and looked into his baby blue eyes and said, "No, not particularly. Live and let live, I say."

"So, and still you accepted my invitation to try out my hot tub while your wife was away? Why, might I ask?"

A long swig at the beer. "Curious, I guess," I answered, "just curious."

"Have you ever been . . . curious . . . before?"

"No, not actually. No, no . . . never before." Another nervous swig at the beer. It was beginning to give me a buzz. It was a lie, of course, and I doubted that he believed me.

"But you're . . . curious . . . now?"

"Yes, I guess so."

"Just how curious?"

"Very curious, I guess. I've had some time to think about it."

With that, Marty moved in until we were touching sides, and the arm he had extended around me wrapped more snuggly around me, and he draped his left hand over my shoulder. His fingers touched my chest lightly, but to me they felt heavy and to be marking a point of no return.

"Curious enough to try a kiss?" Marty asked.

"Yes, I guess so. But I won't be good at it. As I've said, I've never done this before."

His left hand lifted to the side of my head and he turned my face to his. He brought his lips to mine. First a light kiss on the lips, but the one that followed was more firm, and he opened my lips with his. He tasted sweet and I hoped I did as well. His right hand went to my lower belly, and I gave a nervous twitch. But he held me there and I settled back down. He pulled his lips away and, in a low voice, said, "I thought that was nice. Are you OK?"

"Yes," I whispered. "I thought that was nice too." All of my attention was on that hand on my belly, however. He had moved his index finger to my navel and had pushed it in ever so slightly. And then out and then back in, repeatedly, making sure I noticed it. Just this little gesture, foreshadowing what might be coming, aroused me.

Marty brought his lips back to mine; again a light kiss and then a deeper one. This time he took my lower lip between his and ran his tongue over my lip. My right arm was pretty much pinned against his side, but I instinctively raised my left hand up to cup his head and to hold him to me. His upper lip pushed up, opening my mouth to his tongue. I returned the pressure of the kiss for the first time. I liked this. I had had no idea whether I would, but I did, and I'm afraid that my cock liked it as well. I could feel myself grow. Marty must have known that this should be happening about now, because the hand that was on my belly moved downward and explored the basket of my Speedo until he was able to outline the bulge down there. I first felt him get the measure of my cock, which I was pleased gave him a little shudder, and then he outlined where my balls were. But he returned to my cock and was gently rubbing it.

He broke away from the kiss. "Ah, I can see that you *are* curious," he said, "Very nice."

"Thank you, I guess," I answered, nervously.

"Yes, very nice, indeed," he said. While stroking and rubbing below with his right hand, he gently encased his left hand in the hair at the back of my head and pulled my head back. He then buried his lips in my neck, finding an artery pumping blood there. His lips on that artery caused my cock to lurch. He squeezed with his right hand and kept nibbling at my neck, and my cock swelled further. He obviously was a master

69

at this. This was a case where age and experience obviously paid off.

"Yes, very, very nice indeed," he mewed. His kisses traveled around to the other side of my neck, and his right hand came back up onto my belly, but only long enough to push under the rim of my Speedo and to gently pull my cock free.

"Uh, Marty . . ." I murmured.

"Just go with it," he whispered back. "You knew where this was going when you let me kiss you."

I moaned and closed my eyes.

"Here's where you can feel me too, if you'd like," Marty instructed. I tentatively moved my free hand to his chest and ran it from nipple to nipple. He had a good chest. I then ran my hand down to his washboard stomach. Very nice shape for his age. Marty's lips ran through my chest hair and went to my right nipple, where he applied suction. His right hand went down to cup my balls, pulling the Speedo down farther.

"You know where we're headed, but am I moving too fast for you?" he asked. "Everything still all right?"

"Yes, thanks. That feels nice."

"Here, let's get these off," Marty said, and I raised my butt so that he could pushed the Speedo down and off my feet, and he then flipped it away from the tub. While he was doing this, I looked over at Seth. He had pulled himself up on the edge of the tub and had a beefy mitt wrapped around one of the fattest and blackest—far blacker than his own skin—pricks I'd ever seen. He had a look of languid pleasure in his eyes as he watched Marty play me masterfully at our side of the tub.

When Marty came back around, he twisted his torso so we were face to face, chest to chest, and gave me a deep kiss. My right arm went around his back, my hand at his waist, and my left hand slid back down his chest to his belly and then, tentatively on down. I gasped as I realized that he hadn't been wearing any trunks at all. This shouldn't have surprised me, of course. Seth had shown he wasn't wearing a suit. Marty's pubic hair was thick, but not anywhere near as thick and long as the dong my hand found. I gave out little gasps again, and Marty registered his pleasure with his mouth, as I encased the root lightly in my hand and then slowly explored every inch of his tool.

Marty leaned over, fiddled with something on the rim of the hot tub and came back with a big gob of goo in his hand.

"Lubricant, a special kind," he whispered in my ear, as his hand went under the water and he started lathering up my cock with it. "But we still have to be fairly quick," he whispered again, "or the hot water would eventually dry it out and wash it away." We kissed while he slowly hand pumped me up, the lubricant providing additional pleasurable friction. Within a few minutes I was pretty well pumped up. He swung up and around me, suspended over me with his knees on the bench facing me and me between his legs.

"Here, scoot out on the bench a bit," Marty directed. I did so, beginning to understand what he had in mind, and feeling a little thrill running through my body. This was what I had been most curious about. Marty's hand went to my cock, and I felt its head being positioned at his asshole.

"But, but, don't you need something, too?" I asked.

"Oh, I'm well oiled down there already," Marty said. "Seth and I got started before you arrived."

I could feel my cock go into his ass up to the rim of the helmet. Anxiously, I started pushing up.

"Easy, there, big fellow," Marty said. "And I do mean big fellow. Give us a minute."

But in far less than that, I felt I was beyond the first tight area, and his sphincter muscle pulled me on in. Marty did a few up and down pumps while he was skewering himself on me, but, in large, it was a quick slide down my pole. It felt tight and bumpy, not at all what I had expected. Marty winked at me and asked, "How do you like my new sleeve? The first half of the channel you just went up has a sleeve with silicon bumps in it, both inside and out, to give your cock and my hole a ride I bet you haven't gotten from your women." And with that he reached out and grabbed the rim of the hot tub with both hands and I grabbed his hips with both of my hands, and he began pumping up and down, short and long, slow and fast, until we were both panting and I felt like I was going to explode. He was right; I'd never gotten this kind of ride from a woman before, and I'll have to admit that I've been up a few women's asses. I was about to shoot, when Marty rose off me and plopped down beside me again. He took my cock in his hand and held it still. I tried to hand fuck him to completion, but he held me still until the urge subsided.

"Not yet, good neighbor," he whispered in my ear. "Too early for your first load."

After I had calmed down, Marty took another glob of ointment in his right hand and slid it down my belly and along my upper thigh to my crotch. He put the heel of his hand under my balls, made me spread my legs with the pressure from his fingers, and found my asshole with his index finger. He held the tip of the finger on the rim for a moment, but then pushed it and some of the ointment ever slightly into the hole. I flinched and tightened up.

"No? Not yet? Too fast?" he whispered, as he came out of the kiss.

"No." I said. "Yes, I mean too fast. In fact, I'm not sure . . ."

"Nothing you're not sure about," He whispered. "We won't do anything you're not sure about . . . until you are sure. Don't worry." His hand came back up to my cock. He took the dick helmet in his fingers. I found I had been holding his the same way without quite knowing what else to do with it.

"Here, follow my lead," he said. He wrapped his hand around my cock and slid it down to the root. I did the same. Applying pressure, he gently, but steady pumped my cock for about a dozen beats. I did the same in rhythm, and both of our cocks grew. He then slid back up to the helmet, and so did I. Taking that in his fingers, he ran his fingers lightly around the rim of the helmet. I did so as well, and we both gave a low moan, although mine perhaps was deeper and more surprised than his. He put his thumb on the slit at the top of the helmet, and I returned the favor. He brought another finger up and squeezed so that that hole opened more. I began to squirm, but

Marty remained rock solid—and I mean rock solid. All the time, he had my lips in his and was deep kissing me. I looked at Seth. He was stroking himself with one hand and pinching at the nipples on his gigantic chest with the other.

I pulled away from Marty's lips and said. "Umm, maybe we'd better cool it a minute again, Marty. This might be getting a little critical with me."

"Not to worry, neighbor," Marty answered with a little laugh. "I think you can come now. You're a young, virile guy. I'm sure you have reloads if we need them. In fact, I think it's time for a little change." With that, he pulled away, knelt beside me on the hot tub seat, put his hands under my butt cheeks and raised me up. To my surprise and somewhat consternation, Seth was there behind me, kneeling with his knees behind my waist, my butt hanging just below the rim of the hot tub, and supporting my back along the incline of his torso. I could feel his huge dick running up my spine, which, I must admit, was not the least pleasurable feeling I've ever had. He wrapped his arms around me and placed his hands over my chest, where he did some subtle work on my nipples and chest muscles. From time to time, he buried his face in my neck and gave my arteries there a sensual sucking.

Marty, his knees in the hot tub and on the bench, facing me, was between my legs. His hands were encasing and squeezing my butt cheeks. "Gawd, what a nice butt you have," he said, with admiration. "And that prick. Get a load of that prick, Seth." Indeed, I must admit that my cock was very much on display, sticking straight up there in the air.

Marty brought his lips down to my navel, and he kissed and tongued me there, as I squirmed a little and did some sighing and moaning.

"This okay?" he asked.

"Yes, fine," I answered. I wasn't really sure about it, but I didn't kid myself. We were already far beyond what I had imagined.

"This okay?" he asked, as he moved his lips farther down and kissed and tongued along my pubic hair line.

"Yes," I answered weakly. He ran his tongue down along my crotch and around my dick until he got to my balls. He tongued and kissed those. "And this, this OK?" he asked.

"Yes," I moaned. Then he popped one of my balls into his mouth and extended it out.

"No, no . . . yes," I volunteered. He took the other testicle in his mouth. He now had one in each cheek. Again he extended them out and down and applied a little sucking pressure. He started humming and the vibrations on balls that were puffing his cheeks out were driving me wild.

I couldn't say anything at this point. I was holding as still as possible and was beginning to pant. Seth ran a hand down across my belly and encased my cock and squeezed.

"Oh, oh," I moaned. And then, "Yes, oh yes," as Marty popped my balls out of his mouth and was fed my cock by Seth, who was holding it upright. Marty treated it like a Popsicle briefly, running his tongue down to Seth's hand and then around to the other side and then up. He took just the helmet in his mouth and ran his tongue over it and around the rim and into the slit and then sucked it. What a sensation. I'd never felt this during sex before. Then he started deep-throating me, first soft and slow strokes and then faster and deeper, with the beat of the music of his CD.

I was writhing under Seth's bonds, moaning and whimpering, and murmuring that we needed to stop and cool down a bit. It was then that I noticed that Marty had worked his way along and inside my butt cheeks and now had two fingers, one from each hand on the rim of my asshole and slowly pulling the opening apart. I could feel more of the cool ointment.

"No, no, Marty," I said, as I tried to slap at him with my hands. "Get away from my ass."

Seth put me in a headlock that threw my arms over my head, but Marty did move his hands higher on my butt cheeks without losing a beat of his pumping action on my cock.

"Oh, oh, I'm going to come, Marty. Pull off, I can't hold it much longer."

"No problem," Seth whispered in my ear. "Marty can take it. He likes it." And take it he did, three jolts of wad, down his throat. Then he relaxed and looked up at me with a smile.

"There, that was lovely," Marty whispered as he came up for air after swallowing my jizzm. I just lay there in Seth's grasp, panting from my first male cocksucking. "You have one of the nicest packages I've ever had," he went on to say.

I thought that Seth would let me go then, but he didn't. What he did do was drag me farther out of the hot tub, so that my butt was on the rim. I could barely reach the seat with my feet.

Marty rose up on his knees and said, "What I can't understand is your fear for your ass. All I want to do is what a doctor can do. Didn't you know the prostate was the men's G-spot? All you heteros don't know the pleasure you are missing. It's just a little ways in; I just want to show you what a pleasure a prostrate massage can be."

"I . . . I don't know," I answered uncertainly.

"You came for adventure, didn't you?" Marty asked. "Why leave without knowing just how much pleasure you even could be getting with your wife. She could be doing this just as easily as I can. But obviously she hasn't been. You've been missing out. I'll bet you make sure you service her G-spot."

Again, "I just don't know."

But he was right there. My wife made sure I paid attention to her clit.

"Well, let me start and you can always let me know when to stop. I've done that before, haven't I?"

"Well, I suppose." I couldn't think of a better answer. And without waiting for a further answer, Marty pushed my legs apart and was lightly kissing my asshole. It did feel pleasurable. Seth lowered my arms again and again wrapped his hands around my chest and played in my chest hair and with my nipples. I turned my head and we kissed. His lips were bigger than Marty's had been, and his kiss was more bruising and insistent, but the taste was just as sweet. I could feel his hot sausage-like prick on my back, and I snaked my hands behind me in search of it. Seth lowered his shoulders to take the weight off mine and pushed my torso up so that I could reach his rod with both of my hands. I wrapped my hands around it covered from top to bottom without the hands overlapping.

"Raise your legs when I push them up," Marty commanded in a husky voice. I did so, and he got his hands where my thighs met my buttocks and pushed my legs apart. He had his fingers dug into my butt cheeks and he used them to pull them apart to give maximum access to my asshole. He kissed my puckering hole again and rimmed me with his wet tongue. It felt strange but tingly. I felt his tongue enter my channel and I gave a little gasp.

"Okay, so far?" he asked. I broke away from the kiss with Seth to give a hesitant affirmative response.

"This will feel cold, but it will make it more comfortable for my finger to reach the proper position," he said reassuringly. With that, he draped my left leg over his shoulder and came up with another large dab of ointment. This time I felt the cool moisture pushed farther into my asshole than he had done earlier. Marty spent some time working this in, and I could feel my asshole loosen up and expand.

"My, my, my," I heard him cluck.

"What?" I asked.

"Oh, just my, my, my. This is going to be better than I hoped." Not bothering to pursue that point farther, I relaxed a bit under his ministrations to the point that I no more than flinched when I felt a finger at the rim and tentatively push up to the first knuckle into the hole.

"There, does that hurt?" Marty asked.

"N-o-o," I said with an edge of doubt in my voice. "Huh," I said with a gulp, as I felt the finger push further in. I felt my sphincter muscle catch it and draw it even further in. And then I felt the pad of the finger on my prostate. Marty could feel he'd found the spot too, even though I gave him notice by flinching and giving a little gasp. Marty applied gentle pressure and began to rub.

"Here, this will take a few minutes," Marty said. Seth pushed the full length of his torso into me again, trapped my hands between him and me and slid his right hand down to my cock again. As Marty rubbed, I felt almost as if I had to piss, and I could feel a few dabs of cum involuntarily dribble up and out of my cock, but, oh what a sensual and relaxing feeling it was. I almost thought I'd begin to purr. I'm glad I found out about this. Seth rubbed the precum around my cock with his finger. He had propped me up so I could look down the whole length of my body and see him playing with my cock and Marty there between my legs. The pleasure from watching what was going on and the pressure on my prostate began to grow, and along with it my cock began to engorge again.

And then Marty's finger was out of my hole and he was standing on the floor of the hot tub. I could see his erect phallus, and it was leaning its way in, toward my butt.

My intense pleasure flipped to fear, "No! I half yelled. No, I don't want . . ." My voice was muffled by Seth's big mitt coming up and covering my mouth.

"Hey, you came to find out what this is all about. This is part of what this is all about," Marty said with a husky voice. "You came here. As soon as you let me kiss you, we both knew I was going to fuck you. Who are you going to complain to? Who in the neighborhood wants to know what you are a part of now? Your wife maybe? Don't worry; I'll make it a good experience. No, I'll make it a great experience; I can tell from your reaction that it's already gone beyond a good experience. And your hole has opened up incredibly. I've never seen this happen the first time. I bet you could take me and Seth both." I moaned and writhed at the thought. I didn't want to admit that I'd played dildo games with my women partners for years.

He still had my left leg over his shoulder, so he lathered up his dick with ointment and positioned its head up against my asshole with his right hand and pushed in just enough to get the helmet in and to have purchased. Then he grabbed both of my legs at the ankles and split me up and out like a wishbone. I saw him slowly entering me and I began to buck my pelvis, which only increased the pain, so I stopped. What I didn't want to admit, even to myself, was that this felt a whole lot better than the dildos I'd taken up there. Marty held still, while Seth reached over and turned up the music and did a quick turnaround on me. He had my hands by the wrists and was kneeling with my chest between his knees.

"You can scream if you want," he told me. "But I'm going to get rough if you do. And I'm going to get rough if you don't pay some attention to me now." There was little doubt what attention Seth had in mind. From where he was positioned, the moist head of his long dong was touching my cheek.

"Seth's right," Marty said from below me. "I can either give this to you within your tolerances, or I can give it to you really hard. If you service Seth, I'll be as gentle as possible."

"Go to hell," I screamed. I had barely gotten this out, though, when Marty pushed a good five inches up my ass in one slide. I thought I was going to be ripped apart.

"What was that you said?" Marty asked.

I didn't answer, but I opened my mouth and turned it toward Seth's dick and took the bulbous head in. I licked and sucked, and Seth gave little whimpers of pleasure. "Get your tongue under it," he said, and I complied. He entered me about three inches and I thought I'd gag. "Don't think gag," he directed. "Lift your chin to give it a straight shot and push your tongue and under it as far as it can go. And open wide, very wide. Loosen your jawbone. You can do it." I did so, and he slid in a little farther. Then me began to slowly pump in and out, fucking my face but not trying to give me more than I could manage.

Meanwhile, down below, Marty had withdrawn his prick most of the way and was pushing back in. He reached my prostate again with his cock, and he was rubbing up against that and giving me a not-unpleasurable sensation. Other than the one painful punishment thrust, he hadn't been doing more than slowly working his way in at this point, holding for me to stretch to be able to accommodate him. After he had gotten past the sphincter, I no longer felt great pain and the sensation of being stuffed beyond limits, and shortly I could feel I had loosened and relaxed and a felt the whole length of him glide on in. I could feel his pubic hair mashing down on mine.

"There," he grunted, "you did it. You did fine. You've got one sweet, big ass channel." He didn't do any pumping at that point, but he did move his pelvis around, rotating his cock inside me. My prostate liked that just fine, and it served to loosen and widen the canal some more. He came back up on the hot tub seat with his knees, so that now me was hunched over me. He pushed my legs down toward the deck at an almost impossible angle, so that now we was hovering over me, with his ramrod almost on the vertical.

It was then that Seth jerked out of my mouth with a grunt and spurted cum all over my chest, and as that happened, Marty began his pumping action in my ass. In and out, short strokes and then long strokes. Wiggling his pelvis and rotating his dick around, stretching and filling me. Seth changed positions again, without me being able to escape. He turned around on me, putting my head firmly between his knees and kneeling there. His hands went to my dick and my balls. He played with the balls for a while and then got hold of the cock and started stroking and pumping it. He and Marty did some kissing without letting it interfere with their other activities. And then I felt lips on the tip of my cock, and Seth took me on to the root in one slide, showing me that, indeed, it could be done. In turn, I showed him I wasn't taking any of this passively. I pulled his butt cheeks apart and started tonguing and rimming his asshole. I then fisted a hand and started pushing the knuckles at his hole, and, to my surprise, they started working their way in. Seth's only response was to wiggle his ass in pleasure, which I increased by taking his dick in my other hand and starting to milk him.

Marty, Seth, and I came at just about the same time, and, with a combined scream of release, followed by a sigh of relief we all were back in the hot tub, soaking away body fluids. I wasn't really in any condition to look where I was going, however, because when I went to sit down on the hot tub ledge, Seth was under me. I struggled and objected, but he had only of those beefy arms around me and the other was on his dong, which he guided to my newly plowed asshole as I came down. I managed to stop, at first, when helmet of his cock was just at my entrance. But Seth held me there steadfastly and slowly, ever so slowly, my leg muscles gave way and I descended down his gigantic tool, feeling every inch in both length and diameter as I was skewered until my butt was nestled up against his upper thighs. I panted and moaned, while Seth clucked sweet nothings in my ear and nibbled at my neck.

"Oh, Gawd, no, Seth. You're too big. Let me go," I whined.

"You've already taken me in, Glen. From here, just take it and enjoy it. You now know there isn't anyone you can't take. I'm ten inches long and mighty thick, Glen. There aren't many bigger than that. Just relax. That ointment we used is good stuff, and, as Marty said, you've got one incredible ass canal. You could take us both."

When I had stopped panting and groaning, Seth pulled my knees up and into my chest and began gently rocking from front to back. His rock-hard, yet flexible dong was rubbing my prostate and other nooks and crannies up my ass channel in a way that gave me a whole new sensation, and I found that I could accommodate him without pain now. I was lulled into a sense of relaxation, but the two weren't finished with me yet.

I had about dozed off in exhaustion, when I felt Seth standing up. He still had me folded into his chest by the knees, and he bore my weight as if I were a rag doll. He didn't go far, however, he just moved up to where he was perched on the rim of the hot tub. That's when Marty came back into view. Seth leaned back so that my butt was lifted in the air and there Marty was, with more ointment, and spreading it around my now-occupied asshole. I don't know how he was doing it, but he was managing to get a few fingers into the hole above Seth's buried dong.

"What are you doing?" I cried. "Oh, no, not that."

"Such a sweet hole and channel, Glen," Marty cooed. "And so flexible. It opened right up. More than I thought possible for a first time. Have you and your wife been playing rear-entry games? I kinda like that what Seth said—that you could take us both. I find that downright inviting. I think you've been shitting us. I think you've done doubles before."

"Nooo," I moaned and began to squirm.

"Don't do anything rash, Glen. Just hold very still there, for me . . . and for your sake."

And then he did it. I felt the head of his cock at my hole above Seth's rod and slowly, ever so slowly, he was entering me as well. He was half way in when he slowly pulled out again and then in, a little farther than the first time, and then slowly out and slowly back in.

"I knew it," he declared. "You do doubles."

"No," I moaned.

"Well, you do them now," he said and let loose a cackle. "And you do them real good."

Seth was giving little yelps of pleasure at the friction Marty was bringing to bear on his buried cock between kisses he was enjoying with Marty. His cock began to do some involuntary pumping as well. I was zoning out before they were finished.

* * * *

I had fled Marty's hot tub as soon as I had come fully back into consciousness. They had left me there, hunched over in the seat of the hot tub and they were now much more interested in each other than in me.

Marty had called out to me "Great fuck. See you down here tomorrow night," as I struggled up out of the hot tub and left, and I hadn't bothered to retort. I had gotten much more than I had bargained for. I'd played with fire and gotten very burnt. I needed to get my life back in order.

My wife would be gone for nearly a week more. The next day I got up late and soaked in the tub—my own tub in my own bathroom—both because I was incredibly sore and because I wanted to wash the dirt of my indiscretion completely from my body. I had to put this all behind me. The rest of the day I worked furiously at my computer, buried in my book editing, not giving myself any space to think about what had happened and how I had so wantonly volunteered for it. I couldn't blame Marty. I had thrown myself into his clutches.

He wasn't right about knowing how far it would go when I let him kiss me. I knew where it would go—well, not the double part—when I accepted his invitation.

I fixed myself an evening meal that required considerable work and turned the TV to CNN while I ate it, throwing busyness at my mind, not wanting to think about what had happened and how it had affected me.

It was dark when I returned to my home office. I raised my hand to turn on the light, but it hovered there. The glow from the lights around my neighbor's hot tub filtered in through the open window at the side of the house. I could hear the gurgling of the water being whooshed around in the hot tub. I moved to the window, telling my legs no, but being ignored.

Marty was sitting on the rim of the hot tub, naked, his erect cock in his fist. A younger man was sitting beside him, someone I'd never seen before. Perhaps a bit younger than I was. Very well muscled; obviously one of Marty's gym pickups. He also was naked and had a long, thin cock that bent up toward his stomach in its full erection.

The two men were whispering to each other, but they both were looking up—looking up at my window. Waiting for me.

My Speedo was still damp from the previous evening and my hands were trembling as I struggled to pull it over my hips, wondering why I even was bothering with it. And then I was descending the stairs in the dark, walking through the front door, moving toward my neighbor's hot tub.

No More Evening Shifts

There were four of them who entered the store close to closing time, all muscled punks decked out in black leather. I owned the small convenience store but found myself behind the counter this evening because my regular night clerk called in sick.

The hulkiest of the four came up to the counter, puckered his lips, and tossed me an air kiss. He asked me where Jake, my regular evening clerk, was. When I answered, he told me that I was cuter than Jake and that I turned him on. He asked if I wanted to join the group for a good time after closing. I could tell by the way he looked me up and down with that little sneer on his face what he considered a good time to be. I knew Jake swung that way, which had never bothered me, but I told this guy as politely as I could that I didn't. But he kept right on sweet-talking me. I figuring he was just trying to keep my attention while the other three picked out some presents for themselves, and this assumption proved to be correct.

I looked past the guy who was harassing me and saw one of his friends, a big black dude, heading for the door with a six pack of beer.

I brought my handgun up from under the counter where everyone could see it and, as confidently as I could, said in a loud voice, "I think you might want to put that back unless you are going to pay for it. And I have to close up now, so perhaps you guys need to go on to your party."

They left, but not without giving me meaningful looks and a few sniggers. Their bikes were gone from in front when I locked up and walked around to the back of the store to my car, and my mind was so full of business matters that I wasn't even thinking about them. But as I got out my keys to open my car door, there they were—all four of them.

Two of them had me in their powerful grip as the blond hunk who had harassed me and the black dude who had tried to make off with the beer stripped down. They both had strongly muscled bodies and were horse hung. They pulled at their cocks as the other two roughly stripped off my clothes.

The blond broadcast that he liked what he saw—better than the Jake he had expected to find here this evening. One of the guys who had stripped me waved my key ring in the air, and the blond hunk told him to go back into the store and get that beer they had wanted.

"And make it a better brand than the shit Tray picked out the first time."

The other guy and the black dude slammed me down onto the hood of my car, and the black dude mounted my chest. He was holding my arms against the hood of the car with his knees, and he pulled my head up by the hair so that my mouth was touching the big glob of penis helmet dangling from his loins. He directed me to suck him and to be good at it, or I'd regret it. I took his dick into my mouth and did what I thought would please him with my tongue on his glans and piss slit, and he did indeed seem to be pleased. His dick began to thicken and harden. I could hardly get it into my mouth.

Meanwhile, the blond dude had gotten his hand under my butt and was assailing my ass with his fingers. First one, then two, and then three. And he was finger fucking me. I couldn't help it; he was turning me on. My own dick began to harden, and the third guy swallowed it and began sucking me off as he rolled my balls with his fingers.

The fourth guy returned with several six packs of cold beer and a handful of condoms, and they all paused to drink a bottle off. I was in no position to say anything, though, as the black dude was rotating his cock around in my mouth, rubbing his helmet against the inside of one cheek and then moving it to the other.

The blond hunk took one of the condom packets, opened it, and slowly rolled the condom onto his huge cock.

"Sure hope you stand behind your products," he said with a laugh. "Cause I'm going to stand behind you and test this fucker out. You'd better hope your goods hold up to the test."

He then opened a bottle of beer, held it up, and said, "Think I'll try both of your products out on you." He passed out of my view behind me and gave a command, and the other two guys were grabbing my ankles and wishboning my legs. I felt the cold neck of a beer bottle being pushed into my ass, and then, at another command from the blond hunk, my legs were being pulled up toward the windshield, my ass was rotating up toward the sky, the bottle was tilting up, and cold beer was gushing down my insides. I heard the blond hunk and his cohorts laughing at this trick. And then the blond hunk's mouth was at my asshole. He was slurping beer and pushing his tongue into my channel.

The black dude was right over my face now, pushing his dick deeper into my mouth. I felt cold beer being sloshed over my chest, belly, and cock and balls, and one of the other guys, whose hands were still holding my leg up at the thigh, was tonguing the beer off me. He was driving me wild with his nipping and sucking at my nipples.

The blond hunk stopped slurping and tonguing my ass, and I felt his bulbous cock head at my hole. He entered me and I lurched, forcing the black dude's cock down my throat and causing me to gag. The blond guy kept his cock helmet just inside my ass opening for a few minutes, rotating it around, encouraging me to open to him—which, luckily, I was doing. When he was satisfied, he started to slowly but relentlessly feed his long, thick hose into me, stretching me to the edge of endurance.

The pain and sense of being filled to the limit was excruciating, but I couldn't scream, as the black dude was now face fucking me deeply, and it was all I could do to keep from gagging and to try to catch my breath. I could moan, though, and I was doing plenty of that. And the blond dude said he loved my moaning and that I should do it louder for him. He also said he loved my tight ass, and that he knew the others would love it to. The others? I moaned louder.

The fourth guy swallowed my cock with his mouth, and my cock betrayed me, showing that it enjoyed the attention.

The blond hunk was in to the root now, and he started a slow, steady pumping action, which started off deep and shallow and slowly lengthened. The pain was subsiding, and, as it did, I found a sense of pleasure increasing. My cock felt like it was going to explode. And then it did, and the guy who was giving me head took the full wad and licked me off before pulling away.

"Liked that, didn't you sport?" The blond said. "Hardened up and came real nice. I knew you wanted to party with us."

Shortly thereafter, the blond hunk pulled out of me and shot his jizzm up my belly. In a loud voice, he proclaimed it was the black dude's turn, and my jaws were given relief as the black dude withdrew from me, still kneeling above me, although his knees were now off my arms. He barked a command and one of the guys threw him a condom packet, which he neatly pulled out of the air.

"Cap me, bitch," the black dude said, as he put the condom packet in my hand.

My hands trembled as I fumbled with getting the packet open and then rolling it onto his giant tool. He then pulled my mouth back up to his dick, and forced himself back into my mouth.

"Get it nice and wet," he commanded, and I felt the acrid taste of latex in my mouth. When he was satisfied, he hopped off my chest. The other two guys let loose of my legs and the black dude had me flipped onto my belly and his cock moving up my ass chute before I had time to react. He was holding my torso down on the hood of the car with one beefy arm. His efforts to bury his enormous dick in me were causing him to grunt with frustration, and he commanded me to widen my leg stance. I did, and this helped him bury himself to the hilt. He got his big mitts under my chest, grabbed me by the pecs, and arched my back up to him. He had me in a lip lock, and his tongue was now deeply probing my mouth just as his dick had been doing shortly before. He pumped his cock in and out of me like a piston and soon came in a big gush of semen that filled the head of the condom and made me pray that the latex would hold. He then let me fall in an exhausted heap on the hood of the car and pulled away from me.

I lay there, panting, unable to move, as the blond dude signaled to the other two guys and they stripped. They were both thinner and wirier than the blond and black guys, but they quite clearly were strongly muscled as well. They also didn't have the monster cocks of their cohorts. They weren't all that thick, but both were long and one had an unusual crook in it that brought the head up toward the guy's belly when it was erect. Both cocks were very much erect. The blond flipped them a couple of condoms, and they took their time, standing very close together and facing each other, in getting a condom rolled onto the other's cock.

The blond pointed to one guy and said "bottom" and to the other and said "top," and the bottom, the one with the straighter cock, came over to me, pulled me up off the hood of the car, got behind me, and pulled me back down on top of him. He got his feet on the inside of my ankles and pulled my legs wide apart. And his powerful arms held me in a full nelson hold, with my arms above my head. Thereupon, the top guy walked between my legs, spread my aching asshole with two fingers and helped the bottom insert his cock and run it up my canal.

I twitched and grunted, but this cock didn't compare to what I'd already taken in, so I wasn't all that much alarmed. But then alarm started to set in, as the "top" moved into me and started to push his own dick in above that of the bottom. I suddenly realized what the bottom and top business was all about. I was being sandwiched.

I screamed as my ass canal was being stretched and nearly split, and the blond and black dudes answered my response with gales of laughter as they finished off another round of beer.

The top, the one with the crooked cock, pushed into where the helmet of his cock was positioned directly on top of my prostate, and he rubbed me there until I myself was in a sexual frenzy and my cock was oozing precum once more. Then he pushed right on in, and the two of them started a counterpiston action that played my ass passage like a calliope. The hands of the top were wandering all over the bodies of both the bottom and me, and all three of us were alternating kisses. The top's mouth went to my nipples while I was in the lip lock with the bottom, and I just relaxed and gave up my inhibitions. I became adjusted to the action and went with the flow. My cock was rubbing up and down the top's belly, and all three of us came almost in succession—and my cry of enthusiasm was no less heartfelt than theirs.

The top and bottom disentangled themselves, and the black dude picked up my clothes and threw them at me, while the blond hunk opened the driver's door of my car and waved me in.

Relieved that they weren't going to do worse with me, I headed for the door. I wouldn't stop to put my clothes back on; I'd wait until I had driven out of danger before I did that. As I got to the door, however, the blond hunk roughly pushed me down on my side across the seat and center console with his hand, lifted my leg over his shoulder, and fucked me in a side split one last time. Skin on skin. No condom this time. Deep strokes, in which he fully withdrew and then power-dived back into me and up to the hilt. I was moaning and sobbing, which he seemed to be enjoying a lot. And then I was enjoying it too. I had to admit to myself that I loved this hunk's cock up my ass. I started to go with his rhythm, and the blond sensed that I had given in to him at last.

"What do you think now, stud? Want me to pull out of you now?"

"No," I reluctantly moaned, "Don't stop now. I think I'm going to cum."

"Tell me you like it," he commanded after a particularly long stroke that had me gasping.

"Oh God, yes, plow me. Plow me deeper." I felt shame, but the sexual charge had taken me over.

Satisfied, he continued pumping me. He wrapped his hand around my cock and milked me until I came in a splat on the pavement below the door sill. And this time he came in an explosion and a cry of pleasure deep inside me, bathing my insides with his semen.

He leaned over and whispered in my ear. "There, I own you now, you muthafucker—just leaving you a little something to remember me by until the next time. It was a nice party; thanks for providing both the refreshments and the entertainment."

And then they were gone. I just lay there, until I was sure I was alone. And then I pulled myself out of the car, dressed, went back to make sure the door to the store was locked, and drove on home and took a long shower, ashamed that I had enjoyed much of the evening.

However, this was the last evening shift I ever worked in my store. But it was not because I didn't want to; it was because I couldn't trust myself.

No Pole Big Enough

He certainly looked like a big brute when he had arrived in the hotel room, and with all that muscle, he provided me the hope that he could touch me where I needed to be touched, take care of my need, and give me relief. But it hadn't happened. Once again it hadn't happened. I was beginning to think there really was such a thing as wearing your hole out, as having become so used that you no longer could be touched where you were screaming for it and spouting off all that buildup, draining yourself in satisfaction.

I had ordered and paid for a guy who, they claimed, was not only the biggest they had but could keep it working all night—wouldn't finish without me.

I had lived for three years in that remote valley in the Himalayas, where the men were elephant built and could fuck all night. Through long practice, they had reamed me a wide one and had trained me to hold out for hours. And now my sex life was ruined. I had returned to the corporation offices in New York a year ago, and I hadn't had good sex—or what I had been trained to in the way of good sex—since I landed in Manhattan. It was making me irritable. It was getting in the way of my work.

I had tried the bar scene and the classifieds, being very explicit about my need, and then, when I'd never gotten what I advertized for, I had turned to the escort services. This was my third one, and although he had a good ten incher and seemed to have a lot of stamina, I was, once again, left unsatisfied, jittery, and with an ache in my balls that just wouldn't go away.

After the fifth fuck as deep and vigorous as he could manage, he just fell off of me and over onto his side on the bed and cried uncle.

But when he left, he said, "Here, man. Nice tail, but sorry I couldn't do it for you. I've never failed before, but I felt like I was swimming around in there. Maybe you need surgery or something. But Leo told me that if this didn't work, I should give you this card. No charge for the tip. Again, sorry. It isn't that you don't turn me on. You'd be a fine lay if you weren't stretched so wide."

With much regret I took the card, and after we'd kissed at the door and he left, I looked at it. It simply said "Club Pan" and had a telephone number and an address on the other side for a side street in the Village.

Two nights later I was standing at a dimly lit walk-down door under a iron porch giving access to the main level above of a nondescript brownstone on a dark Village street. A blinking sign saying "Club Pan" was beside the door. So I at least was in the right place. I had called the number on the card the night before, and, after I had very directly told the man on the other end of the line what the nature of my problem was, he told me he thought they could help me. He also told me not to wear any clothes I was fond of when I came to the club. The one-evening visit I had prepaid for was quite expensive. But I was willing to try anything now for relief.

After giving my name to the pair of dark flashing eyes that opened a window in the door, I was let into a small vestibule that was completely black—walls, floor, and ceiling. But what arrested my attention was the half man who ushered me through the door. He was costumed as some sort of nymph—horns on his head that were cleverly attached so there was no indication they weren't naturally his and the hairy legs and hoofed feet of a goat. He was pretty cute, actually—very slender, with black curly hair, including his pubes, which were exposed. He had a long, thin cock dangling out of pert little balls, and he had a little goatee that jerked up and down when he talked. He was giving me a very enticing look, and I wondered if he was the one who was to try to service me. If so, I didn't think this was going to work. He did have nice length to him, but I doubted his would hit my walls at all as it slid up me.

He led me past an entrance down into some sort of club room where a performance was going on. I could see as I passed that the room, which stepped down to a stage area, was dark except of the glitter of gold cylinder-type decorations hanging from the ceiling. I caught just a glimpse of the stage in passing, but there appeared to be small figures dancing on poles at the four corners of the stage, with other, more muscular nymphs then this one—satyrs really—embracing the pole dancers. And a young naked man was tied to an X-shaped contraption in the middle of the stage and seemed to be in the middle of being fucked by another satyr.

As the nymph guided me farther down the corridor, I rather regretted that I hadn't been taken into the club. I needed warm-up if there was any hope of bringing me to the orgasm I needed.

We entered a room that was all white and had a curtain at the far side with some sort of framework in front of it, sort of a large, sturdy window frame, also in white. The nymph told me to stand in the center of this, and I hardly had noticed the velvet restraints at the four corners of the frame before he had my arms spread and my wrists tied to the upper corners and then my legs spread and my ankles tied to the lower corners.

He left the room, and the curtain in front of me slowly opened. A diminutive figure was perched on a low bench nearly against the far wall of the room that was revealed to me. He was dressed in what looked like a Roman toga. He couldn't have been more than four and a half feet tall, but he wasn't by any means either a dwarf or a child. He was a perfectly formed little man. Some creature of the mythical woods, I supposed, just as the nymph who had let me in and satyrs I had seen down on the stage were—or were pretending to be. It was all in keeping with the Club Pan motif, I figured. But I really had no idea what it meant as far as filling my hole to satisfaction and giving me a needed orgasm.

The little man, who had downy reddish-blond hair and a beatific expression on his handsome face was playing a haunting tune on some sort of piped instrument. I watched him for a couple of minutes and listened to his playing and wondered what possibly could happen out of this in the way of a solution to my problem.

I blinked my eye, and in the moment of that blink, another figure had entered the other room. He looked like one of the satyrs I'd seen down on the stage. He wasn't terribly bulky or tall, but beside the young man playing the pipes, he looked like a veritable monster. He was hung like a horse. And he was ready for action in that department. His rod curved up from his belly like a crescent moon, and it was capped with a big reddish, angry-looking bulb. He strutted around the room, giving an evil leer from under his bushy eyebrows. He was swaying to the music on cloven hoofs. His legs were as hairy as a goats, and he had massive pecs with patterns of hair circling his nipples and trailing down into his bushy pubes. He snorted and moved around the room to the music coming from the pipes, giving off an air that was many things at once: cruelty, sensuality, power, grace, danger, domination, and brutality.

I found myself both fascinated by him and shrinking from his visage as far as my bonds would allow, just as the small young pipe player seemed to be doing on his bench.

But then, as I watched in horror and absorption, the haunting piping stopped and the frightened squealing began. The satyr had drawn near the bench and just grabbed the little man by the front of his toga at chest level and lifted him up with the strength of one hand. The pipes went skittering off across the floor, as the little man howled his shock and surprise.

The satyr was ripping at the little man's toga, unwrapping him in ripping fashion like a child getting into a Christmas package. As I had surmised, this was neither a dwarf nor a child, but a fully—and very nicely—formed adult who just happened to be about half adult sized. Without further ceremony, the satyr, turning sideways to the window so that I got a full view of what he was doing, held the young man in front of him with strong hands encircling his waist, crouched a bit, and brought the young man's hips over his hairy thighs. He positioned that bulbous mushroom cap at the young man's hole, and I thought there would at least be some preparation, although surely the young man couldn't take him with or without preparation. But I was wrong on at least the first count.

With guttural animalistic sounds of lust and expectation, the satyr was skewering the writhing young body down on his tool. The satyr pushed the torso of the young, howling man down toward the floor and turned then, full frontal toward me, so that I could see the head of the cap poise a brief moment at the rim of the hole and then slowly get stuffed inside as the satyr pulled the young man's hips up into his groin.

The satyr was doing the impossible: Stuffing an improbably thick and long cock inside an impossibly small ass. If it all went in, I was sure it would reach the young man's stomach. And slowly and surely is was all going in, and the young man was faltering. His arms and legs were dropping and I could see the whites of his eyes. He was either passed out or near to passing out. And this was all being done for my benefit. And I'd like to claim that it was frightening me or disgusting me, but I began to feel stirring inside me that I hadn't felt since I'd left that mountain valley in the Himalayas.

I kept telling myself that this was all being done for me, that these two probably did this nightly. And sure enough, when the satyr had bottomed his dick inside the young man, I saw the little man's face begin to flush. And then, as the satyr began to play the young man's body, making it slide up and down on his cock, I saw the little man's eyes come alive once more and now he was crying out again. But he was crying for the fuck now. The fright was gone and he was crying out for the plowing.

The satyr stiffened and gave out a loud sigh, and the little man was exclaiming that his insides were being bathed in cum. I expected the satyr to withdraw then and this phase of the demonstration to be over, but he just resumed pumping the little man's ass on his hard cock, all the more vigorously now thanks to the added lubrication.

I was no longer alone in my own room. Two hulking presences were beside me. And the first sensation I got was the musky smell of their lust. Two more satyrs. But this time, big towering specimens, over seven feet tall each and with swinging cocks that put the satyr's on the other side of the window to shame. They both took hold of the clothes I was wearing and literally ripped them off my body.

Mean, determined looks on both. Cold, piercing eyes staring out from underneath bushy black eyebrows. Sharp, flashing white teeth.

One showed me the monster dildo in his hand and, while the other moved to my front and started teasing my nipples and then my cock with those sharp teeth of his—never piercing anything with them but with the continual threat of being just on the brink of doing so—the other thrust the dildo in my ass. It was thick and long, but not of filling proportions in my present stretched state. Still, the satyr worked it around inside me in circles so that I felt the first flutterings in months of an arousal that might reach a climax.

I looked in the other room and the satyr was still fucking the young man. The little man cried out in ecstasy for a second time as I watched and the satyr's body gave a lurch and I knew that there had been a second ejaculation. But still the satyr pumped on.

The tormenting satyr in front of me stood and turned and released my wrists and ankles. But I wasn't free, not by any means. The dildo had been withdrawn, and my ass canal was now descending on the huge, throbbing tool of the satyr at my rear. He had lifted me off the floor with his strong hands and just sat me down on his cock.

He was monstrously big. Bigger than the escort I'd been sent earlier in the week. Both thicker and longer. I splayed my legs out, my feet finding leverage on the window between this room and the next. The satyr worrying my nipples now dropped and swallowed my balls, vibrating them with a maddening hum and sucking hard on them. I was crying out in ecstasy myself now. I hadn't had a fuck like this for a year.

The plowing in the other room was still going strong, relentlessly. There was an obvious third spouting, and the little man's eyes appeared to be swimming in semen and he was babbling to himself, completely lost in the experience, stuffed impossibly to the gills. The obvious inference to me was that, as ordered, these satyrs were determined to stuff me on a similar scale and to continue fucking me until I had my elusive orgasm.

That was all very nice, I was thinking, but this satyr wasn't going to quite be able to satisfy me. But that's not what they had planned. Now the satyr at my front was standing and then going into a crouching position, his thighs crisscrossing those of the satyr at my rear and his gigantic, hard tool now poised under me as well.

Thick fingers were at my hole now, spreading me further apart, giving purchase to the second gigantic cock. Sliding in alongside his fellow satyr's, fingers remaining just inside the rim. Two monster cocks inside me now, as well as a couple of fat fingers. I arched my back against the hairy chest of the satyr at my back and accepted the thick-lipped kissing of the satyr at my front as the two counterpumped me.

I looked into the other room. They were still fucking away. But the satyr had turned the young man. the little man was facing me now, his feet against the window on the other side of mine, but between mine, the satyr's arms wrapped around his prey's belly. The soles of the little man's feet were scrunching in and out, no doubt in the rhythm to what was churning in his tight little ass. The satyr was behind and crouched below him and I could see that giant cock pumping up into the impossibly small hole. The little man's face was slack jawed, but his eyes were dancing and just swimming in the cum that was building up inside his body. He was staring right at me and looking totally content and fulfilled, loving the stuffing and the never-ending fuck. His eyes were telling me that I could be content in this way too with what was being done to me on this side of the window. And I believed him; I believed there was hope. I watched the scrunching of the soles of his feet to the rhythm of his fucking, and I believed I could be well stuffed and fucked forever too.

This . . . was . . . just . . . about going to do it. Plowing. Relentless plowing. I was sighing and purring and crying out for it and doubting I could take any more of it, my mind flashing back to the Himalayan mountain valley and the giant mountain men with their monster tools. I was panting and groaning and tightening. The satyr reached down and squeezed my balls hard and I shot off all over his hairy belly. For the first time in a year.

And then so did the two of them. Deep inside me, lathering my insides with their combined jizzm.

I looked into the other room. Still fucking away.

I felt great. They had done me. I had had the ejaculation I had paid for. The release that I wondered if I'd ever had again. I lowered my legs from the window, ready to be released and to leave. Determined to do this every week now, no matter what it cost.

But the satyr in front of me still held the cruel piercing look in his eye. And it contained that edge of lust still as well. They weren't releasing me. Their cocks were alive again. They were pumping me again. They pumped and pumped and pumped. I whimpered and cried for mercy and ejaculated, miraculously for the second time. And so did the satyrs. And then the cruel smile again, and they once more were pumping and pumping and pumping and . . .

I looked through the window and they were still fucking there as well. Endlessly

Mooaaann.

Pirated

I had thought we were well away, safely bound for Boston through the gate of Gibraltar at last from taking on a precious load of ivory from the Barbary Coast, and that I could now entrust the helm to Nelson and go below for some long-overdue randy business. And I was also just about home free with the tasty wench the lads had brought on board for me from Tripoli when the attack started.

After some mouth play, the wench hadn't objected in the least when I'd unlaced her bodice and started giving her ripe melons the attention they deserved. We were entwined together in the window seat of my vessel's fantail, and, forward lass that she was, she had unbuttoned my codpiece herself, fished out my Johnny, and was making it thick and hard with her stroking hands. I bunched up her crinolines, was delighted to find she was wearing no undergarments, and dove to her luscious pink clit with my lips.

When she was wet and wild, I stood away from her and stripped off my breeches. I was now standing completely naked before her except for my black leather boots, and she was admiring my manhood. She entreated me to come into her quickly and deeply, and I was making my final approach when all hell broke loose on the deck above me. It was clear that we were being boarded in the night, and it seemed equally clear that my men were outnumbered. We had been warned that the Barbary pirating was on the upswing, and I knew that our new nation was on the point of taking up arms with the North African chieftains responsible for this outrage. But right this moment, that gave me no solace.

I had no time to do more than grab up my short sword and turn to the door, when that same door burst open and Black Ned, my Nubian cook and valet, spun into the room. My slight but well-formed and flinty Nubian companion was being closely engaged in hand-to-hand sword combat by a swarthy pirate twice his size. Spinning in behind Black Ned's assailant was one for me too, a muscle-bound Scandinavian giant twice the size of Black Ned's opponent, stripped to the waist and covered in tattoos. A black giant of a man tried to swarm in behind him, but was stopped in the doorway because the cabin was hardly big enough to hold the combatants and petrified lady already in attendance.

Black Ned ran his opponent through the gut with his sword, leaving no doubt that the man had been dispatched. At the same time, my sword tip found a soft spot near the abdomen of the Scandinavian. As both men fell, the black giant found room to enter and pierced Black Ned's side with his sword. I pulled my own sword out of the Scandinavian and sliced at the black giant's sword arm just as he was preparing to finish Black Ned. This assailant turned to me with a look of surprise and malevolence in his eyes, and I was about to run him through when the doorway was filled with yet another figure.

We now were joined in company by the apparent pirate band leader, a magnificent figure of a man, dressed fancier and more ruffled than his compatriots and honored with the benefit of two flintlock pistols rather than cutlery. I heard a loud noise and saw a puff of smoke enveloping the visage of this late-arriving figure, and all went black.

When I became half conscious again, my first sensation was of a burning sensation in my scalp above my ear, where the ball had grazed my head and laid me out cold. My next memory was of the screaming from the adjacent cabin of the wench I'd nearly won. Clearly someone else was reaping what I had carefully sown. My third memory was the most painful of all. My hands were tied off with rope above my head around a leg of my captain's desk in the center of the cabin, and I was stretched out on the desk, belly to wood. I felt an excruciating pain in my intestines and soon became aware that the fancy pirate chief had his cock up my ass and was churning away inside me.

He and his men had caught me in a distinct disadvantage of total nakedness other than my leather boots when they had penetrated my cabin, and the pirate chief must have taken a instant liking to what he saw, obviously preferring me to the woman other members of his crew were playing with in the adjacent cabin. Now he was penetrating *me* deeply, and I was not at all accustomed to being used in this way. He pulled my head back toward him with a grip on the hair I had tied off in a tail, arching my back. With his other hand, he brutally turned my head to his face and possessed my mouth with his churning and searching tongue until I was near unto gagging. He continued to pump away madly at my ass. At length, he let loose of my head and moved his hands down to my pecs on either side and dug long fingernails into the aureoles surrounding my nipples.

To try to block out the pain from my brutal taking, I looked into the corner of the cabin, where the black giant, a rough bandage around his sliced arm the only clothes he now was wearing, was force-feeding a long and hard, but not terribly thick cock into Black Ned's mouth. Black Ned was on his knees, his chest was covered in blood from his own wound, and the black giant was holding a knife under his chin to encourage Black Ned to give him good suck.

I screamed and writhed back and forth, successfully causing the pirate chief's long and thick cock to dislodge from my ass, but the struggling served me not. The pirate chief turned me onto my back on the table and rendered me unconscious again with two heavy fist blows to the face. When I regained consciousness, he was fucking me in the ass again, but this time I was below him on my back and he was wish-boning my legs out and up from my body. When he saw that I was conscious, he pushed my legs down along my body, my toes point toward my head, and brought his own torso down on top of mine and attacked my nipples and my mouth with his teeth. He was looking into my eyes and grinning a silly grin and clearly enjoying the yelp I gave with every deep thrust he made with his cock.

All I could hear from the other cabin was weak sobbing of the woman and boisterous laughter from more than one male voice. But then I heard a piercing scream cut off at its apex, and I started to struggle once more to get out of the clutches of the pirate chief and to do whatever I could, albeit belatedly, to right this wrong being done to the woman I'd been about to do my own wrong with.

The pirate chief's fist went to the wound in my head, and I saw fireworks, felt maddening pain, and fainted once more.

This time when I awoke, I was out on the open deck, strung up with rope around both wrists, which were tied off on the rigging of a mast overhead. Black Ned was similarly tied off, facing me, not more than twenty feet away. The pirate chief stood between us, at a right angle to us, his legs splayed out a wide stance, a satisfied smirk on his face, and his arms crossed on his chest, a flintlock in each hand. He was stripped to the waist, showing a magnificent barrel chest, and his horse-hung cock still dangled from his open codpiece. I wondered that all of that had been stuffed up me, but the searing pain in my ass canal left me little doubt that it had been.

I watched in horror and fascination as the black giant fucked the slight Nubian, Black Ned, from behind with his long, long cock. With their disparity of size, I thought that surely the cock was making its way into Ned's stomach. The black giant was bent at the knees and was swinging Black Ned's butt back onto his battering ram of a cock with beefy hands lodged unto the smaller man's thighs. Black Ned obviously wasn't enjoying this treatment nearly as much as the black giant was.

Seeing that I was awake again, the pirate chief came around behind me and entered me again with his cock, sliding in to the hilt and sending ripples of pain—and, yes, of pleasure

102

too—around my ass walls. Two of his men held my legs out while the pirate chief plowed me yet again. The pirate chief wrapped his arms around me, buried his lips and teeth into the side of my neck, and his hands, now bereft of his flintlocks, locked onto my manhood. I was greatly embarrassed that my cock hardened up for him and that I spilt my seed on the rough planks of the vessel's deck.

The black giant grew bored with his fucking of Black Ned and pulled away from him. The pirate chief suddenly tensed and bathed my insides with his cum. He then pulled out of me as well and returned to his stance between us. Waving a reacquired flintlock in Black Ned's direction, the pirate chief declared that Black Ned had killed one of his best men. "What then," he asked his assembled men, "should we do with him?" The word "death" rang around the deck.

"How about death by belaying pin?" the pirate chief asked in a ringing voice, and boisterous assents were given all around. At a signal, one of the other pirates brought out a belaying pin that was well over a foot long and several inches thick, which I watched only so far in his journey to Black Ned's passage, and then I had to look away.

After Black Ned had been dispatched, the pirate chief's flintlock then turned to me, and he told the two men I had wounded and who now were naked except for the dressings on their wounds that they could have at me together if they liked in compensation for their wounds. They obviously liked, because the Scandinavian approached me from the rear, with his long, thick manhood at attention, and the black giant, with his longer but thinner cock, also at attention, approached me from the front. Other ruffians lifted and spread my legs wide apart, and two assailants I had supposedly wronged both entered my ass with their ram rods and began fluttering their hands all over my body and each other. The cocks of the two pumped me in counter piston action until both pirates had come, almost simultaneously.

I thought I had been stretched and filled to the limit, but when the two were finished with me and had pulled their dicks out of me with a sucking sound, the pirate chief asked his crew what should be done with the captain of the ship they had just taken. I once more heard the sickening word "death" being proclaimed to the winds.

The pirate chief looked around the deck, obviously searching for something, and then all eyes, including mine, went to the railing around the bridge over my cabin. Each separate section of the railing was topped off by a newel post. Each post was topped with a round, wooden ball of some four inches in diameter that was commonly used to contain tie offs of ropes from the rigging.

"Death by post ball," the pirate chief declared in a ringing voice, and all voices but mine agreed with a great deal of mirth. I had no illusion how they planned to use one of those four-inch post balls, and I began to jabber and sob.

"Or perhaps you would prefer this," the pirate chief announced with a laugh. He then walked back over to me and slid the cold barrel of one of his flintlocks up my ass. With a sickening sensation, I heard him pull the trigger, which was followed by a dull click. The pirate's crew roared with laughter at this excellent joke, and my knees gave way and I almost fainted again.

The black giant and the Scandinavian were untying my ropes from the rigging and starting to manhandle me up the stairs to the bridge, when there were new shouts heard at the far side of the ship, and we all turned to see yet more sailors, armed to the teeth, coming over the sides.

The harbor master must have noticed the earlier attack on my ship and sent out the small contingent of American marines, I reasoned, as I tore myself from my now-elsewise-occupied tormentors and backed to the far railing.

Looking down into the murky nighttime water, I saw that there were other small, open boats on this side of my vessel. Reinforcements were preparing to come up this side as well, I thought.

I climbed up on the rail and dove into the water, my presence now completely ignored by the pirate chief and crew who had ravished me and killed my companions. They had themselves been caught by surprise and were now fighting for their own lives.

The water was cold, and I was weak from the recent assaults on my body, but I managed to dogpaddle to one of the open boats, where strong arms pulled me up into the boat.

There was only one sailor in the boat. He must have let off his comrades on the other side of my vessel and been sent around on this side for safety and to pick off any of the pirates who had tried to escape this way. He was even bigger and more heavily muscled than the Scandinavian pirate had been. He didn't look the least bit like an American Marine. He was stripped to the waist; was covered in tattoos, including a prominent death's head; had a big ring through one ear; and obviously was ready for action.

Zounds, was he ever ready for action! It hit me instantly that this was yet another Barbary pirate, just one serving a different master than the one who had originally attacked my ship. He leered at me, and chortled a, "And what do we have here, my lovely?" as he quickly tied off the ropes still around my wrists on hooks at either side of the bow of his open boat. He pulled my pelvis up onto a wooden seat of the boat, allowing my shoulders to hit the bottom of the boat and my head to bounce off the bow's gunwale. Through the piercing pain this head bounce caused in my head wound, I saw him standing above me, unbuttoning his codpiece, and rolling out the longest, thickest cock I'd seen that night— already hardening fast. He knelt down below my buttocks, and I felt a thick finger roughly entering my ass.

The sailor grunted in surprise and pleasure. I needed no preparation for him; my ass was already swimming in the cum of several who had gone before him, and I was lathered up enough to accommodate him. He grabbed my legs in strong hands and hung them over his shoulders, and I screamed in surprise and pain as he thrust himself into me, plowed his engorging dick to the depths of my ass canal, and started a relentless deep fuck that went on forever as the din of battle roared over our heads.

Rest Stop

We were tooling down the highway in the early evening at a pretty good clip in my BMW Z4 Roadster when Perry started to get frisky. Perry was this hulking blond roommate of mine who also was on the football team, but who was a couple of years older than I was and played first-string tailback. I'd just started college this year and was still warming the bench, although I'd impressed the coach pretty much with my catching and running ability.

I was headed home for spring break, and I really needed a break. Between the studies, trying to keep my football scholarship, and my part-time job as a model for men's wear catalogs, I was really zonked out and needed a break.

Perry had asked me for a ride to the house of a friend of his in a town near mine, and, fool that I was, I had agreed. He was a cocky bastard—always on the move and exercising his mouth and topping any of the guys who appealed to him. The coach never said anything about this, because he was topping Perry. With Perry's status on the football team, and his hunky good looks, he didn't have too much trouble getting his cock in his ass of choice. But thus far I had held off all of his advances myself. I'd fooled around with guys in high school, but not all that seriously—just some mutual cock handling— and I just didn't want Perry to have any power over me.

I guess my stonewalling had only increased his determination to get into my pants, though, because he admitted to me as we tooled down the highway that he'd only asked for this ride because he wanted to do me. If I'd known that, I wouldn't have been wearing the comfortable sweat shorts and T-shirt I had on for the journey.

"Hey, I like you in that T-shirt, man," he turned and said to me, "Sets off your pecs and biceps real well. You're turning me on, Dale. Let's have the shirt off. See, mine is off."

"Cool it, Perry. Just sit back and relax. We're still several hours from home."

"Can't cool it, Dale. You're making me hot." He ran his hand up under my T and slowly worked his way up from my belly to one of my nipples. I slapped at the hand with one of mine, causing the car to swerve a bit on the pavement.

"Whoa. Hold steady, Dale. Look, you've got me excited."

I instinctively looked down in his lap, and, sure enough, his pants were tenting at the crotch, which was quite a feat, considering how tight his jeans were. I already knew he had an oversized package, because he had been careful to show it to me several times in the locker room shower.

"Knock it off, Perry." I didn't give you this ride just so you could proposition me again.

"Yes you did, sport. I didn't need this ride. I've got a car of my own. I assumed you knew that and were game. I asked for the ride because I'm dying to fuck you."

"Well, it isn't going to happen," I answered with irritation. "And put that hand somewhere else."

"Of course, anything you say, Dale," Perry answered with a laugh. His hand slowly moved back down my torso and across my belly and under the waistband of my shorts.

"Ah, very nice," he was saying as his hand got the measure of my cock.

"Stop That! We're going to crash," I yelled. And, indeed, the car was weaving in the lane. I pulled over to the slow lane and brought the car down to the speed limit.

"OK, OK," Perry answered. "That's not what I'm really interested in anyway." And with that, his fingers went under my balls and glided across the perineum in search of my asshole.

"I said stop."

"Open your legs to me," Perry commanded in a husky voice. The fingers of his other hand got entwined in my hair, and his lips went to the side of my neck. He was tracing my carotid with his tongue. For some reason, I responded to his command. I shifted my left leg over to where it was touching the door, and widened the stance on my right knee as well as I could while still keeping my foot on the accelerator. My pelvis rolled up as if on its own accord, making it easier for his hand to move under my balls. His middle finger found my asshole and pushed in up to the knuckle. I gasped and felt like my legs were turning to jelly.

"No, don't. Perry," I pleaded in a suddenly hoarse voice. "I'm trying to drive."

But he paid me no heed. His mouth traveled down my torso and swallowed my cock, which was engorging under his attention. My pelvis instinctively tilted up farther to meet his mouth, and he was able to get a second, and then a third finger into my asshole and to push them deeper. I felt him rubbing on my prostate. I was melting.

"God, at least let me pull over somewhere," I pleaded. Luckily I saw the sign for a turnoff into a rest area in the next mile, because he just kept on sucking and rotating his fingers in my ass.

The car was barely creeping along and I was fighting to keep it between the lines as we took the exit to the rest stop. I bypassed the well-lit car park and pulled behind the building into the truck parking lot and over to an area that was as far away from the trucks parked there as I could get.

The top was down on the roadster, and I propped my left leg up on the top of the windshield and just lay my head back on the head rest while Perry finished blowing me off and playing with his fingers in my ass. After I'd come and he'd licked me off, he brought his lips to mine and gave me a deep kiss. The fingers of his left hand were still entwined in my hair and he was holding my head back on the armrest in a hair lock.

His heel of his right hand was still lodged under my balls, and his fingers were up my ass.

"Climb over here on my lap," he commanded in that husky voice of his. "I'm going to fuck you now."

"No, you're not," I responded in a strong voice. "Not here and not now. Possibly not ever! I have to piss, so I'm going into the men's room, and then we're going on and you're not touching me again. Or I can bail you out right here." Without waiting for a response, I brought my left leg down, threw open the door, adjusted my shorts, and marched off to the building with the restrooms.

I was standing at a urinal, pissing, when a hulking, dark-haired dude, very hairy, but handsome in a sultry Spanish sort of way, came into the restroom. I'd seen him moving in my direction from a group of trucks across the lot as I headed for the facilities, so I assumed he was one of the truckers putting in here for a rest. He smiled at me when he entered the restroom and then moved over to the urinal at the end of the row and unzipped his pants. He rolled out a thick, but not unusually long, pecker, and held it and showed it to me before turning to toward the urinal. I got a good look at him but shifted my eyes to the tiles in front of me to let him know I wasn't interested.

Then Perry entered the restroom and unzipped himself and pulled his long cock out before he'd come anywhere close to the urinal. He took the urinal right beside me and made sexually insinuating comments all of the time our cocks were streaming. He made quite clear that he was claiming we'd had sex in the parking lot just before I'd come into the men's room. I could have died from the embarrassment.

He was finished before I was and, without zipping up, came in back of me, kissed me on the neck, and rubbed his cock on the small of my back.

"Sure you don't want some of this, honey?" he asked sweetly. "You got me worked up, and I'm dying to get my nuts off—like you were happy just now to let me get your nuts off."

"Just stop, Perry. You're embarrassing yourself as much as you're embarrassing me."

A stall door banged open across the room, and both Perry and I jumped in surprise. The dark trucker at the end of the line of urinals didn't flinch, however, so he must have known someone was in that stall.

I quickly pulled my shorts up as I turned to see a mountain of a man sitting stark naked on a toilet in the stall and pulling at one of the most enormous cocks I'd ever seen. He was all muscle, with flaming red hair, worn long, in a pony tail.

"If cutie there don't want you, Blondie, come over here. I'll give you a blow job you won't forget for some time. God, look at you. You work out most of the day?"

"First-string college tailback," Perry responded with pride.

"Figures; come over here and give me a taste of that. I could tell you what a tailback is good for."

"Sure, any port in a storm."

I looked on with fascination and horror as the man mountain pulled Perry into the stall at his side and went down on his cock expertly, getting Perry to moan and gasp with ecstasy within seconds.

The guy at the end of the urinals watched for only a minute and then made like he was coming over to do the same to me, but I waved him away and stepped back. Taking the hint, he left the men's room.

"At least close the door in case someone else comes in," I said, as I pushed the stall door closed. Upon reflection, I decided that Perry getting his rocks off this way was better than continuing to hit on me for the rest of the trip, so I finally shouted at him over the door, "I'll give you fifteen minutes and then I'm pulling the car around to the car lot. If you're not back out in twenty minutes, I'm tossing your bag out and leaving you here."

I took the hoarse mumble I got back as agreement. So, I marched out of the restroom facility and back to the car and sat there for fifteen minutes. I noticed that the Spanish-looking guy from the men's room was sitting on a picnic table nearby and watching me. After the fifteen minutes, I turned the key in the ignition, planning to drive around to the front of the facility. But nothing happened. The car didn't start. The engine didn't even attempt to turn over. I tried it several times—nothing.

The Spanish-looking truck driver strolled over to the car, put his hand on the window ledge, and looked down at the dash board with a concerned look on his face, as if maybe he could tell from a dark dash what the problem might be.

"Got a problem?" he asked.

"Yeah, it won't start," I answered. "Guess I'll have to look under the hood."

"Sounds like that would be a waste of time. I think you need a mechanic."

"Yeah, you're probably right. Guess I'll have to call AAA."

"Doubt they'll be out here too fast," the trucker said. "And this might not be a good place for you and your friend to be after dark. It'll get dark soon."

I had to admit he was right. The truckers I'd seen here had been pretty direct about what they wanted to do with Perry and me.

"I'll tell you what, though," he said. "I know of a mechanic living nearby. I know that he works on Bimmers too. I can drive you there and back, and he can get this baby fixed quick like."

"Hmmmm, I don't know. Maybe."

"All I'd ask is for the same consideration your friend was giving that trucker back in the men's room."

"What? I don't—"

"Just let me suck you off, like's happening with your friend, and I'll help you get this car fixed up."

I was pretty scared now. "I don't think I can leave my friend like that. In fact, I think I'd better go over and check with him before making any decisions about getting the car fixed."

"Oh, I don't think he's in any mood to be going anywhere for the moment. We have plenty of time to connect and get your car fixed before he'll be ready to go, I think."

"What do you mean?"

"Get out of the car, and come on over here, and I'll show you what I mean."

I got out of the car and followed the Spanish-looking trucker over to where a group of trucks were parked together. Beyond their trucks, shielded from the rest facilities, there was a picnic area, with tables, and I saw what the trucker meant. I saw Perry stretched out on a picnic table, totally nude. A beefy black guy with flowing dreadlocks who I'd never seen before was standing over Perry's head, his torso arched over Perry's and his mouth working Perry's cock. Perry's mouth, in turn, was working the black guy's cock. Perry's legs were splayed out, in the grip of the redheaded monster from the toilet stall, who had his dick up Perry's asshole and who was pumping away at Perry's ass. I thought idiotically for a second that Perry was being shown the redhead's definition of a tailback.

I stood there in horror and fascination—watching Perry get sucked and plowed at both ends.

The Spanish-looking trucker stood close behind me. I felt his arms go around me. He pulled my T-shirt off, and he had his big, beefy hands covering my pecs. I could feel the hardness of his cock at the small of my back.

"It looks like your friend is used to this," the man whispered in my ear. "But I'm willing to bet you aren't ready to party like that. Come with me. I'll blow you in the privacy of my truck's sleeper cabin, where none of the rest of them can see us. And they we'll go get your car fixed and you and your friend can get out of here. How about it? If you won't come with me, there's no telling what will happen to you out here."

One of his hands had traveled down below my waistband and to my crotch, and he was gently pulling my cock. Between that sensation and what I could see going on on the picnic table, I was hardening and lengthening pretty solidly. I felt trapped, wondering what would be the lesser of the evils of this situation. I made my decision as I watched the huge cock of the redhead stroke in and out of Perry's asshole. Perry was used to this; I certainly wasn't.

"OK, I guess that would be best," I whispered, as my eyes went back to the brooding line of Trucks and I wondered what lay in wait for me in one of those foreboding cabs.

"My truck's just over here," the trucker said. He led me over to a huge semi with a large cabin behind the driving compartment. He opened the door to this cabin, and I saw that there was a short-lengthened twin-sized bed in it along with some shelves, a compact john, and a small refrigerator and cooking unit. The bed was covered with pillows and there were shiny hold bars on the cabin wall at either end of the bed.

"There, stretch yourself up on those pillows and get comfortable," he said in a friendly voice. I laid down, with my legs sort of dangling off to the side, and he pulled off my shorts and briefs and knelt between my legs. I tensed up as he gently took me by the balls and the root of my cock with his mouth and ran his tongue over and around my cock helmet. I could see him tracing a thick vein running up the side of my cock with his tongue.

He took his mouth away and said, "Easy there, we'll go slowly. You have a beautiful cock. In fact everything about your body is beautiful." He went back to running his tongue around my helmet and then down the sides of my cock, while his free hand went to my belly and then on up my torso, tracing my muscles lightly, stroking me into relaxation. He surprised me. He was a trucker, but his attentions were a lot less rough and insistent than Perry's blow job had been.

He slid his mouth over my cock, and I began to moan and sigh softly for him. His free hand went between my thighs, and I opened my stance for him, as he gently massaged my leg muscles and stroked my inner thighs. I groaned and arched my back. But when the tip of one of his fingers went to my asshole, I tensed again.

"A blow job; we agreed on just a blow job," I said with alarm.

"OK, OK. I was just trying to add extra pleasure to it." His mouth slid over my cock and just kept sliding until I felt his lips at my root. He had deep throated me and I felt warmth and pressure at all points on my cock. I gasped and grabbed his head with both of my hands. He was cupping my butt cheeks with his hands and pumping me with his mouth now in long, relentless strokes. I writhed under him, alternately struggling against him and meeting his rhythm, until I felt like I was going to explode.

He had a finger at my asshole again, and I no longer cared. He held it there for nearly a minute, just covering my hole, and then I felt him moving around the rim in a circular motion, rubbing me, and then he moved it back to the center. All the time his mouth was going up and down on my cock and his tongue was at my piss slit, the tip pushing its way in.

He didn't have to penetrate my ass with his now well-lubricated finger. I pushed my butt cheeks down on him, pulling his finger in myself, all the way to where the pad of his finger rubbed up against my prostate gland. I moaned loudly, and tensed, ready to shoot my load.

But then his mouth came off my cock and he held me there, very still, until my breathing became normal again and I had passed the urge to ejaculate.

I looked at him with a question mark written all over my face. The deal was that I would let him suck me off, but when he'd brought me to the brink, he hadn't collected on the deal. I needed to get this over with, get my car fixed, and get back on the road.

"What . . .?" I started to ask.

"Shush," he said. "I don't want you to come yet. I want you to come inside me. I want you to fuck me."

"That wasn't the deal," I objected, as I tried to struggle up from the bed and head for the door. But then he got serious with me. He backhanded me across the mouth to stun me, and then he produced a pair of handcuffs connected with a good three feet of chain, and cuffed one of my hands, drew the chain through the slot in the hold bar on the side of the truck at the head of the bed, and then cuffed my other hand. He whipped out a black rubber gag with a mouthpiece that looked like a thick, four-inch cock with a bulbous head and stuffed the dildo in my mouth and tied the gag at the back of my head.

Then he opened a drawer, took out a handful of condoms, and opened one packet and rolled the condom on my dick. He climbed up astride my lap and tried to sit on my cock. I fought him, though, not allowing him to get my cock into his hole. In frustration, he pushed his hairy torso down onto my chest, put his mouth very close to my ear, and pinched my nostrils together with his fingers. I couldn't breathe. The gag completely filled my mouth, and I had to keep my nostrils open to be able to breathe.

"Now relax and don't fight me on this or I'm going to snuff you," he whispered in my ear. "Nod your head to let me know you're going to cooperate."

I held out for as long as I could, but when I felt my lungs were going to burst, I nodded my head and he released his hold on my nose.

I was still pumping air into my lungs when I felt my cock at his hole and being slowly encased in the clinging warmth of his canal. I just lay there, letting him do the pumping, but increasingly enjoying the friction of my cock against his ass walls. He had one hand pulling at my balls when he could get to them in a pumping down stroke and the other hand planted on my sternum, with one thumb squarely pushing and rubbing on one of my nipples. He was riding me like he'd ride a bull in arena, letting me know that he liked my length and thickness just fine.

This went on for several minutes before I heard the door to the truck open and a jumble of arms and legs and engorged dicks filling the sleeper behind the cab. Perry and his redheaded and black monster friends were joining the party. They'd all been tossing off beers.

"What?" I heard Perry bellow. "That was my lay. I was going to be the first to fuck Dale."

"Well, you can still be the first," my Spanish assaulter tossed amicably over his shoulder. "I've got him fucking me now. I haven't had more than one finger in his ass yet. Here, here are some condoms. His hole ain't busy."

I stared, aghast, as Perry laughed and opened a condom packet with his teeth. He rolled the sheath on his big cock, and

I lost sight of him behind the bouncing torso of the Spaniard. But then the Spaniard was being pitched forward again onto my chest, and I could see a grinning Perry beyond him. The redheaded guy and the black guy were at either side of me, each with one of my legs in a beefy hand, and they too were grinning at me as they wishboned my legs up and out.

Perry's head disappeared right before I felt a wet tongue penetrating my asshole, pushing it open and making it wet. This didn't go on too long before I saw Perry's head come up again and felt the palm of a hand under my tailbone, lifting my butt. All the time this was going on, my Spaniard continued to ride my cock like a rodeo star.

I bit down on the mouthpiece, trying to scream, as I felt the big head of Perry's cock at the entrance of my hole. And then he was pushing into me. Searing pain at first, but when he was a good five inches in, he went still and waited for me to adjust to him. The last two or three inches of penetration was more pleasurable than painful, and after he was in to the hilt, Perry started to stroke me, at first deep and shallow and then with longer strokes, almost exiting altogether before he slid back in to the hilt.

At some point I felt the truck began to move, and both the Spaniard and Perry matched their rhythm to the rhythm of the tires on the pavement.

I heard Perry exclaim with pleasure as the black guy got behind him and appeared to be fucking him from behind. But minutes later, I heard Perry exclaim more in anger and fear as I saw the redheaded guy trying to throw his leg up and between Perry's back and the black guy's belly.

"No, no doubling," Perry was screaming.

"But you've got the hole for it," The redhead was saying. "I know you've done it before."

"Oh, all right," Perry tossed off. "This is your luck day. Have a ball."

In a flurry of activity announced with a slurping sound, I felt Perry being pulled out of me. The redhead and the black guy were manhandling him, and I saw him being handcuffed to the hold bar at the other end of the bed and gagged just as I was. The black dude was under him, penetrating Perry's asshole from behind, and the redhead's belly was sliding against Perry's, and his cock was snaking in, with some difficulty, on top of the black guy's dick in Perry's hole. Perry was writhing and throwing his body about between them, but they had him double skewered and handcuffed and gagged, and it was quite clear that they intended to play him like a pump organ.

I would have felt sorry for him, but he had invited all of this and got me involved in my own predicament as well.

Watching the two muscle-bound truckers double Perry was more than I could take. I ballooned out the head of my condom, shooting my load deep inside the Spaniard. He sat back on his haunches, letting my cock go soft inside him. His eyes were locked on mine, and I could see that his eyes were swimming in desire. His cock was engorged. And I became aware that he hadn't cum yet himself.

I watched him anxiously as he slowly reached over and picked up a condom packet, opened it, and rolled the sheath onto his cock.

He rose off me and turned me around on my belly.

"On your feet," he commanded, "No, chest still on the bed. And spread those legs. You'll want to." I did as he ordered, and I felt his cock sliding into my ass canal, which had already been widened and lubricated by Perry. He arched his chest down over my back, and I felt his chest hair tickling my shoulder blades. As he pumped me, he had his hands over my pecs for a while, playing with my erect nipples. At length, one hand went down to my cock and balls. He rolled the used condom off my dick and milked me. I came for the second time, and he for the first, almost simultaneously.

Not long after that, I felt the truck stop and then the door to the sleeper cabin open. A guy I'd never seen before, short, middle-aged, and a bit paunchy stood at the door.

"Thanks for rolling us around so we didn't get noticed," Jake, the Spaniard chimed up. "I'll take the wheel now, and you can take your pick of one of these studs."

As Jake was sizing the situation up and the Spaniard was dressing and leaving the sleeper, I looked over at Perry. He seemed to be unconscious, although there was a sloppy grin on his face, and the two monster truckers still had their cocks buried deep in his hole, although their languid looks and the deep kissing they were engaged in with each other told me that they had both flooded Perry's insides and essentially were done with him now. I hadn't seen that either had taken the time to use condoms.

I guess both Jake and I realized that this meant he was going to pick me. He grinned at me and took his time taking his clothes off. I hunched up the best I could in the back corner of the sleeper, folding my thigh over my privates.

He wasn't in all that bad shape for an old guy, even with the beer belly he sported. Most notably, though, he was a true bear, furry from head to toe and sporting a full beard and shoulder-length hair. He'd been dark-haired at one time, but much of that had gone to gray. I thought it had been the beer belly that caused me not to be able to see his cock, but after he was undressed and was fiddling with a condom, I saw that his cock appeared to be stubby in repose, but it had a gigantic girth of almost four inches. Fascinatingly enough, also, the bulbous helmet was pierced with a gold stud.

He lost patience with the condom packet and threw it aside. Then he reached out and grasped my ankles and opened my legs up. He came down on his knees between my legs, and let one of his hands roam around on my body while he pumped himself up with the other hand.

Miracle of miracles, his dick was reaching a prodigious length while retaining its ass-splitting width, and I started to moan in mixed fear and anticipation.

I thought about objecting, but I was still struggling with trepidation versus desire when he bunched up some pillows under the small of my back, lifted one of my legs and wedged it against the edge of the side window in the sleeper, and entered my ass with his ram in a side split.

It immediately became obvious that he'd been doing this for a whole lot longer and with a whole lot more skill than either Perry or the Spaniard who had plowed me earlier, because he had me interested and working with him almost from the beginning. The stud in his dick helmet played my prostate so well and so long that I was spewing precum in greater quantities and pleasure than when I had ejaculated. Then he dragged his stud along my ass walls, sending ripples of pleasure through my body. He could feel that I was enjoying this fuck, and he released the gag from my mouth, and we kissed deeply. I lowered my mouth in search of his nipples, but I couldn't reach them, so he released my hands as well, and pulled his dick out of me and allowed me to work my tongue and mouth down his hairy torso and down to his cock and balls, where I gave him head for several minutes. At length, he lifted my body and turned to where he was sitting on the edge of the bed and then he brought me back down on his dick, with me facing him. I arched my back as his hands guided my pelvis up and down and his lips played on my torso.

The truck had stopped again, and the redhead and black dudes had extricated themselves from Perry, unbound him, and left him in a heap in the other corner of the bed, when Jake was finally finished with me and had bathed my insides with his man cum.

The Spaniard returned to the sleeper and he and Jake scouted up Perry's clothes and redressed him while I painfully dressed myself. When I emerged from the semi sleeper, I saw that we were back at the rest stop, parked right next to my Bimmer.

"You can go now," the Spaniard said, as he and Jake moved Perry's unconscious body to the passenger seat of my car. "Just don't tell anyone about what happened or you'll be regretting it. And, for Chris' sake don't pull into the truck area of a rest stop in the evening unless you are looking to get fucked. Not that I wouldn't welcome having you visit me at a truck stop again real soon."

"But my car," I said. "You were going to help get a mechanic."

"There was nothing wrong with your car that didn't get fixed by another visit under the hood," the Spaniard said with a laugh. "As I said, don't go messing around in areas like this at night unless you are looking for the kind of ride you don't get in a car."

Then he and Jake climbed up into the semi and drove away. As far as I could see, the other two guys who had done us weren't anywhere around. But I didn't take any chances; I revved up the Bimmer, roared out of the rest stop, and took the first turn I could find off of the Interstate and on to a secondary road that was heading toward home.

I was one sore dude for several days, and, I'm glad to say, that once Perry woke up, he was pretty quiet and didn't try to hit on me again for several weeks.

I do regret that I didn't get a number or anything for that old guy, Jake. As long as I kept my eyes closed, he reached my itch better and longer than anyone who has tried since that night at the rest stop.

Saddled

I immediately was suspicious. Leon was smiling today and talking nice. Just yesterday he'd propositioned me for the hundredth time and I'd turned him down for the hundredth and one times—I'd turned him down before he asked the first time. The most recent time I'd turned him down he'd gotten pissy and I'd given him lip back and he'd pulled back a lucrative assignment. A faded, and largely harmless, movie star gig that would have paid my rent for the rest of the month.

And yet he'd called me in again today. Usually after one of these fights with my pimp, I would be left in limbo for a week or more. I decided he must be short of staff.

"You ride a horse, don't you?" he asked, using his fat lips to shift his smoldering cigar from one cheek to the other.

"Yes, of course," I answered, thinking that maybe that's what narrowed down the pickings to me.

"Thought so. Pack your bags for the weekend." And, with that, Leon slapped an airplane ticket folder down on the coffee table. I picked it up. Destination Dulles Airport, the international airport located in northern Virginia that services the Washington, D.C., area.

"Where from there?" I asked.

"You'll be picked up. Client doesn't want to say."

"And the driver will know me by . . . ?"

"Oh, yeah, you'll be a platinum blond." Leon was smiling. I didn't think this was all he had to say. But I stood

123

and turned for the door. If I had to dye my hair before I had to be at the airport, I'd best get to it.

"All over." Leon said. I turned, and he was grinning. Well, OK, that made sense if the hair color was a fetish of the client's. More time, though. Still Leon seemed entirely too pleased. I stood there, knowing I hadn't heard it all yet.

"Except, there is to be little all over. You're to shave everything but your head and a V at the bush."

"A V at the bush," I said in a deadpanned voice.

"Yes, pointing to the goods."

"Well, OK, I've had to do worse," I said. I took one last look at Leon before I turned and left the room. He still had a sloppy grin on his face. I still had the uneasy feeling that I didn't know everything he found amusing. But it wasn't my job to know everything. I got paid very well for doing what I did and shutting up about it.

My plane was two hours late landing at Dulles, apparently because bad weather at both the Chicago and Atlanta airports, which were nowhere near was I was traveling, had the jets stacked up in holding patterns across the country. I didn't mind the extra time in the air, though. Our flight wasn't crowded, and I made friends with a distinguished-looking man sitting beside me who I'm sure I recognized from the television as in some sort of political job. We had enough time to chat that the delay earned me an extra $100, when I let him slip into one of the johns with me and give me a blow job, him sitting on the can, beating his meat into a paper hand towel and me with my butt perched on the small sink and my heels dug into the rubber-matted floor to counteract the slight pitching of the plane. He seemed turned on by the platinum-blond V and licked it down into swirls of curly waves, so I guess that wasn't such a bad idea after all.

He managed it all within a confined space without getting cum, either his or mine, on our clothes or any of the surfaces in the john. I'd have to guess he'd done this several times before.

I hadn't been standing at the baggage area for long—I didn't have more than I could put in my carry-on, but this was where I was told to stand—before I was approached by an extremely well-turned-out coffee with cream young guy, complete with contrasting dark brown chauffeur's livery and a big welcoming smile on his face. He was maybe three or four years younger than I was, shorter than I was by a couple of inches, and a little stocky—but in a solid, four hours-a-day in the gym sort of way. Bullet headed, totally bald, big hands, big feet in his slicked-up black shiny shoes. All promising.

He seemed to have no question who I was. I was standing in front of the designated pillar just off to the left of the baggage belt—and there was the platinum hair that I had moussed up into slight spikes. The West Coast surfer look to go with the tan I'd worked on so hard. I struck the pose for him, and I could tell in an instant he was interested. I often found the clients barely fuckable, but I occasionally, like now, was able to develop other side prospects while on a job. That gym-muscled look, the big hands and the big feet. And the bald head. Testosterone building up somewhere. The promise of being big elsewhere as well.

He took my bag, even though we both knew I could handle it without any huffing, and led me up the ramp to where a black Lincoln limo was parked right at the door, its engine idling, daring an airport cop to give it a ticket and find out who he or she had inconvenienced.

Eric wasn't exactly chatty, but he willingly gave me his name as we nosed out of the airport spaghetti pattern of roads and onto Route 28—at least according to the signs—and headed east toward I-66, a major highway running east to west from the center of Washington, D.C., out to California.. He didn't ask me my name, however, and he shut down when I asked him the name of the one who had sent for me. Good. Eric didn't fuck and tell.

When he turned west on Route 50 before we got to the intersection with I-66, he was friendly enough to tell me where we were going.

"Middleburg. We'll still be in this suburban congestion for a while, but it won't be much more than half an hour now before we reach Middleburg. Five Oaks. It's just on the other side of Middleburg."

Ah, information. I liked to have my bearings. At least something to process if a client was being too rough and I wanted to head for the exit.

"Middleburg. Middleburg. I've heard of that before, but I don't—"

"Maybe from back in the Kennedy era," Eric said. He had his eyes looking at me in the rearview mirror. He looked very interested. He obviously had been told not to say much, but he wanted to be friendly. He was assessing me just like I was assessing him.

"You may be too young," he continued, "but you may have heard about Jackie Kennedy and her horse riding both when her husband was president and then for years later. They had a retreat out here in Middleburg. They ride to the hounds out here, old southern style. The closest place to the White House that she could do that."

Ah, yes, I remembered hearing that now. Horse riding. Another piece of the puzzle Leon had tossed out on the coffee table. I was riding to the hounds this weekend, maybe. I wondered if Leon had any idea what the difference was between western saddle riding in California canyons and riding to the hounds in Virginia. Well, I'd cope. I always did.

"Thanks, Eric," I said. "Thanks for the information."

"Don't mention it." He was giving me a big smile in the mirror. Some sort of understanding established. I had a friend here if I needed it—maybe a very friendly friend. I took the plunge.

"Later, maybe, Dude?" I said and flashed him a smile.

He understood. He was a player.

"I'd like that," Eric answered, the grin I could see in the rearview mirror going from ear to ear.

After driving through Middleburg, one of those "quaint" little country towns that looked like it had barely cleared the eighteenth century and was obviously dripping in old money, we drove for maybe six more miles. The scenery was quite an attractive and calming switch from the frenetic pace and arid conditions I'd left that morning—rolling Virginia countryside of majestic oak trees, well-trimmed pasture land, and endless sweeps of white-painted wood rail fencing set against the backdrop of bluish-shaded mountains to the west.

"It's some sort of chemical breathed into the air by the trees."

"Excuse me? What is?" I asked.

"The blue color of the Blue Ridge. It's something in the trees reacting to the air that does that."

"Oh, uhh, thanks." More information. Not particularly useful information. But the point was to keep information coming. And his eagerness to provide information now seemed connected to his interest in something else. All good and promising.

We turned off to the south and drove not more than a half mile more before we turned right between two massive stone columns with marble eagles perched on top of each. A bronze plaque in one of the columns announced we were at Five Oaks.

"The five oaks are all gone now," Eric suddenly piped up from the front seat. He hadn't spoken for several minutes and I was afraid that he'd thought better of talking to me. We'd both been sitting and enjoying the scenery—and at least I was contemplating what Eric had to offer under that dark brown chauffeur's livery.

I grunted my acknowledgment that I'd heard what he said and appreciated the bit of conversation. He went on, "There are more like a hundred oaks now. Northern money."

Another piece of proffered useful information. A client who was rich and on the make in the South while being carpetbagger. Grasping and probably anger issues. I sensed bondage and maybe a bit of SM. Well, with the fees we charged, we did see more than a bit of that. Leon knew I had my limits. But maybe that was why Leon was so nice all of a sudden after our fight and had that sloppy grin on his face when we parted. Maybe he knew my limits were going to be challenged.

We drove for maybe another quarter mile on a freshly asphalted two-lane road running between some or all of those hundred oaks, which must have been pretty mature when they were planted, because they were quite impressive now.

I heard where we were headed before I saw it. The baying of hounds. We turned a corner and there it was, a massive, stately brick building, a traditional American Georgian four over four over an English basement with wide portico held up by four hefty white columns. Newer, but still old, two-story brick wings jutted out from either flank of the antebellum center structure. And gathered on an oval lawn in front of the house was a swirl of sleek, lean horses; equally sleek riders in scarlet coats and tan breeches; and an undercurrent of teeming lean hounds, some black, some brown, but most white with brown splotches on them. Everything was chaos and loud gossiping and obvious preparation for a fox hunt. I thought I'd stumbled onto an MGM set. I expected to see Elizabeth Taylor and Rock Hudson stride down the stairs from the portico and mount their fine fillies at any moment.

I had only a glimpse of this, though, as Eric pulled the limo around the side of the house and wound his way through a sea of Mercedes and Jaguars and BMWs, many with horse trailers attached, all parked willy-nilly around under the trees at the side and back of the house. Eric pulled up to a detached five-car garage, hidden neatly behind huge boxwoods at the back corner of the house. He retrieved my bag from the trunk and ushered me, without a word, as if he knew we now were being closely monitored, into a side door of the house.

We were in a narrow, Oriental-carpeted hallway that split the width of the house. From down the hall, a distant patch of light, I could hear the din of conversation and the braying of a loud voice for someone to get out there and get the hunt in order. We continued walking toward the voice and eventually arrived in the broad center hallway of the center structure.

The braying voice belonged to a distinguished-looking, trim, yet solidly built, handsome in a matured way man, carefully barbered hair with gray sweeps at the temples,

128

standing at the foot of a sweeping curved staircase rising to the upper story, several paces short of a double door with wide side windows looking out onto the portico. The doors were open, and I once again saw beyond those the swirl of scarlet jackets and fine horse flesh standing in a frenetic swirl of braying hounds. The man, who obviously was in charge—who obviously was in charge no matter where he was—was alone in the foyer by the time Eric and I reached it. He turned, saw us, and scowled.

"You're late," he said. "Almost missed it. Eric take him to the scarlet room. Dress quickly and come down. We have a horse ready for you. You should be able to make the last trumpet."

That was it. That was all he said, and then he was out the door. I didn't have much doubt this was the client and that he was the dominating type.

We started up the stairs, Eric ushering me to go first. Half way up we were accosted by another equestrian hurrying down the stairs, pulling on white kid gloves, decked out like the rest, a black velvet-covered helmet already on his head.

The same man who had just walked out the front door onto the portico.

"You're late," he said in the same disapproving, "to be obeyed" voice. "Dress quickly and get out there." He swept by me, brushing against my sleeve. Eric, probably well accustomed to this, deftly turned to let him pass without contact.

Twins. There were two of them. Identical twins. Another possibility for Leon's grin.

Eric escorted me up the stairs and down a long transverse hallway deep into one of the wings. The silence of the house contrasted with the muted sound of the developing hunt filtering through thick brick walls. He stopped at the last door down on the hall at the back of the house, opened the door, and set my carry-on inside, and then he stepped back to let me enter. When I had moved through the door, it clicked behind me, and I was alone.

Scarlet was a good name for the room. It certainly was scarlet—the carpet, the drapes on the windows, the bedspread and drapery on the solid mahogany four-poster canopy bed set between two windows looking into the back yard. The spines on the books in the bookcases beside the fireplace. A rich-looking Bergama oriental rug spread in front of the fireplace had a scarlet background. Even the burnished wood of the walls as well as the fireplace mantel and surround were a rich red mahogany.

I could see riding clothes laid out on the bed and a pair of gleaming black leather riding booths at the foot of the bed, with a black leather riding crop balanced on the toes. A riding shirt, a scarlet jacket, a black velvet-covered riding helmet, and a pair of tan breeches that flared at the hips and had leather ovals at the inner thighs—the three-quarter-length breeches that were called jodhpurs. And an athletic supporter with a sturdy cup made out of some sort of hard plastic.

I walked over to the foot of the bed and looked up into the canopy frame. Just as I thought. A steel-cage structure inside the wooden frame that gave the bed stability and would take a lot of weight. And in the upper corners at the top of the pillars at the foot of the bed, leather leads and ankle restraints tucked up into the canopy. I walked around to the head of the bed as I started shedding my clothes. I saw the black leather bands around slats at the headboard and looked between the headboard and the wall. Sure enough, wrist restraints tucked down there. I opened the drawer of the nightstand beside the bed. Piles of condoms, tubes of lube, a collection of dildos, leather blindfolds, and gags with rubber balls for the mouth to prevent the subject from biting his tongue or pulverizing his teeth by gnashing them.

Scarlet room. A very good name for it. Well, forewarned and all that. At least the fee was appropriately impressive.

I dressed quickly, and it all fit well—Leon obviously having given them my measurements—except that the jodhpurs were skin tight. They were so low slung the top of my platinum V spilled out in curls over the waistband that were quite noticeable before I got the shirt and jacket on, and I wasn't so sure that the seams of the jodhpurs would hold under the strain of my thighs and glutes.

The hunt wasn't anything to write home about. It was probably quite exciting, and I'm sure catching glimpses of the fox as she gave us a merry chase across the manicured pastures and through the sylvan glens was thrilling for those who were paying attention. But I was doing everything I could just to stay horsed and not make a fool of myself among all these avid equestrians. This wasn't anything like riding the range in the West.

Luckily, no one noticed what a novice I was. And in the hour of cooling down from the blooded excitement of siccing a pack of frenzied hounds on a tiny red fox, when we were all standing around and stroking the flanks of fine horse flesh on the lawn of Five Oaks, each sipping his or her preferred form of southern comfort, I was amused to see that I had become a center of attention. Several of the women—and men—had taken a fancy to me and were floating around me, trying to solve the mystery of Bob and Bill's houseguest.

I had gleaned during the hunt that my hosts were, indeed, twins named Bob and Bill and were fabulously wealthy and extremely powerful in whatever they did and, other than joining in the hunt, were reclusive and seldom in residence at Five Oaks.

While I was spinning lies about my devised-on-the-fly Kentucky roots and charming the pants and panties off my admirers—or at least so it seemed they wished, as evidenced by the young beauty with the thick southern drawl who tucked a card with her telephone number in my waistband—one of the twins stood off to the side and assessed my every move through slitted eyes. The other twin had disappeared as soon as the first riders to depart started loading their horse trailers.

Eventually, the crowd had thinned down considerably beyond a hopeful handful clinging to my elbow. At this point, the twin must have had enough, because he rudely cut through the ring around me and took me by the arm and said he wanted to show me something in the barn.

I could hear the something he wanted to show me as we approached the barn, which was set off a good hundred yards from the house.

When we entered the structure and my eyes adjusted to the dimness and the straw chaff floating in the air, I saw that the missing twin had a naked Eric bent over a bale of hay, topped by a horse blanket, and was riding him hard from the rear.

Eric was doing a good deal of grunting and groaning and praising of the twin's performance, but I sort of had the idea that he was doing it to please and because it was expected of him. The glistening of the light sweat on Eric's undulating muscles under the onslaught of "no slouch himself" twin was a real turn-on. The twin was holding Eric's cheek down on the horse blanket roughly with a hand spread out on his bald head, and Eric watched me as I entered the barn.

"See you started without me, Bob," the twin who had brought me into the barn said. That cleared up for me who was who.

Then Bill turned to me. "Strip off the jacket and shirt. Leave the jodhpurs and boots on."

I stripped slowly, exhibition style, but, in my mind, I was doing so for Eric, not for the clients. Eric rewarded me by widening his eyes and smiling big as I pulled my shirt off and slitting his eyes in an obvious reverie of lust. He grunted and twitched as Bob pulled back almost full length and jammed his cock back inside the chocolate muscle man with great force.

While I was slowly shedding down to the jodhpurs, Bill had more quickly stripped down and had moved deeper into the dimly lit barn.

"Come over here. Now." There was no question that Bill was to be obeyed.

I moved back into the barn, and my eyes opened wide in surprise. Bill was astride some sort of padded pommel horse contraption supported by a grounded center pole, like they used in gymnastics, although it looked more like what they had in some of those pseudo-Western bars with the mechanical horse rides. It had a saddle strapped to the top, stirrups and all.

Bill was in the saddle, completely nude. He was angled up at the back of the saddle and was pulling on his meat. His cock was long, if a bit thinnish. And it already was very hard.

"Climb up, facing away from me," he commanded.

I put a foot in a stirrup and swung my other leg up in front of me as gracefully as I could and over the contraption. Bill held me by the hips as I swung over, helping me to hold steady. I came down wedged in front of him in the saddle, with his long, hard cock throbbing up the small of my back. When I was saddled, Bill reached down at both sides and activated straps across my ankles in the stirrups so that I now was trapped there.

Then he began to make love to me as my butt was firmly wedged against his pelvis. Big beefy, hairy arms encircled me, and he was kissing the back of my neck and running his hands all over my torso, palming at last one hand over one of my nipples and digging below my waistband and inside the supporter cup with the other hand to cover my cock and balls and bring me to the game down there. He was moving his pelvis up and down, dry fucking the small of my back with his dick. He was the client and this was kind of nice anyway, so I moaned for him and moved my body against his. And I turned my lips to his and we kissed deeply.

"Raise up in the stirrups," he commanded in a hoarse voice, and I did as he directed.

I felt the back seam of the tight jodhpurs split as his fingers tugged at the edges, and I no longer had to wonder if the seams of the breeches would hold. They probably weren't meant to hold on the breeches I'd been given. He drew a tube of lube out of a side pocket on the pommel horse contraption and palmed my belly with one hand while the lubed fingers of the other hand slid through the slitted seam and worked inside my ass. I heard a condom packet being ripped open and saw it land on the floor of the barn shortly before he was tipping me forward and then pulling me back onto his long, throbbing tool.

As he slid into me, I groaned and grunted for him and gave a little cry of invasion and arched my back and threw my arms and head back, pulling his lips to mine in an "Oh fuck me!" maneuver that I knew worked so well with the clients at this point.

We writhed together for several minutes, with me declaring how good he was, how filling he was, how I'd never had it this good.

And then the surprise was on me. The pommel horse was shuddering and the other twin was now swinging up into the saddle as well. Facing me. Grabbing me by the hips, as Bill palmed my pecs and leaned back, tipping our hips up. Forcing the head of his cock at the entrance of my channel, already stuffed with Bill's cock. Pushing a lever somewhere that caused the stirrups to rise and spread, opening my legs further. Giving Bob's cock room to force itself inside me, alongside Bill's. No more acting at this point. I was double stuffed and stretched to the limit. I cried out and groaned and grunted.

And Bill holding his cock steady and hard and deep inside me, Bob began moving his cock in and out, rubbing against my walls, caressing his brother's cock, moving deeper, ever deeper. I was panting and trying to catch my breath. Hands roaming all over me and over each other, lips kissing me and each other. A cacophony of moaning and groaning and sighing.

I glanced wildly to the side as I sensed movement inside the barn at the periphery of my vision. A chocolate mass of fluid muscle coming into view. Eric approaching closer. Watching the fucking in the saddle on the pommel horse. A magnificently compact body of glistening muscle. Eric was stroking his own, huge, thick cock as he watched the twins double me. He was licking his lips. I had a brief vision of being tripled and almost fainted from the shock of how sensually, if physically impossible, I felt about that.

Another switch was thrown and the pommel horse began to gently rock back and forward on the center pole. A heightening of sensation, an effect on the cocks inside me that went beyond the control of the twins.

Was it me or was the rolling increasing in intensity, becoming bucking? No, it was. Oh Gaaawd. The twins crying out in passion. Me joining them in chorus. Bucking, bucking, bucking. The cocks fucking, fucking, fucking, sent churning by the bucking horse. Oh, Gawwd, oh Gawwd. Losing it. Shoooting Offfff.

Not ending there, however; the mechanical contraption continuing to buck and roll until long after the twins had played my channel like a counterpunching piston engine and made their deposits and finished with their shouts of climaxing lust in two-part harmony.

Off the horse now, unentangled. Bob just grabbed up his clothes and strode out of the barn. Bill motioned to Eric and, between them, they moved me over to the bale of hay with the horse blanket on it and laid me gently down on my back.

"Clean up here and then bring the car around at six," Bill said to Eric in that "to be obeyed" tone both the twins had. "We're going into Middleburg for dinner." And then he was gone as well.

Eric dipped a cloth in a nearby trough of water and came over and started dabbing my face and torso with the cool cloth. I put my hand on the back of his hand and let it slide up his forearm and across his bulging bicep, pulling his face down to mine, taking his lips in mine. I spread my legs and wrapped them around his beefy thighs and pulled him into me. Big hands, big feet, bald head, all panned out in this package. The power of him was swinging like a baseball bat between his legs.

I threw my head back and arched my back and cried out for him as he entered me with the thick, thick dick of his. I bucked hard against him, riding hard, enjoying him as he was enjoying me in waves and waves of freely offered fucking.

* * * *

I was toweling myself off after a long, languid bath in the well-appointed bathroom off the scarlet room that evening when I heard the soft knock on the door.

When I opened the door, Eric entered with a supper tray for me. I'd been told I had to stay in the room for the remainder of my stay—and to expect visitations. I moved to embrace him, but he leaned away from me, put a thick finger up to his lips, and then pointed to the corners of the ceiling. I looked up and saw the small flickering of pinpoint lights. Of course. What happened in this room was being video recorded.

I let him go with regret, ate the dinner, and put the tray outside the door. Then I unwrapped the towel from my waist and threw it into the bathroom and went back to the canopy bed. Stretching myself out on the bed on my back, I masturbated and writhed sensuously on the bed for the benefit of the camera for a short while before sinking into a semiconscious doze. It had been an exhausting assignment. And I was pretty sure it wasn't over. I couldn't remember whether I had ever been as inventively and fully fucked.

When I woke, the room was dark except for the flickering light from the fire in the fireplace and the pinpoint of lights from the cameras. One of the twins was at the fireplace, perhaps having just lit it. He was naked, facing the fire. His legs were spread, and I could see his long cock dangling between his legs, picking up the light coming off the fire. He turned at hearing me stir, and I began to learn that the twins were not identical in their preferences.

He, who I later guessed was Bill, motioned me over to the fireplace.

"Kneel on the carpet here and suck me," He commanded. His voice wasn't as hard edged as it had been earlier that day.

While I sucked on his dick, bringing it to life, and fingered his balls, he poured himself a glass of wine and held the glass in one hand and cupped the back of my head with his other hand. I was pleasing him. I certainly knew how to do that well.

When he was fully engorged, he pulled my head back off his cock with his fingers in my hair. I twitched with surprise at sight of the wine bottle in his hand as I arched back. He tipped it, letting wine spill down over my chest. Then he put the bottle down, came down on his knees in front of me. Wrapping one strong, beefy arm around the small of my back as I was arched back on my knees, my head reaching back almost to the floor, he started to lick the wine down my torso, until his lips reached and swallowed my cock. I just lay back supported by his forearm around the small of my back, my arms hanging at my side and staring into the flickering fire in the fireplace as he sucked me to ejaculation.

Then he turned me onto my knees, my chest flat on the carpet, my eyes still glued to the firelight, as he opened a condom packet and crowned himself. The packet fluttered to the carpet beside my face, and then he crouched over my hips and took me doggy style in long, smooth, slow strokes.

While he was fucking me, I heard someone enter the room. Eric, perhaps? And when Bill had ejaculated and pushed me down on the carpet and moved sensuously on my body with his as he kissed my neck and shoulders and we both watched the fire until we had calmed down, he escorted me to the bathroom, where a warm bath had been drawn. We went into the tub, facing each other, and then we both drank wine, while I let my toes bring his cock back to life. With a little cry of passion, he grabbed my butt cheeks and pulled my hips into his pelvis. I let my legs rise out of the tub and planted the soles of my feet on the tiles on either side of his head. He held my hips with his strong hands and I used the leverage of my feet on the walls to fuck myself on his regenerated tool.

One satisfied client.

The other twin, Bob, I'm sure, was a whole other story. He silently entered the room late that night. I was barely awake as he bound my wrists over my head at the headboard. I was quite awake, though, as he was trussing up my legs in the apparatus at the foot of the bed that spread my legs wide and lifted both them and my pelvis.

He roughly gagged me with the rubber ball gag I'd seen in the nightstand drawer earlier. Then he lubed up and used a progression of ever larger, ever more knobby dildos on my ass channel while I writhed on the bed and tried to scream around the rubber ball filling my mouth and pushing my tongue down.

That little excitement over, he jerked the gag off. He wanted to hear me when he was taking me himself. I watched him take a strap-on cock enlarger out of the drawer. It had suction cup-like knobs running around it in a screw pattern. I watched as he lubed himself, rolled on a condom, and then strapped on the apparatus. I begged him not to do this, just as I knew he wanted me to do. I trembled for him and stammered my fear. And I knew this excited him. He walked over to where I had left my riding clothes and took up the riding crop I'd dropped there.

He was flicking it as he approached me between my spread and raised legs, and I whimpered for him. I cried out as he wanted me to and arched my back up and down on the bed and struggled as best I could while still giving him the sensation that he was fully in control as he screwed his enhanced tool inside me. I grunted and groaned for him as he started stroking inside me and flicking my butt cheeks and flanks with the riding crop.

After a while, he pulled out of me, freed his long, hard cock from the enhancer, pulled off the condom, and climbed up on the bed and straddled my chest. He fed his cock into my mouth and I sucked him expertly, as I knew he expected me to. He pulled out of me and shot all over my chest with a throaty cry.

Then he moved to a nearby short-backed boudoir chair and just sat there, watching me, naked and all trussed up, and fingering and pulling on his cock.

I could see that he was beginning to breath heavily and getting big again, and I wondered what he had planned for round two.

But, inexplicably, he stood and started releasing me from the bonds.

"You can go clean yourself up now," he said in a low, hoarse voice when I was free.

I stumbled off the bed, sore and exhausted from my full day of making money the old fashioned way, and started to hobble toward the bathroom.

But that was the signal for round two. Bob grabbed me by the hair from the back and propelled me to and astride the chair he'd been sitting in with a fist in the small of my back.

The breath went out of me as I fell across the chair. He was at me like a thundering animal in full rut. Yanking my head back with a fist in my hair and thrusting hard between my butt cheeks with his long, hard cock. Fucking me and fucking me and fucking me.

I gave him what he wanted. Complete subservience and cries of being cruelly split asunder—which wasn't all that much off the mark.

Another satisfied client.

* * * *

The next morning Eric drove me back to the airport in the Lincoln limo. I missed the scheduled flight and had to rebook for later, because Eric stopped the car near the end of the drive and joined me in the backseat, where, first, he pushed my head down between his legs for me to suck him as he sat back in the seat and spread them, and then lifted me and sat my channel down on his thick tool while I rocked back and forth on top of him to our eventual mutual satisfaction.

It was only when the plane was half way back across the continent that I realized why Leon had really been grinning. The twins had first fucked me through a slit in the jodhpurs and had at no point commented on the platinum hair, shaved chest and pits, or the V of the bush. They didn't give a flying fuck about this. Leon had told me to do that just as his own private joke. Well, fuck him—but not in this lifetime, I hoped.

Seven- and Eight-Inch Drills

Ad placed by Andre (eight slender inches) and Mike (seven thick inches) in the local weekly newspaper:

- - - -

Power Drills: GBM's, Strong, hard, silent seven- and eight-inch power drills seek tight BWM or SWM who seeks filled fantasy experience for multiple drill role play says-no-but-wants-yes bottom. Call Mike at 945-6036.

- - - -

Ad Rob saw instead in the local weekly newspaper and decided later to respond to:

- - - -

Power Drills: Set of strong, hard, silent power drills for sale. Multiple-drill set, including seven- and nine-inch power drills. Call Mac at 945-8279.

- - - -

Telephone number Rob called after scanning through the paper the next day for the number he wanted to call: 945-6036.

A very friendly voice on the other end of the line told him to come right on over and gave him the address.

Mike answered the door.

"Hi, I'm Rob. I called about the power drills you have."

"Well, hello, Rob. Come on in. God, you looked ripped, man. What a lucky day. So, you want to be drilled? Hey, Andre, com'on down here. The bottom who called is here?"

"Huh, excuse me? The name's Rob Buxton, actually. Oh, the drills. Yes, I came for the drills. Can I see them?"

"Wow, Mike, we've got an anxious one," the beefy Andre said as he appeared at the door. "Well, let's not keep him waiting. Com'on in, dude. Nice butt, man. Do you work out?"

"Uh, yes," Rob answered a little confused. "So, where are the drills? In the garage?"

"Anywhere you like it, Rob," Andre answered with a laugh. "God, I'll bet you are cut too. Let me see your pecs next to Mike's here. Mike, off with your T. I'll help Rob here. There. Yep, you're just about as ripped as Mike, and he's workin' out all the time. So, you want it in the garage. Come on through here."

"So, is that where you keep the drills?" Rob managed through his confusion.

"Sure, a lot of the time," Mike answered. "We're always workin' on Andre's truck. Sometimes we stop doin' that and work on each other." Mike and Andre shared a laugh. Rob continued to look confused.

"So, ever done this before, Rob?" Andre asked as they bustled through the kitchen and out to the garage. He hesitated on the way to pick up a tube of KY.

"Huh, shopped for drills, you mean?" Rob asked. "No, not really."

"Sweet." Andre said, as they entered an oversized garage with a cleared area in front of a pickup truck that was backed into the front part of the garage. "There, Mike, pull that saw horse over there and spread those old burlap sacks over it."

"And your ad said you had a seven inch and an eight inch. Is that right?" Rob asked.

"Yep," Mike answered. "I've got the seven inch, but it's very thick. Andre's got a more slender one, but it's over eight inches."

"So, can I see them and examine them."

"Absolutely," Mike and Andre said in unison. And they stripped right down. Rob stood there in complete shock, as Mike walked over and stripped him right down too.

"Sweet," Andre said with a whistle of appreciation. "God, he's beautiful. And he's got some length too. So, me first, I guess, as I'll set him up for your thickness. Here, pull him over the saw horse and get him in one of your head and wrist locks."

Rob woke up to what was happening and started to struggle, but not early and strong enough. Andre and Mike were two strong black dudes. Mike pulled Rob over the saw horse on his belly and got a head lock on him between two strong thighs. Instead of going for Rob's hands, however, he reached under with his long arms and got a hold on Rob's balls and said he'd crush those if Rob didn't quiet down. With the other hand, he reached around and alternated exploring Rob's nipples and pecs and stroking his own cock hard.

Rob quieted down a bit, but he was objecting and whining and whimpering in fear, as, behind him, Andre, of the slender eight-inch cock, was fingering KY into Rob's asshole with one hand and stroking his own cock to KY-lathered hardness with his other hand.

"Nice job with that role playin', dude," Andre said. "That's really helping me get hard. The fantasy of fucking a straight white dude who didn't see it coming. And I'm going to fulfill the fantasy you had of being filled and drilled when you answered our ad right now." And in he went up to the rim of his helmet. Here he stopped, because the hole was still too tight, and he rotated his cock just inside the hole to loosen it up.

"Ahhhh! No. Gawd, that hurts," Rob screamed and writhed in pain.

"Ahhhh, Ahhhh, Ahhh," he continued to scream, as Andre managed to get in past the sphincter. And then, "Ahhh,

Ohhh, ohhh," as the helmet of Andre's cock dragged along Rob's prostate, giving him a new, much more pleasant sensation. And then Andre was in solid, and he let his cock slide the whole eight inches in.

Rob was panting and groaning, but his ass was adjusting to the new experience. Andre pulled out to drag his cock head over Rob's prostate a couple of more times, and Rob's writhing and moaning began to have some sounds of pleasure mixed in with the sounds of pain.

Mike released his headlock on Rob and pulled his head up by the hair until Rob's mouth was at the level of his half-hard cock. "Here, make this hard, pretty dude. I'm next in your ass."

Rob tried to resist, but Mike pushed his cock between Rob's lips with the comment that if he didn't suck him off or if he did any damage to the cock, Rob would regret it mightily. Rob did open his mouth enough for Mike to start face-fucking him but didn't get any more actively involved in giving him head than he absolutely had to.

Meanwhile, Andre had buried his cock in Rob's tight ass again up to its hilt and began a deep-fuck piston motion that had Rob bouncing up and down on the top of the saw horse. To keep from being bounced off the saw horse, Rob grabbed Mike's butt cheeks and held on for dear life, an act that caused Mike's cock to harden faster. Andre was holding one of Rob's hips with one hand and slapping his butt cheeks with the other one. He was loving the ride, and he spun out his drilling operation for more than twenty minutes before he couldn't hold off his climax any longer and shot his load over eight inches deep inside Rob. Mike was going slower with his face fucking, because he wanted to save his load for his own turn in Rob's ass. Rob wasn't doing much else other than whimpering and moaning quietly, waiting for the assault to stop, but having mixed feelings about being fucked deep in his ass by such a well-built black stud, never having had the sensation before, and not finding it nearly as unpleasant as he assumed he would.

When Andre pulled out of Rob, Rob was able to make a break for it. But he only made it as far as the kitchen, where Mike took his turn with him on the kitchen table. Andre held Rob's arms stretched above his head across the table, while Mike slapped Rob down on the table top on his back, grabbed his calves and wishboned his legs out, and thrust his thick cock into Rob's asshole, drilling right down to the full seven-inch mark. Rob screamed in pain, feeling his ass canal ready to split with the thickness of Mike. But Mike paid him no mind and just pumped away. After a couple of minutes, Mike dropped one of Rob's legs and turned him to his side and side split him for several minutes.

"Hey, Andre," Mike said after a while. "He's opened up real nice. I think there is room for you too." Pulling Rob off the table top, Mike hopped up in a sitting position on the table himself and pulled Rob back into his lap, neatly impaling his asshole again, and sliding back to full depth. Rob was sputtering and moaning as Andre came around the table, pushed Rob down onto Mike's chest and wishboned his legs back out. He saw where there was a bit of room for another dick above the one Mike had buried in Rob's hole, and Andre worked his way in, accompanied by Rob's screams, first for mercy and then in ecstasy, and Mike's grunts of pleasure in having a cock running up beside his.

No sooner had both Andre and Mike come again than they heard the doorbell. They let Rob fall to the kitchen floor in a heap, and Mike quickly pulled on T and shorts and went for the door. A young red-headed man stood outside the door.

"Hello," he said, as Mike opened the door. "I've come about the ad in the paper about the seven- and eight-inch drills you're selling. Is . . .?"

"Sure, dude. You're in the right place. Come on in," Mike responded with a big grin on his face.

Snowball Effect

I couldn't resist Michael Dabney's proposition in the Checkers Lounge at the LA Hilton Checkers hotel during the Entertainment Industry Advertisers' Association convention—well either of his propositions, really. I'd never done it with a black man before and that had become somewhat of a special fantasy of mine. I was attending the EIAA convention, because I'd been working with a small firm that had exclusive contracts with a few actors' agencies for commercial TV work. Dabney worked for a much larger and more influential black-owned firm representing the recording and advertising portfolios for black singers—mostly bad-boy rap artists.

"But why me?" I asked.

"You mean other than trying to get your luscious body in bed?" Michael asked. But he was smiling that enigmatic smile at me that I found so engaging, and he was so glib and given to turning of phrases and playful double entendres that I didn't take him seriously. Besides, he was far more luscious than I was. Not American black, but a transplant from the Caribbean and all hot sexy looks and lean and trim body, emphasized by his graceful, fluid movement. And he had a smooth, rich voice and an expert grasp of the disarming sales pitch technique. He could talk the chastity belt off a nun, which in today's world probably still is a lot more difficult than talking a priest out of his cassock. Which probably was why he

147

was head of the marketing department for Johnson Brothers, the rising black advertising firm in the music industry.

"No, I mean that I'm a white guy and Johnson Brothers is an all-black firm representing black musicians only. Why are you offering me a job under you?"

"You mean besides the desire to have you under me?" he asked. That enigmatic smile again. "Well, being all black has put us at a barrier to advancement," he continued after that pregnant pause that put me off balance again. "Our clients are all black, but the industry is pretty much white—and some of it is pretty racist white too. Clarence and Maurice Johnson want their business to grow. They think having a white guy in place to work with sticky situations will enhance our business. We've been over the likely candidates in the field, and we think you are our white guy."

"I guess I should feel flattered," I said with a laugh. "And how much would a token white guy be worth in your firm?"

I whistled at the number Michael tossed out. It was nearly three times what I was making in my current position.

"And you wouldn't be token," Michael said. "We think you'd be worth your weight in gold with companies who aren't giving us the time of day now."

"Because of my résumé?" I asked, trying to keep the sarcasm out of my voice.

"Yes, that—and, of course, because of your terrific bod," he flashed back. I still couldn't read whether he was toying with me, making fun of me.

"My bod," I said in a flat tone.

"Just being honest here. Advertising is all about appearances. Sexiness sells. We wouldn't have anyone on our marketing staff who didn't come across as sexy. And you're sexy plus—in a white way, of course." That disarming teasing smile of his again. I think he could tell me I'd had spinach in my teeth throughout an important briefing and I would just nod and give him a silly "happy smile."

I knew that sex sold and was important in the advertising business already, of course—I'd let many a woman and man who wanted to to lay me on the way to closing a contract—but it wouldn't have taken more than a glance at the suave, achingly sexy Michael Dabney, Johnson Brothers' marketing director, to see the truth of that.

I said I'd think about it. And when Dabney pressed, I said I'd most likely accept the offer.

And that's when I realized that he wasn't joking with me with his suggestive double entendres. Because that's when he hit me with his other proposition.

Michael was an astonishingly attentive lover. He held me in his arms just inside the door into his hotel room and kissed me deeply—and expertly, I might add—while his hands were stripping me of my clothes—also quite expertly. He then guided me to the bed and lay me down on my belly and gave me a deep massage from neck and shoulders to the soles of my feet, taking his time and making sure he'd covered every inch of my backside with his sensuous massage. Then, I already being fully aroused, he turned me onto my back, and lay, shirtless but still with his trousers on, stretched beside me on the bed, his arm encasing me, and glided his free hand all over my body, becoming increasingly intimate. All the time he was kissing my lips and the hollow of my neck and my eyelids and running his tongue into my ear cavities. His hand went to my engorged cock, and he began stroking me off slowly while still holding me closely in place with his other encircling arm.

"Now doesn't that look nice?" he murmured to me. "My milk chocolate on your milky white body. Don't they meld nicely?"

"Umm, umm," was the best I could respond under his attention.

"And how about some milky white cum on my chocolate thigh?" he whispered.

I couldn't answer, as I was arching my back and panting shallowly to try to prolong the pleasure before that happened.

He made love to my body in this manner for more than a half hour, until I was writhing under him and begging him to fuck me—and ejaculating in great gobs of milky white cum under the attentions of his stroking hand and his thumb rubbing back and forth on my piss slit.

Then, as I lay there all mellow and moaning for him, he stood up and slowly dropped his trousers and briefs. He was a true black. His skin was the chocolate color of the Caribbean quadroon and his features delicately European, but his cock was black as coal and hung low—except that now it was at full staff.

"Want to watch a black cock moving in and out of that nice white hole? I know I do," He murmured.

I moaned at the mere thought of that image. I'd fantasized about being taken by a black man, and here it was, happening in reality.

Smiling down at me, he took my hips in his hands and pulled me down to the foot of the bed. Then he knelt between my spread thighs. His mouth went down on my ejaculate-slicked cock head, and he was sucking me into his mouth. The image of my whiteness being pulled between those full, brown lips had me hyperventilating. At the same time a moistened thumb went to my asshole and he was beginning to open me to him.

I undulated my pelvis in involuntary response to his attention, fisted the bedspread, and cried out for him to fuck me—the foreplay had gone on for an eternity, and I was burning for him to finish me—to bury that luscious black cock in me and pump me hard.

He moved his lips and tongue to my asshole and by the time he was finished there, I was so open that he merely stood between my legs and slid that long, black tool into me. He pumped me deep for a few minutes as I moaned and groaned and arched my back and pulled his torso down to where we could kiss. After we parted, he put a hand behind my neck and raised my head so I could see that black cock appearing and disappearing inside my hole—and I began to pant and melt.

He turned my body on his cock so that I was belly down on the bed, cock hanging off the end to be found by his stroking hand, and fucked me from the rear in deep, long strokes. I turned my head and sought his mouth while he thumbed my nipples with his free hands, and I felt him jerk and could feel the strong flow of his come even though he was sheathed.

* * * *

Strangely enough, Michael was mostly business with me once I had joined Johnson Brothers and, although we did fuck again on occasion, it certainly wasn't as often as I was willing to be taken by this master lover—nor was it as intense or as fulfilling as that first encounter was. Over time, I developed the suspicion that the lovemaking was mostly just part of the job offer pitch—and testing me out, perhaps on just what I too would be willing to do to close a deal. Still and all, it was the best attention I've ever gotten—and it fulfilled every fantasy I'd had of sex with a black man. And it wasn't like I hadn't done the same thing myself several times to close a deal.

Michael must have talked around the office about me, though, because there wasn't much in the way of checking out preferences or willingness on the part of one of their premier clients, the black rapper Sledge, when the firm assigned the marketing department to help find a home for his newest album recording. Michael asked me to take a crack at getting him into Top Ten Records, which had just started including rap artists in their offerings, but wasn't yet into the heavy leather type of music that Sledge put out. Michael made sure to let me know that Sledge liked his men, what he liked from his men, and that I would be expected to accommodate him if it would help me make him happy with whatever deal I could negotiate.

I make an appointment with Top Ten Records, whose name pretty much said it all as far as market position was concerned. I didn't really think there was much hope, because they were an old-white boy, tight-assed sort of organization that only went for surefire projects. But, miraculously, they showed interest, even though a flagrantly bad-boy tricked-out Sledge, complete with minimal clothing coverage of his heavily muscled and obscenely tattooed body and his fake fur coat and platform shoes, insisted that he attend the session. One of his homeboys drove us from our offices over to Top Ten Record, and I was shocked to see how much floor space there was in one of those Hummer stretch limousines.

After the meeting, with Sledge euphoric over how well the talks with Top Ten had gone, I got a personal lesson in why Sledge had all of that floor space in his limo. As I was starting to climb into the back outside Top Ten's entrance, Sledge pushed me in and onto the floor of the vehicle with a meaty fist to my back. And then he showed me his appreciation for the extraordinary sales job I'd been doing for him by pulling me up to my knees with a fist in my hair and gagging my throat with a big, black cock with a heavy-duty silver ring in its head. He stripped my trousers and briefs off as I was trying my best to suck him, and when he was satisfied that he was prepared, he simply picked me up and slammed my butt into the seat at the back of the Hummer and spread my legs wide with his hands.

"Lay down nice for me, white bitch," he said. "Gonna ream you a whole new hole with black cock. Your ass is mine. You put on a good show in there; so's now put on a good show for me. Nice tight hole." He was digging the fingers of one hand deep into my ass while pulling my lips up to his bulging nipples on a hard chest with a fist in my hair.

I whimpered and gasped as he then fucked me hard and deep until I was crying out. He was so good at rough cocking, though, that I was soon crying out for more. He laughed a deep-throated laugh as he felt me give in to him and then to clutch his bulbous buttocks to hold him deep inside while I sighed and murmured my involuntary ecstasy.

Sledge kept declaring that he owned my white ass while he was jackhammering me—and perhaps he did in the cutthroat world of entertainment advertising. I certainly wasn't in a position to naysay him without backing in my own office, which I wasn't likely to get if this cushy Top Ten Records deal went through. So, in effect I was fucking myself by having won him a chance at the deal.

After he was done with me and the Hummer was pulling back up to the building in the low-rise parklike office campus that housed the Johnson Brothers offices, he grunted at me to dress and then we went back up to marketing division's second-floor offices. He just sat there all smiles and all innocence as I reported on our success to an appreciative Michael Dabney, while I tried to cover my embarrassment of having a twitching butt that was asking for more attention from Sledge's cock ring.

I had to walk Sledge back to his limo and found it hard to walk a straight line as out of joint as my legs were from Sledge's power cocking. When we reached the foyer, though, Sledge saw a couple of muscle-bound homeboys lounging at the door to the shipping department and went over and chattered with them for a while in low tones that I couldn't have deciphered even if they were loud enough for me to hear. I didn't need an interpreter, though, to figure out that Sledge was talking about me. He kept sniggering and pointing to me, and the two bulky black homeboys were muttering back to him with big, knowing smiles on their faces.

When he returned to me he palmed my butt as we walked to the car and he smiled back at the two shipping clerks with a "I own this white boy's ass" look that they fully appreciated. I thought I was seeing him to the door, but he wasn't finished with me. He took me back to his place and pounded my ass so hard all night that I called in "ravished" the next day and had to soak in the tub for hours.

The day I returned to work, I made the mistake of stopping by the shipping department when leaving on my lunch break to drop off some outgoing packages that I just as well could have let an office boy take care of. And before I knew it, I was lunch for Ham and Sly, the muscle-bound shipping clerks. Without so much as a "May we fuck you, kind sir," they lifted me and hustled me out of the shipping dock and over to the picnic table they'd set up for themselves in a copse of trees next to the building.

They stripped me, and Ham fucked me hard and rough doggy style, while Sly pushed his thick cock between my lips.

And when Ham was done, he turned me and changed places with Sly. Once again, though, I melted at the image of being fucked by big black cocks and watching hard, chocolate muscles rippling against my white skin as they worked me.

Each of my fuckings at the hands of the black dudes of Johnson Brothers was getting rougher and involving more. I likened it to a snowballing effect. We were building to something it seemed—something that made me tremble with fear. So far, although I objected to the lack of choice after my taking by Michael Dabney, I must admit that I thoroughly enjoyed the plowing by these hunky black studs.

I just wasn't sure I liked being taken for granted like this—or how much rougher it could get and I'd still be able to endure it.

While Sly was standing being my legs and pistoning my ass and Ham had already finished getting his blow job, I had a chance to look up at the building. Several of the windows had black guys standing in them. More than one of them had his dong out and was pulling on it while watching me being spiked and squealing for mercy on the picnic table. The two Johnson Brothers themselves were standing at the window of the corner office on the third floor. I saw more black men in my future at Johnson Brothers.

* * * *

As I looked up at that window, I realized that I'd never seen Clarence and Maurice Johnson alone—I only saw them in tandem. They attended meetings together; whenever they were in the lunchroom, they were together; whenever they left for lunch, they left together. When one went golfing from the office, so did the other one. It was almost like they were Siamese twins. They did look like identical twins. The same meaty, but nicely proportioned build. The same bull necks and bald bullet-like heads. The same smirky smile, following a tandem track, as they watched me walk in the corridors in the days immediately after my public fucking on the picnic table by the shipping department.

Days later their secretary called me and told me to meet them in the lobby—that they wanted to take me out to lunch and give me my three-month initial performance evaluation. I wasn't surprised to see them both there in the lobby, wearing identical business suits and smiles as I exited the elevator.

Their limo drove us way out into the Watts area, deep into a section I've never dared travel in before. I probably should have felt safe in the limousine, but I was sitting in the center of the backseat with a big black man about twice my bulk hemming me in tight on both sides, each looking at me with an identical "could eat you up" grin. I was relieved when the limousine pulled up in front of the restaurant—although there was really no reason I should have felt relief. The block looked derelict and the street was littered with—well, litter. The sign over the one-story, windowless building hunkered between a sleazy-looking liquor store and a parking lot read "Club Doblar" in green neon lights, with the light out on the "B."

The light inside was dim, the furnishings something out of a 1950s burlesque house—and all of the clientele other than me looked very, very black—and very, very male. I felt all eyes on me as we were guided to a table near a small stage with a curtain in back of it.

The Johnson brothers ordered drinks—identical brands of beer, and, being keyed up and on edge, I made that three of the same.

The lights went down even lower—except for the spots on the curtain—and then the curtain drew back and I gasped in shock.

I wasn't the only white man in the establishment. There was now a young white guy on the stage as well—completely naked. And there was a naked black guy under him, working his ass with a black cock, and another naked black guy saddled up over his spread legs, and the audience was getting a clear shot—to the accompaniment of bump and grind music, of a dance of double penetration by the black guys in the white guy's ass.

155

I started to pant and continued to gasp, as the Johnson brothers, one on each side of me, came in closer to me and were wrapping their arms around my shoulders and running their hands all over my body—and eventually meeting their fingers at my crotch.

The eyes of the white guy on the stage were as big as saucers, and his mouth was formed in a big "O" of consternation and emitting a yip, yip sound of being stretched to within an inch of endurance, as the black cocks buried themselves deeper into his hole and started a rhythmic pumping in concert with the bump and grind music.

I wasn't around for the finish, because the entertainment had gotten the Johnson brothers all hot and bothered and I was being hustled through a door covered with a beaded curtain at the back of the room and through a dim, narrow corridor. I was pulled into a small room with a red-velvet-covered dais in the center and full-length mirrors on the walls and ceiling and beeping video cameras at various levels on the walls.

Clarence was working my lips with his and undressing and squeezing and prodding me with what seemed to be a dozen hands, while brother Maurice was stripping himself and laying down on the dais on his back and working up his cock.

Before I knew it, Clarence was sitting me down on Maurice's cock, facing away from his chest, and Maurice wrapped his arms around me and pulled my shoulder blades back to his chest and was stroking his cock up inside me and making me moan and groan. Clarence stood below us and stripped down and worked up his cock. And then he was moving in, straddling Maurice's thighs and pushing mine up and spreading them with his hands. And his cock head was at my already-filled hole as well. And I was crying out and being invaded by a second cock—and pumped and pumped and pumped. I watched myself get double fucked by my hulky black employers, the Johnson Brothers, from all angles in the mirrored walls and ceiling as the video cameras beeped away. My mouth formed a big "O" just as the white guy's on the stage had, and I was yip yipping my stretching and the feel of two cocks in counter fucking motion inside me.

I was indignant and in shock, yes. But if I said I didn't enjoy it—not least just because I survived it—I'd be lying. So I won't say any more about that experience.

I will say, however, that two days later, when I was invited up to the Johnson Brothers' office near closing time and was met by a naked Clarence and Maurice—and introduced to their third brother, an equally naked larger version of them named Roosevelt—and I could see the videos of my double fucking in the Club Doblar running on a couple of TV screens in the background, I decided that this had snowballed far enough. I beat a hasty retreat and mailed in my resignation letter from New York City.

Stalker

From the moment I saw Gideon in the locker room, my life was focused on becoming his lover. I hadn't been at the Mount Holly prep school for more than a week before I first laid eyes on him, although I began to hear about him from my first evening. And what I heard about him very likely set me up for this obsession of mine.

Mount Holly was a post-high school, two-year prep school for athletes who had been offered college scholarships but whose grades were not yet up to par for entry into the Carolina coast universities the school fed into. I had actually started out at another of the feeder prep schools, Jackson Hall, up in southern Virginia, but I was pulled out of that after two months because of the coach-students sex scandal that threatened my promised basketball scholarship. I had never been linked to the football coach and student players involved in the scandal, but it had been that same coach who had taught me to take the cock and had made me realize which way I swung. I'd always suspected as much through my high school days, but it was Coach Vance who had taken a special interest in giving me late-night instruction on my ball handling—and in handling his balls and cock as well.

Although my parents had moved me to Mount Holly in a panic, my already having felt cock inside me in my previous school and that fact having been broadcast, I had no intention of not seeking it out here. And so it was with particular interest that I had heard on my first night in the dorm that the upperclassman and football team quarterback, Gideon Grant, was the premier cocksman of the school—that his appetites were voracious and that he could get any tail he wanted on the strength of his extraordinarily good looks and cut body, his self-assuredness, his position as top jock in an all-jock school, and his supersized equipment.

The football and basketball teams were practicing the same afternoon on my first Tuesday at the school, the football squad out on the playing field, and the basketballers in the gym. Basketball practice finished first, and we'd showered and were sitting on the benches in front of the team's lockers with towels wrapped around us. I was becoming more deeply introduced to several of my teammates—all of them ogling the new guy and considering the possibilities—when the football squad entered—or more accurately burst—into the locker room and past us in a swirl of muddy sweats en route to their own locker area on the other side of the entrance into the shower room, where clouds of steam were trailing out into the division between the two teams' changing areas.

I knew in an instant which one was Gideon Grant. It was as if he walked in his own spotlight, surrounded by a swirl of sycophants, but isolated from them in a circle of untouchability. He'd stripped off his jersey upon entering the locker room, and he was all blond radiance, tall and bulky, but perfectly cut. A powerful body that demanded attention. I instantly knew I wanted him to fuck me.

He stopped when he drew up beside the group I was chatting with, and the cacophony of laughter and raunchy banter that had accompanied the football team's entrance into the locker room quickly tapered off to near silence. He was surveying us, and I nearly melted on the spot. But I was sitting, straddling the wooden bench, and a couple of the other guys were standing, leaning up against their lockers. And one or two had already dropped their towels—for my benefit, I thought, so I don't think Gideon's eyes took me in at all. If they had, I'm sure my chances would have been good at catching his interest. I'd never had reason to question my ability to get a man to notice me. Coach Vance certainly hadn't wasted any time in getting me alone on a weight bench.

"Charlie," Gideon called out—and even his rich baritone voice turned me on. "Can you give me a hand in the shower?" It was a question, but it didn't really come out as a question. It came out as a statement with a foregone conclusion.

Charlie, who had been standing behind me and a bit to my right, a hand on his open locker door, his towel dropped to his feet, and in the process of reaching into his locker for his briefs, gave a little jerk and turned and smiled a shy "caught-in-the-headlights" smile. But he was quick enough to follow Gideon into the shower, stepping over the sweat pants and jock strap and cleats and socks Gideon was peeling off along the way—and leaving his own towel where it lay in front of his locker.

I waited only a few minutes before I disengaged from chatting with my team mates and meandered purposely over to the tiled frame of the doorway into the shower and peeked in. Charlie was down on his knees in front of Gideon, who was standing under the spray jet of water and soaping himself up—and clearly enjoying the blow job Charlie was giving him.

The other football players who were piling into the shower acted as if the scene was completely natural and were going about their business in a swirl around Gideon and Charlie, although their business did include lascivious looks, randy talk, and feeling each other up in an easy, familiar way as if this was how all of their practices ended—and no doubt that was how a good many of them did end.

I couldn't help myself. I ran my hand up under the edge of my towel and slowly masturbated, aching for Gideon to pay me the attention he was paying the gurgling and groaning Charlie.

When Gideon and Charlie came out of the shower and went into the team room rather than back to their lockers, I moved with them. And I was there, watching and coupling with them in spirit, as Gideon gently pushed Charlie onto his back on top of the metal conference table in the center of the small room, spread Charlie's legs, and slow-fucked him with one of the meatiest cocks I'd ever seen. Charlie gasped and moaned and begged for the fucking, while Gideon made love to him as slowly and languidly—and totally—as I could have hoped for in Charlie's place. It surprised me that an athletic hunk like Gideon would make love like that rather than roughly taking Charlie, and this revelation only added to my quickly developing obsession that it would be me.

I watched Charlie, eye's slitted and sighing and moaning, as Gideon paid attention to his nipples while his dick slid in and out of Charlie's channel in long, slow strokes, and I noticed that I wasn't the only one taking an interest in the scene. As the other footballers left the showers, several of them entered the room, brushing past me, and formed something of a line along the wall and watched . . . and waited.

At length, when Gideon had grunted and his firm butt cheek globes had jerked, signaling his climax, I learned what the others were waiting for. Gideon pulled out of Charlie's channel, gave him an affectionate pat on the hip, and turned and walked straight out of the room, past me, not seeming to be looking at me at all.

But I'll have to admit that in that moment, I was not looking at Gideon walking close to me in all of his naked magnificence, because my attention was riveted to the center of the team room, where the naked football players were lining up behind the black fullback who was insinuating his pelvis between Charlie's spread thighs. I heard Charlie cry out and arch his back in response to the thrust of a jet-black cock inside the hole Gideon had already stretched before I turned and padded back toward the football team's side of the locker room. Gideon's taking had just been prelude to the team putting Charlie on the string.

"Hi," I said as I moved toward the bench where Gideon was now sitting and pulling socks onto his feet. "I'm Sean. Just arrived this week. New to the basketball team."

"Hello, Sean," Gideon muttered, but he didn't even look up.

"I've seen you play," I said, reaching idiotically for any small talk I could muster. "I've come from Jackson Hall—you guys creamed us last year."

"Yes, yes, we did," Gideon answered. "Gonna cream Jackson Hall this year too. Bunch of wimps."

"Yes, I agree," I said. "I never . . ."

"Pretty agreeable, aren't you buddy?" Gideon said, and now he looked up at me. "And pretty anxious to get an eyeful too, aren't you?"

Oh god. I'd gotten off on the wrong foot already. I'd been standing there with my tongue hanging out, watching him get serviced, and I'd left the impression I salivated over him. The fact that it was the truth was beside the point.

"Gotta go . . . Sean, was it?" Gideon said, now fully dressed and ready to stride out. "Welcome to Mount Holly, Sean. Try to learn not to look too needy, though. That's got Jackson Hall written all over it."

And then he was gone. As I passed the team room on my forlorn, worst-introduction-possible trudge back to my locker, I looked in and saw that Charlie now had a footballer at his head with his dick face-fucking Charlie's mouth and there was a Hispanic lineman between his legs now. And then, when one guy laid on his back on the table and Charlie was lowered on his cock face up and I saw another of the guys approaching Charlie from the front and beginning to work a second cock inside Charlie's hole, to the tune of loud moans and groans from Charlie, I couldn't watch anymore and had to turn away. I'd have half a notion of trying to intervene, assuming that this was more than Charlie had agreed to, but as I walked down the corridor, I heard what clearly was Charlie's voice shouting out, "Yes, Yess. Gititgititgitit! God! Move 'em both!"

Welcome to Mount Holly, I thought. But my next thought—and the one after that—was of Gideon Grant and his magnificent body and cock and of how I was going to go about winning him over to me.

I blush to think how obsessed I became with Gideon Grant in the following weeks and the lengths I went to to try to get him to pay attention to me—and to want me as badly as I wanted him.

I transferred to some of his classes; I found out where and when he studied in the library and tried always to be near him. I mapped out his schedule for moving around campus and followed him—to the point that he noticed I was there and scowled at me and tried to vary his movement schedules. But I always caught on to the changes, and, although I tried to be more discrete in following him when I saw how much it annoyed him, follow him I did. I dressed like the guys did who Gideon paid attention to. I tried to change my sport from basketball to football to be close to him, but the coaches would have none of that. I should have been flattered that the basketball coach said I was too valuable to his team, but all I could think of was all of that lost time I'd be in the gym and Gideon would be out on the practice field.

I tried every angle I knew of to get close to him—to let him know not only that I was available, but that I was good, worthy of being selected. I even seduced his roommate, Jonas, with the hope that Jonas would tell Gideon what a good lay I was.

Jonas was among those who had gangbanged Charlie that first day I'd seen Gideon in the locker room, so I knew he was attainable. He liked to study in the park. So I started sunning myself in the park not too far from him. And then one day I volunteered to exercise Professor Taylor's dog for him, and I took the dog to the park and played Frisbee catch with him wearing nothing more than skimpy silken gym shorts.

By that day, I had gotten Jonas to study me as much as his books. I worked my way over to the edge of the woods, and when I could see that Jonas was looking at me real good, I leashed the dog to a tree and turned and looked real hard at Jonas. He was up on his feet before I had pulled my gym shorts down to my knees. I then turned and walked into the forest.

Jonas caught up with me in a shady glen of ferns and fucked me like he hadn't had sex in a month. And I gave him everything he wanted and treated him like he was the king of the mountain, pulling him down on top of me, giving his cock special attention as I crowned it with a condom, and rolling my pelvis up to him. Telling him what a big man he was, pulling him into me, and working his throbbing cock with the muscles of my channel so that he fucked me with a frenzy and drained his balls in a fountain of cum.

We met in the woods frequently after that, but, alas, I never got the impression that whatever he told Gideon of our couplings had any effect on Gideon's attitude toward me at all.

The closest I came to having sex with Gideon by way of Jonas was the day I maneuvered Jonas to take me in their shared room. I was up on my knees, my chest flat on his bed, and Jonas behind me and between my thighs, probing me deep, when, as I hoped, Gideon came into the room. He watched us briefly and then stripped down—and my groans and moans at this point were for him rather than Jonas. But when Gideon had worked his cock hard as he watched us, instead of taking Jonas's place, he stepped up behind Jonas. And soon Jonas was writhing and groaning and grunting, and I sensed that his thrusts inside me were being driven by Gideon's cock inside Jonas.

I was given no time to revel in this nearness of Gideon, because Gideon pulled Jonas off me and turned him onto the other bed, and the two of them were deep into their own world of long-practiced sex, leaving me unfinished and frustrated. When I left the room, they were still going at it, and I don't think Gideon even knew who had been there with Jonas to begin with—and worse, even if he knew, he obviously didn't care.

I should have given up. I should have just stopped pursuing Gideon Grant. It was clear that if he was going to choose me, it wouldn't be because of what I was doing. But I couldn't stop. He had become an obsession for me.

I thought that at least I would connect with him one Saturday night when he and a group of guys from the football squad went off campus—and off their training—at a bar in town that definitely was off limits to the college students because it was a well-known male pickup joint. I followed them, however, at a distance. And I couldn't help myself when they went into the bar. I went in too. They were settling themselves around a table near a front corner of the room, and when I entered I tried not to make it too obvious I was following them and walked straight back to the bar and ordered a beer—which, of course, I wasn't supposed to have. But Gideon had me tied up in knots and I needed something to either calm me or numb me—I'd settle for either at the moment.

After taking the beer from the bartender and taking a swig, I turned and there he was, on the stool next to me, looking at me with a half smile, and looking oh so radiant—Gideon Grant.

"You've been following me," he said.

"Have I?" I squeaked. "It's a small campus. Maybe . . ."

"No, you've been stalking me. That's not nice. What do you want?"

I had no shame. "You, just you. Like I've seen you take other guys," I said in a small, pitiful voice.

"I don't like being stalked," he said gruffly. "If you get fucked, will you leave me alone?"

"If you want me to afterward," I responded in the bravest tone I could muster. An audition was all I wanted. I just knew that after he'd fucked me once, he'd want to do it again. That was what I was counting on, what I was living for.

"Come into the back room," he said. And he stood and turned and motioned to the guys who had come in with him. They all stood up.

I was frightened then. I wasn't thrilled about having an audience, but if that's the way Gideon wanted to do it, that's the way we'd do it. I'd take him anyway I could get him.

Things started going off the rails as soon as we'd gotten into the back room, which had a pool table in the center and a few straight chairs scattered around.

I had expected Gideon to start working me as soon as we were in the room and stripped down, but he didn't. I felt the fear creep up my spine as, naked now himself—as the rest of the guys crowded in the small room were getting naked as well—Gideon turned a chair and straddled it backwards, facing me with a sneery grin on his face.

"Get him ready, why don't you, Pete?" Gideon muttered in a throaty voice. "He'll want to be wide open."

A beefy black lineman from the football team turned me roughly toward the pool table and pushed me down on top of it. He went on his knees behind me and his tongue went to my hole and a fist grabbed my balls in a bunch, and I didn't have to be told he'd crush them for me if I struggled. Another of the guys came up under me, crouched between the pool table and my spread legs and swallowed my cock and worked it with his teeth and tongue.

All the time Gideon was sitting there, pulling on his cock, and giving me a wicked grin.

I couldn't wait until Pete had opened me up with his tongue. I wanted Gideon inside me so bad.

"OK, when you're ready, Pete," Gideon said in a low, menacing voice. "You can go first."

Pete go first? The realization of what was going to happen now went racing through my head. A repeat of what Charlie got back there in the locker room on the first day of practice. Only Charlie had gotten Gideon first. When was Gideon going to fuck me? I didn't care what any of the others did—as long as Gideon fucked me. My obsession knew no bounds.

One after the other, Gideon's football team chums fucked me on the pool table—the first couple from behind and then I was turned onto my back and a couple took me missionary style.

All the time Gideon sat there, smiling that sneery smile of his and working his meat. His cock was gigantic and gorgeous. I couldn't wait to have it inside me. I had nearly worked through the roster of those present. Gideon's turn couldn't be long in coming now. It was what I had been waiting for, what I had endured this gangbang for.

And then I was being lifted from the table, the team's star fullback's cock still deeply encased inside me. He was holding my pelvis to his, his wide palms on my butt cheeks. I had my fists locked behind his neck and was climbing his hips with my thighs, trying to stay in place as he rose in a standing crouch. He was spreading my cheeks with the palm of his hands, and I felt the presence of someone coming close in behind me. And I opened my mouth wide in surprise and pain and started to bellow as a second hard cock was worrying my hole, trying to enter. I went rigid.

"Relax, sport," the fullback was whispering in my ear. "If you don't relax, you're gonna be split for sure."

And so I relaxed—or as close to that as I could. And I looked over to where Gideon was sitting. But he was gone now. For the briefest second I assumed he was the guy behind me, the bulb of his cock now inside me, the fullback's cock holding steady, as the second one fought for entrance. But then I saw Gideon over by the door, pulling on his T-shirt over his shorts. And moving for the door.

He wasn't even going to stay and watch me being stretched to the limit by two cocks. He was that contemptuous of me. I should have hated him. But I didn't; I wanted him now more than ever.

But I couldn't think of that right now. All of my senses were focused on the second cock slowly moving up inside me. And the embrace of two meaty bodies, the two men now in a deep kiss over my shoulder. And then the slow pumping of the second cock started, and I was moaning and groaning and begging for mercy. The first cock started a countermotion pumping—and I was crying out. Opening to them. Feeling what I'd never felt before inside me. Exulting at taking two cocks and at the sounds of passion coming in stereo on either side of me. And crying out now for . . . the . . . fuck . . . of . . . my life. All the time knowing still that it would be so much better when Gideon was fucking me.

I couldn't put my legs together for two days following my visit to the tabooed pickup bar. I had to hobble around campus to my classes, to the library, and to basketball practice, where the coach excused me from floor practice for three days with a smile that told me that he knew exactly what had happened to me and a look I knew so well that told me that he'd be sniffing around me himself for his share in the near future.

And all of the shuffling around campus was because I was still following Gideon Grant. I was obsessed as always—no, more so. There was nothing rational about it. I had no excuses for my behavior. It was just what I had to do. If someone had told me three months earlier that I would become a stalker, I would have told them they were crazy. But even now, knowing it was me who was crazy, I didn't care. I lived for Gideon to look my way, to beckon to me with his hand, to take me to paradise.

The Candy Shop

For some time Dwight had told me that when the time came, when I'd reached eighteen, and if I was still interested, he'd take me to the Candy Shop for the first time. I tried to tell him that he was candy enough for me, but Dwight was an honorable man. That's the only reason why we ever needed to discuss the Candy Shop at all.

The Candy Shop was out on Route 96, beyond the edge of town, and just inside the next county—a much poorer county than ours that needed the revenue and was willing to turn a blind eye. The building it occupied originally had been one of those full-service trucker stops. A gas station out front, whose pumps now had plastic bags permanently over the handles and their gauges zeroed out and just sat there under sagging awnings, rusting away. Inside the storefront had been a combined convenience store and short-order cook counter with a dining area off to the side with a widescreen TV where the truckers could stop to watch and bet on televised sporting events to break up the monotony of their long hauls and to catch up on the gossip of where the cop speed traps were along Route 96. In the back were a communal shower room truckers could use on long, time-sensitive hauls for a minimal fee and eight small rooms where, for less than they would have to fork out for a motel, they could rent rooms with clean sheets and towels by the hour. This served their schedule well. They rarely were able to pull over for a whole night; they had to sleep in three- and four-hour snatches in order to get their loads to their destinations on time.

It didn't take too long before the girls behind the food counter and at the convenience store register were augmenting their incomes by adding a fringe benefit of a fuck to go with the by-the-hour rooms. And there were few truckers who didn't appreciate this release of tension in addition to a couple of hours of sleep in a real bed. But this led to the whole operation being shut down, as the local residents put their own sense of morality over the smooth operation of trucking operations.

The place remained dormant for a couple of years and then the Candy Shop moved in, and the commissioners of the poorer county, seeing the folly of letting a revenue-paying business go bust like the trucker stop had done, turned a blind eye on the Candy Shop as long as it was bringing in revenue.

And bring in revenue it did.

When Dwight drove me out there, there must have been more than two dozen cars parked there, although we didn't see them until we'd swung around to the back of the building, where just about everyone going to the Candy Shop parked his car—out of sight of those driving down the highway.

As we came around the side of the building, though, I saw that there were maybe half a dozen guys milling around the old gas pumps and eyeing everyone coming into the Candy Shop. When we showed up, most of them broke off their discussions and ogled Dwight and me up and down. Three of them came up to Dwight and started talking to him, and four of them surrounded me. They asked me if I'd come for candy and said I didn't have to go into the store—that any of them would be happy to give me a ride in their car and some candy as well.

"Haven't seen you around here, son," said one guy, who looked like a trucker left over from the building's last life. "First time to the Candy Shop?" he asked.

"Umm, yes," I said. I looked over at Dwight, who seemed to be having a little difficulty with those three guys

172

trying to get up close. I wasn't really worried about him being able to take care of himself, though. Dwight had been football player and had kept in tip-top shape. I was sort of worried, though, because there were three of them and they were all white. Dwight was what you'd call a mulatto—his father had been black and his mother white, which had left him with the facial features of a Caucasian but with a rich coffee-and-cream brown skin color. One of the guys around him was pretty drunk, and was talking about dipping in the chocolate in a fairly loud voice. The other two seemed to be less belligerent—one had his wallet out and was fanning a wad of bills out where Dwight could see it.

From the looks Dwight was giving me, I think he was more concerned about those four guys trying to make small talk with me, though.

Another of the guys had put on a big smile when I said it was my first visit to the Candy Shop. He was a surfer type with dirty blond stringy hair and shorts and flip-flops. No shirt; he had a good tan and a good build, so I didn't think I was far off on the surfer supposition. "First time for the candy?" he asked. His voice had a hopeful edge to it.

"Yeah," I said. "Just turned eighteen last week and Dwight here wouldn't let me have the candy until now."

The surfer dude sucked in air and then turned and waved to the other guys over at the gas tanks. "First time for the candy over here guys. And a just-ready batch. Anyone who's interested, let's pool our resources and see what kinda deal we can make."

Dwight stepped in at that point, however. "Let's go on in to the store, Jason," he said. He had moved away from the group of guys he was talking with and put his hand on my arm and guided me toward the store entrance.

"Hey, man. We've got money," one of the gas pump guys called out. "More than enough for both of you."

"Sorry, guys," Dwight called out over his shoulder. "Gotta do this right. This here's my boy."

"I was doing fine, Dwight," I hissed at him was we walked away from the group. "They weren't bothering me."

"I swear I have no idea how I've gotten you to eighteen untouched," Jason muttered back. "Do you want to do this right or not? The first time is all important."

"I know it is," I shot back. "So, what are we doing here at all? You know what I want."

"It's just too important," Dwight answered. "You have to be sure. It only happens once. You need to see the choices before you make one."

That was always the problem with Dwight and me. Dwight had always been more of a father to me than my own dad had been—but that's not what I'd ever wanted from Dwight. I'd had what you could called a really screwed up home life, but Dwight—who my mother had seen as the cause of it all—was actually the only steadying force in my life for the past three years. And I had known from the beginning what I wanted from Dwight.

Dwight and my dad had been on the same semipro football team, one that had spent more time on the road in small cities far from home than they'd spent at home. Mom blamed what had happened between her and Dad on those separations—and on Dwight. That's not the way I had seen it. Dad did what Dad wanted to do because he wanted to do it. And if it hadn't been with Dwight, it would have been with someone else.

I could see that and Mom couldn't, and she and I fought so much over that point that I guess it was easy for her to leave me with Dad and Dwight when she packed up and left the state. We still talked occasionally, but not much at all in the last two years. When Dad had been killed in that freak busted play on the football field in Richmond and Mom had called and told me she was sending a ticket for me back to Fresno and I told her I wanted to stay with Dwight—and why I wanted to stay with Dwight—she hung up on me and hasn't spoken to me since. All there were were occasional terse e-mails asking if I'd changed my mind or threatening what she'd do if there was a hint of Dwight stepping out of line with me. For some time, I was terrified that she would step in and do something to make me come to her, but that hadn't happened.

And now that I was eighteen, there was nothing she could do about it.

In the meantime, Dwight had been a dad to me. He'd quit his football career, which showed some promise to stepping up to the NFL, and had settled in as a football coach at a small college—all to give me a settled life in school. He'd even made sure I got a place in the college for the coming fall.

And in all that time, even though I told him what I wanted from him, he hadn't laid a hand on me. I'd seen him with Dad and that's what I wanted too—and not just with anyone; only with Dwight.

Dwight wanted me to be sure, though, and he wanted my first taste of candy to be perfect. So, here we were, walking through the door of the Candy Shop.

We walked in, stood inside the door for a moment, and scanned the store. The store was laid out in a long rectangle with a counter cutting it in two almost in the middle. On the side the entrance door was on were a series of small malt-shop type tables with café chairs. Several of the tables were occupied—all by men, mostly one per table. Half of the section of the counter separating the two sections was made up of glass-fronted cabinets with displays of candy in them. The rest of the counter was set up as an ice cream shop.

A couple of men stood behind the counter, ready to take orders, but, somewhat strangely, there were several guys sitting in the large space behind the counter, in the area that had once been the truckers' dining area, who were sitting and watching a big screen TV, probably the same one that had been there when the truckers' rest stop occupied the space. They didn't appear to be involved in selling candy or ice cream at all—they were just sitting there waiting for something to happen. There were all types of men and even a couple of guys who looked as young as Jason was. Those younger guys looked a little nervous and fidgety.

Jason started toward an empty table, but Dwight put his hand on his arm and murmured that Jason should stand over by the candy displays for a while until he got an idea of what he really wanted.

As Jason moved over there, a middle-aged man walked up to the candy counter and perused the display. A salesman came over and stood behind the counter.

"What is your pleasure, sir?" he asked.

"Umm, I'm not sure. I'm checking out what you have."

"Well, we have available quite a variety today," the salesman said. "We have the nut-centered chocolates in white chocolate and a limited supply of the milk chocolate. The dark chocolate should be available in an hour or two if you wish to wait for it."

"Routine, customer bottom," Dwight whispered to Jason.

"Umm, no, I don't think so," the man muttered. "Perhaps something . . . well, a bit more special."

"There's the rope candy over here—the licorice or strawberry twists—we have a vanilla version as well. And the pull toffee of course."

The customer took a step away from the counter, almost visibly recoiling. "No, no. Not that, thanks."

"SM and bondage," Dwight muttered.

"Well, perhaps the cream centered, then. We have both white and dark chocolate on hand. And I think the milk chocolate will be coming back in shortly."

"I thought you'd stopped that line altogether," the man said.

"Well, I thought . . . since you mentioned special," the salesman answered. "We do still make those available. Of course we provide certificates—and the customer, of course, as well, needs to provide recent certification. But, we do still have that line, yes."

The customer looked dubious.

Meanwhile, another customer had sauntered up to the counter and drawn the attention of one of the other salesmen. He asked for vanilla rope candy and turned over a credit card. After running it through a machine, the salesman went back to the area behind the counter where the men were watching the TV and spoke with a swarthy-looking fellow who was on the thin side but all ropy muscle, bulging biceps, and angular facial features. That guy flashed a look over at the customer and nodded his head. He stood and moved toward a door at the end and inside the counter as the salesman guided the customer to a door on the storefront side of the counter.

When the swarthy guy went through the door behind the counter, a young blond guy in gym shorts and an athletic T came into the store through the same door. He was moving toward the section with the TV, when the salesman intercepted him and said something to him. Then the salesman called out "Vanilla Shake Number 6" and one of the guys sitting at the café tables stood. He went through the door the previous customer had gone through and the blond went out again through the door the swarthy guy had used.

Jason looked at Dwight quizzically, and Dwight whispered back to him. "Customer tops; Caucasian bottom. You're not really interested in any of the shakes, though, are you? Or am I wrong. That's why we're here. It's all your choice. I may not like it if you pick any of the string candy, and, even though I caution against the cream filled, it's your choice; You were tested and I've brought the certificate. Remember, we both got tested. Maybe barebacking the first time is the best way—as long as it is safe. It's certainly the most incredible feel."

"The cream filled?" Jason asked. He had noted that the middle-aged customer and salesman had discussed that briefly.

"Bareback, customer bottoming," Dwight answered tersely. "Customer doing the barebacking is some form of ice cream Sunday, I think. But . . ."

"Oh," Jason responded.

Jason turned his attention back to the middle-aged customer, who was still hemming and hawing at the candy counter.

"Do you wish to make a selection, sir?" the salesman asked politely, only slightly seeming to be trying to jolly the man along in the transaction. "If you wish to think about it further, you are certainly welcome to sit at one of the tables over there. Or if there's a particular piece of candy you have spied over there in the television room, I would be more than happy to tell you what kind of candy it is. Some can be more than one kind of candy, I'm sure you'll be happy to know."

"Well . . . I wondered . . . I heard," the middle-aged man said, evidently having something in mind but not being able to get it out. "I've heard of there being something . . . well . . . very special on offer."

"Ah, yes," the salesman said, with a smile on his lips that didn't extend to his eyes. "Perhaps you are referring to what we have under the counter here. We have here our double-dipped chocolates. We usually offer them in various combinations: white covering either milk or dark chocolate with either a nut or cream center. Or there also are double-dip shakes or Sundays. We, of course, don't have all combinations at all times, but if this is your interest, we could see if we have what you want."

Jason was trembling, so Dwight thought he'd figured it out, but he leaned over and whispered, "Threesomes," anyway. Jason just nodded.

The middle-aged man was shaking his head though and looking a little perturbed.

"Or would you perhaps mean our very, very special cherry chocolates?" the salesman went on to ask.

The middle-aged man took a handkerchief out of his pocket and wiped his forehead, but he was smiling. "Why, yes. That's exactly what I've heard about—that latter, the cherry chocolates. Do you . . . ?"

"Why, yes. We do have just two on offer today. And a choice. White or milk chocolate." The salesman had half turned and he was gesturing over to the TV area, a finger pointing to the two young men of about Jason's age, one Caucasian and one a light-skinned black, who were sitting and fidgeting and looking just slightly scared.

"Ah, yes. Nice, very nice. White . . . white chocolate, I do believe."

"Good choice," the salesman said. "A bit pricey though, of course."

"Do you take American Express?"

"Yes, yes, of course."

Moments later, credit card verified and signed for, the Caucasian youth went through the one door, the middle-aged man had gone through the other door, and the salesman approached Jason and Dwight.

"Yes, may I help you? Did you come for candy . . . or did you perhaps come to apply to be candy? I'm sure we would be happy to employ you—both of you. Shall I call the candymaker down?"

"Buying," Dwight said. "My young friend here is interested in some candy. But I understand there is a tour—for a fee? I want to make sure he chooses just exactly the candy he wants for his first time."

"His first time?" the salesman was practically salivating. "He has never had candy before? And such a handsome young man. Beautifully formed."

"No. Do you have such a tour—for a fee?"

"Of course, we would be happy for you to tour what is being made in the way of candy at the moment. We have several varieties being prepared. And, this being the first time for our very . . . lusciously sweet . . . young friend here, we would be happy to waive the fees. Please, please, just go through that door over there and take your time watching the candy being prepared. There are several rooms in operation and there are one-way windows in the walls into the rooms from the corridor. Please, please make yourselves comfortable."

While Dwight and Jason were walking back toward the door in which the middle-aged man had recently entered, the salesman was scurrying off toward a door beyond the television waiting area.

As they were walking through the door, Jason said, "I already have made my choice. We don't really . . ."

"This is important, Jason," Dwight said. "There can only be one first time. I want you to be very, very sure. So I want you to see what is really involved in this."

The first room they looked into was where the Vanilla Shake Number 6 customer had gone into with the young blond man who had obviously gone straight from one session to the

179

other. The blond was bent over a massage table, and the Number 6 customer was fucking him from behind in strong deep thrusts. The blond was gripping the edges of the table hard to keep himself in place. His head was turned away from the viewing wall, so Jason and Dwight had no idea how he was taking the thrusts, but customer Number 6 seemed to be enjoying himself.

In the next room, the swarthy man from the candy pool was fucking his customer in much the same vein, except that the customer's wrists and ankles were bound to hooks on the massage table and the swarthy string candy man had a riding crop that he was lightly beating on the customer's buttocks as he fucked him from behind. There were thin red welts already across the customer's back and his butt cheeks and he was making a good bit of noise.

The third room was where the middle-aged man and the Caucasian youth had gone. They were not very far into their session, but they had had time to strip and the youth was on his back on the massage table, and the middle-aged man, who was a little paunchy, but who had quite a thick and long—and very hard and rosy red—cock was standing on a stool that put his pelvis at the level of the youth's butt cheeks. The youth's near leg was hanging down over the foot of the massage table and the man was holding his other leg up and out with a fist around the youth's ankle. The man's dick head was just inside the rim of the youth's hole, and the youth was panting hard and arching his back and scrabbling at the edges of the massage table with his white-knuckled hands. He was crying out and groaning and moaning loud enough to be heard in the corridor.

Jason watched in fascination, knowing that this would soon be him too. He welcomed it; he had been looking forward to it, and only Dwight's strict substitute parenting had made him wait until now. Well, that and he didn't want to do anything that might have taken Dwight away from him. Jason could never be sure what his mother would do—whether she would make another stab at "saving" him before he turned eighteen, even though he'd told her in no uncertain terms what he wanted out of life.

As Jason and Dwight watched, the man managed to work his dick inside the virginal hole several inches. The youth was writhing and begging for mercy, but when the man half-heartedly asked him if he should stop or at least take it slower, the youth cried out "no"—that he could not get his fee unless the candymaker was assured that the customer had gotten full value and that the youth had applied for this.

As the man bottomed inside the youth and began to slowly pump him, the youth's writhings gradually turned to undulations of his own hip action. The man moved up onto the surface of the massage table with his knees, moving them under the youth's buttocks and thus raising the youth's hips. Then the man grabbed the youth's hips and pulled him back and forth, slowly on the impaling cock. The youth shuddered and his cock spouted off up onto the man's belly. The man pulled the youth's torso up to his and they were kissing when the man's turn to shudder came.

Dwight had to pull Jason away from that window and to the only other room in operation at the moment. Here, there was a threesome that appeared to be just finishing—or at least changing positioning. Two men, one Caucasian and one a deep brown, were standing in the center of the room, facing each other, both of them bent at the knees in a half crouch. And between them was suspended a third, older man, impaled on both of the other two men's cocks. The customer looked absolutely wilted and totally used, but there was a sloppy grin on his face.

"Double dipped white and dark chocolate," Jason murmured.

As they watched, the two men pulled the customer off their uncrowned cocks and laid him gently down on his side on the massage table.

"Ah, cream centered too," Dwight said.

The dark-skinned man had moved to other side of the table and stepped up on a stool. He pulled the customer's pelvis to his, lifted the customer's leg, and thrust his dick into the customer's ass, as the Caucasian candy man stepped up on a stool on the near side at the head of the customer and presented his cock for sucking.

Dwight pulled Jason away from the window. "I rather hope . . ."

"Don't worry, Dwight," Jason said. "No, that doesn't appeal to me. I've really made up my . . ."

"Come back out front, Jason," Dwight interrupted him. "We can sit at a table for a few minutes, and you can think this through."

Jason wanted to complete his sentence, but he decided not to. He just shrugged and followed Dwight back out into the shop front. Dwight would have to face up to reality pretty soon anyway.

They were met by a small delegation. There to greet them, big smiles on their faces, were the salesman they had talked to and an officious-looking gentlemen who obviously was the chief candymaker. And fanned out around them, wearing smiles that were a bit more lust filled, were a half dozen of the customers who had been sitting at the tables contemplating their choice of candy.

The chief candymaker stepped forward. "I hear this is our young friend's first candy," he said. He was looking at Dwight for affirmation.

"Yes," Dwight answered.

"You wouldn't perhaps have a certificate on him, would you?"

"Yes," Dwight answered. "Both of us have a clean bill of health certificate in hand. But I . . ."

The candymaker was quivering with delight at that news, and the men fanned around him were ooing and ahhing and jockeying a bit with each other for frontline position.

"Well, perhaps I have a little offer—for both of you handsome men—you are both premium candy, worthy of our gourmet line. Perhaps you don't have to spend any money here today at all. Your young friend here has already elicited several cherry chocolate offers—at as much as four times the going rate if cream center is included. Which we would, of course, split. I don't know when I've seen as ripe a cherry for plucking as this. And you yourself, sir, have been the subject of a couple of requests—also at a very good rate—premium milk chocolate nut or cream centered, as desired. Perhaps if we could . . ."

"I'm sorry," Jason spoke up before Dwight could answer. "I'm very interested in a cream-filled milk cherry chocolate. But not in this candy shop, thanks. I have my own candy shop. Come, Dwight, take me home, please. I made my choice of candy before you brought me here."

Not very much later, a naked Jason was stretched out in the center of Dwight's king-sized bed, and Dwight was making love to him, chocolate on white, and slowly kissing and tonguing him from ears to toes, exploring every crease and curve, while Jason sighed. Jason's proud, young cock was already at full salute and his hips were undulating in the instinctive dance of the fuck when Dwight's lips went down over his cock head and his tongue flicked in and out of Jason's piss slit.

Anxious and long suffering as he was for this moment, Jason came almost immediately, and Dwight swallowed his essence and sighed in appreciation.

Young and virile as he was, however, Jason didn't go soft. Dwight turned him on his belly and Jason raised his pelvis, his weight supported on his chest and on his knees, as Dwight's lips and tongue went to his young, virginal ass opening and one hand played with Jason's taut nipples and the other slowly worked Jason's cock, rubbing the bulb across the red satin sheets Dwight had not used since he had last fucked Jason's father just like this.

Jason began to moan from deep down inside his chest. This was how he had watched his father being taken by Dwight. This was exactly what he'd wanted Dwight to do to him for years. This was the perfect first time.

Jason came again as his cock head was being fucked against the sheets and Dwight's tongue was fucking him deep in the ass.

And still Jason didn't go soft. He had dreamed of this for years. He had been building toward this almost forever. The mere thought of Dwight fucking him kept him hard.

Dwight was covering Jason close from behind with Jason on his knees on the red satin sheets and the underside of Dwight's hard cock stroking up and down in Jason's butt crease, rubbing across the puckered hole Dwight had already opened and slathered with his tongue.

The moment of deflowering had come, but Jason gave a little laugh and turned underneath Dwight and scooted down across the sheets until his mouth found Dwight's big, thick, hard cock. And Jason opened his mouth and brought his lips over Dwight's cock and sucked him inside.

Dwight, taken completely by surprised, groaned and then moaned and then sighed as Jason palmed his butt cheeks and started Dwight's hips in a languid face-fucking motion. Dwight soon took up the motion himself, slowly fucking his cock in and out of Jason's open mouth. It wasn't long before he started to shudder, though, and reaching down and grabbing Jason by the waist, dragged him back up the bed until their pelvises were in parallel.

Jason gave a little laugh and spread his legs, and Dwight, trembling from the effort not to spill his seed carelessly, moved his bulb to Jason's puckered hole as Jason raised his hips to meet him.

The momentous occasion was too much for Dwight, though. He barely had his bulb inside Jason's opening, with Jason arching his back and crying out at the hugeness of the bulb inside his virginal rim, than Dwight shuddered and came in great globs of cum at Jason's entrance.

Losing control then, and with his own cum as a natural lubricant, Dwight started slowly entering Jason, as Jason writhed under him and sobbed and moaned and groaned and grunted at his first glorious, long-awaited taking.

Like Jason, Dwight remained hard and was quickly reloading. Half inside, he stopped, wanting to give Jason's walls time to stretch to him, but Jason had waited for this too long. He dug his nails into Dwight's ass cheeks and pulled Dwight deeper inside him. And when Dwight had bottomed, it was Jason who pushed Dwight's hips up a bit, drawing his dick almost to Jason's entrance, and then Jason who moved his pelvis in a slow, but increasingly rapid, pumping action. Jason fucking himself on Dwight's impaling staff, as Dwight held position above him, but dipping his face down to Jason for deep kisses on the lips and nuzzling in the hollow of his young lover's neck and then down further to suck on Jason's taut nipples.

They came nearly simultaneously—and in the next fucking as well, as Jason stretched out on the bed on his belly and Dwight rode his ass hard, skin of dick sliding upon skin of ass walls in an elating barebacking and the constant and prodigious flow of lubricating and filling semen—and the third time as well, when Jason lay on his back at the foot of the bed and Dwight held his legs wide and stood between his thighs and pistoned him to a frenzied completion as their eyes were locked in love. They fucked on through the night until almost dawn.

Before sleep stole up on them as Jason's ass was spooned into Dwight's belly, Jason murmured, "Surely you knew it was you and only you I wanted."

"I barely dared hope," Dwight answered. "I've held off all these years, but it was hard."

"But surely you knew," Jason repeated.

"I did hope," Dwight said. And then he gave a low, throaty laugh. "And yes, I prepared, in case it might be so. That's why I got the health certificate too—so that we could bareback, if my dream came true. And why I put these red satin sheets on my bed this morning. I wanted your first time to be special and to be completely your choice. But, yes, I did hope it would be me who plucked your cherry chocolate."

Jason laughed.

"But do you have any idea how much money we passed up in that candy shop?" Dwight whispered.

"I don't care, Daddy." Jason murmured. "Your dick inside me is worth all the money in the Candy Shop to me."

The Exchange Student

"Do you think we'll ever get him to do it, Alex?" Max asked. He moved his palm over the basket of his Speedo and made adjustments for what was expanding in there.

"I doubt it, Max," I answered. Turning onto my side on my chaise lounge, sitting close to his, beside the pool, I reached over and ran my hand under the waistband of his drying bathing suit. I found what I was searching for and pulled it out of his Speedo and fondled it while Max leaned over and gave me a deep kiss.

When we came up for air, I looked over across the pool, where Miguel, the pool boy, was raking the surface for debris with a long-handled pool rake. I wanted to see if he had his eye on us. And he did. Pretty good, I thought, for two fifty-something geezers. Both Max and I worked hard on our bodies. You don't run a highly profitable hands-on construction company from the front lines without keeping yourself in good shape. Max and I did it all—from adjusting architectural drawings, to constructing the houses, to decorating and furnishing them. And we did it as a couple—as a committed couple—and had been doing it that way for over twenty-five years. And no one—not the clients nor our contractors nor the guys we hired to work with us—most of whom were just like us—ever had a nasty thing to say about it—at least not to our faces.

Of course few of them knew the whole of it—what we really liked.

We'd built up a good business, lived in a mansion, and had no trouble hiring a pool boy who was happy to take cock from us. It's just that this one wasn't coming around to taking us both at once—which was our favorite fetish an which was what not everyone knew about us.

"It would be so nice if he'd do it," Max murmured. "Nice young guy like that; great butt. Luscious brown body and beefy dick."

"Yeah, but he's been pretty definite about it," I answered. "Takes us separately well enough."

"Just not quite 'it,' you know."

"Yep. But speaking of which, do you think this Thai exchange student we're scheduled to pick up tomorrow will—"

"Said he would in the e-mails. That hookup service claimed to match up with what we wanted."

"Yeah, still . . . claiming something just to get to the States is one thing and delivery is something else."

"Yeah, Chances are he won't even show. Well, we'll know tomorrow."

"Yeah, maybe. Or maybe he'll lead us on like Miguel here just to spin out how long he can stay in the States."

"Hey, about we just jump him and fuck him together right here. Together we're stronger than he is. Once it's done, he'll know how hot it is."

"Yeah, sure. Bad idea. We haven't had trouble up till now, and this is no time to start—especially with a willing bottom on the way. I know you're just joking anyway. We've never had to force anyone before. Money covers pretty much everything."

Max sighed and stretched out on his chaise as I slow-pumped him to a more-than-respectable length and girth.

"Is he watching us?" he asked, his voice getting thick with want.

"Yes." I answered. "And he looks interested. The way he's holding that pole but watching us rather than what he's doing, I wouldn't be surprised if he fell in."

188

"And then we could fight for who went into the pool to save him? If we save him together, maybe he'll take us together then," Max answered with a laugh. The laugh turned to a long moan, though, as I dipped my head down to his pelvis and let my lips open over the head of his cock and my tongue flicker at his piss slit.

"Or, I know, maybe he'd be willing to take you along with me."

"Don't even think about it, buddy," I answered, squeezing his balls until he yelped.

"I've done you with another guy before. That's how we met."

"Yeah, twenty-five years ago. I've gotten a lot more delicate down there since then. Another bad idea."

It was quiet for a couple of minutes other than the low slurping and gurgling sound I was making and the moans Max was emitting as I closed my mouth over Max's cock and pulled him deep inside me. I had cupped his balls in my hand and I squeezed gently and deep-throated him and held it there. Max was gasping and raising his hips to my face, and I felt the fingers of both of his hands run into my hair as he held my head steady, his throbbing cock buried to the root in my throat. I held until I felt a gag coming on and then I retreated—but only until my lips were covering just his cock bulb—and I applied pressure and flicked at his piss slit with my tongue.

Between gasps and jerks of his pelvis and the bunching of his fists in my hair, Max muttered all of the things a man will when he's getting a good blow job, and then his groans started again as I slowly swallowed him whole for a second time and held there as long as my gag reflex would allow. The third time I did this, Max lurched and cried out.

"Oh god. You do that one more time and I'll come."

I did it again, but, although he jerked and gasped as before, he didn't come.

"Liar," I said, as I came up off his cock. And then I laughed and pulled my mouth off his cock. I turned my head to see what Miguel was doing, and, sure enough, the pool rake had been dropped into the water and he was standing there, sort of crouched down a bit, his eyes bug eyed and trained on what I was doing to Max across the pool, and the front of his baggy swim trunks pulled down under his ball sac and his plump brown cock in his fist.

"You want to come or do you want to do Miguel?" I turned my head back to Max's face and whispered. "He looks about ready for it."

"We could try again," Max whispered back.

"OK. Let's give it a go. No reason not to try."

I pulled away from Max and rummaged around in the gym bag next to my chaise and fished out a couple of condom packets. I held them up for Miguel to see and gestured to Max. Miguel stripped off his swimming trunks, and by the time he had walked over to the diving board and leaned over it with his hands gripping the side of the board, Max was up and crouched behind him and working between the young hunk's butt cheeks with his tongue and fingers.

I laid back and pulled my cock out of my Speedo and pleasured myself to greater length and width as I watched my beautiful, full-muscled, gray-haired man arching Miguel's head back with a fist in his black curly hair as he pumped the Latin's ass hard with his thick cock.

After a while of this, Max leaned over and whispered something in Miguel's ear and must have gotten the response he wanted, because he changed positions with Miguel. Max was now lying flat on his back on the diving board and Miguel was straddling his pelvis with his hips, facing him, and riding his cock.

Max turned his head to me and smiled, and I understood what he was suggesting. Rising from my chaise, still fisting my cock, I stripped my Speedo off and then approached the fucking pair from the rear.

I stood over Max's thighs, straddling the land end of the diving board and moved my hands around under Miguel's armpits and latched onto his nipple rings. Nicely brown bodied and tightly muscled, he had an intriguing swirl-effect tattoo all on one side of his torso that led down from the hollow of his neck on one side and covered his shoulder and biceps and ran

190

down his side, ending in a snake tail pointing down from his navel to a very nice appendage that now was encased in one of Max's fists.

I brought my lips to the hollow of Miguel's neck where the tattoo started and nibbled him there, and he groaned in acceptance and raised his tattooed arm and cupped the back of my head. I was pinching and prodding his nipples and pulling at his nipple rings, and I held my cock against the small of his back and let the rhythm of the rise and fall of his own pelvis in countermotion to the fucking of Max's cock inside him, raise friction between my cock and the small of his back.

I moved the fingers of one hand down to his entrance and inserted them on either side of Max's moving cock, leaving little doubt what direction we were headed here.

For the briefest moment I thought it was going to work. I had Miguel pitched a bit forward toward Max's chest and I was moving my cock head down along the small of his back toward my goal—and Miguel was breathing hard and moaning.

But then he was muttering opposition and wriggling around and saying, "No, no. One at a time."

And not wanting to force the issue, I just stopped and held there, holding him in place as Max's thrusts became more rapid and deeper. I turned Miguel's face to me and captured his lips until he pulled away with a cry and creamed Max's chest, followed soon thereafter with Max lurching and filling a condom inside Miguel.

And then Max came out from underneath Miguel, and we turned Miguel on his back on the board and Max splayed himself over Miguel's body. They 69ed noisily as I crouched between Miguel's spread thighs and fucked him to my completion in the wake of Max's visitation there.

Miguel left quite pleased and with more money in his pocket than he thought he'd be making today, but I, for one, wasn't completely satisfied. And I didn't think Max was either.

We were hoping for better the next day when Max and I both appeared at the international arrivals area of the airport all showered and slicked up and trembling in anticipation.

It had been Max who had found the "seniors" Web site, ThaiMandate, on the Internet. It was a Southeast Asian-based one and provided a meeting ground for "seeking" men. And both Max and I understood that nearly all of the young guys—mostly Thai because of the origin of the site—posting there were looking for a sugar daddy to get them to a promised land—preferably the United States. Digging deep into the site, Max discovered a service it was claiming to run—called an exchange student program. Anyone who would front the money to get a young Thai guy into the States with enough evidence he was coming there to study at a college—plus would help him get enrolled—could have the services the two mutually agreed to—for a nice finder's fee, of course.

Max and I had plenty of money to burn, so we thought, what the hell, we'd give it a go for the right services.

We went over the profiles of all of the presentable young-looking guys and narrowed our choice to a solid, husky, handsome guy named Dao. A good part of why we picked him was because he said he bottomed, was interested in men between 50 and 70 (a sure sign of a hunt for a sugar daddy), and that he enjoyed "group" and experimentation.

We started a correspondence with him through the Web site's chat room and exchanged more pictures—his photos showing more intimate poses than the ones connected to his profile, and we being careful to always both be in the photos we sent him including nude shots and our full erections. Eventually, we got down to "will you take double?"

After his "no problem" response, we were off getting him enrolled in the local community college that would take anything that was breathing as long as it had the up-front tuition fee. And then we were negotiating with the folks behind the service, who, of course, took an up-front cut and then another cut off all of the legal and documentation fees to get Dao into the States on a student visa, and cleared to live with an American family under an exchange student program. Everyone understood that there would be some exchange of services for hosting the exchange student—but the authorities had no reason to be told that those services involved the "student's" spread ass.

When the customs area at the airport was emptying out, Max and I got a double surprise. All along we'd both thought this just wasn't going to happen—that it was a con—but the whole idea had made us hard and the great fucks we gave each other while contemplating it were well worth the expense—it had rejuvenated our sex life. So, our first surprise was that there was a young Thai guy coming out of Customs and signaling at the sign we were waving with "Dao Chula." on it. (There hadn't been room to run the tongue-twisting Chulalakornampat segment of his name.)

The second surprise—although we should have taken that possibility into account too—was that Dao wasn't the robust Dao of the pictures he'd sent. He was a very nice-looking young man, but he couldn't have been as much as five feet tall and he was as thin and willowy as a seedling.

He smiled bravely and just looked at us with a confused "I don't speak English" look on his face as, trying not to look too dismayed and angry, we attempted to sort out that we had every right to expect something else—a strong, broad-hipped guy able to soldier two cocks at once.

We had been duped. Not in any of the ways we had contemplated, but in a way we should have thought of. Internet posters do the "bait and switch" thing with photos all of the time. The joke was on us, and we'd assumed it might be, so Max and I quickly recovered—we'd already agreed that it would make a good story for the other guys in our circle of friends no matter what happened. It was too late to reticket Dao, so we decided to just take him home and make the return travel arrangements the next day. We'd have an expensive laugh over it, but that didn't mean we'd send him to school or give him a free pass into the States. Besides, he was a cute little piece. Unless he lied about everything, we'd each give him a ride that night for a return on our investment.

Once back in the house, we showed Dao the room where he could spend the night—but just one night, we tried to make clear. He wandered down the upstairs hall, looking into bedrooms and baths, with that "I've died and gone to heaven" look in his face. We left him reveling in one night of the American dream, and I went downstairs and into the kitchen to start up the celebration dinner we had planned to either mark how clever we'd been or to cover our defeat in style. Following behind me, Max, muttering his disappointment, grabbed a couple of beers from the fridge in the kitchen and then went out onto the sun porch that overlooked the swimming pool and our expansive backyard.

It was about twenty minutes later that I first heard the sounds. I thought Max had turned on the TV out on the porch or popped in one of those porn movies we had handy to help put our new conquests in the mood. But the sounds didn't stop, and they intruded into my attention while moving around and slicing this and putting that into the oven.

And I finally walked out to the porch to see what Max was doing.

Max was sprawled in one of the deep-cushioned rattan chairs pointed out toward the pool. Naked as a jaybird. His legs were bowed wide and his arms were hanging loosely down toward the floor over the arms of the chair. His head was slung back, resting on the back edge of the chair. The expression in his face conveyed sheer ecstasy.

Straddling his hips, also naked, and riding Max's cock like a rodeo champion was the thin, willowy Dao. He was looking as happy to be there as Max was.

I looked on, astonished, as Dao lifted himself nearly the whole length of Max's extra-long cock and then slammed down again in a repeated move that seemingly would take Max's dick bulb up under the diminutive Thai's chin.

Seeing me, Max opened his mouth and, after emitting a long, drawn-out moan of supreme satisfaction, muttered, "Nothing wrong with his English. Told me in no uncertain terms that he could take us both together. Doubles. Two dicks in one hole. His hole. Our dicks. Clear, no translation problem. Swears—and fucks—like a sailor."

And he was absolutely right. I was stripped in record time and not long afterward, crouched between Max's spread legs and behind the little Thai's back, I had raised his buttocks in the palms of my hands and pressed my cock head to his entrance above the root of Max's cock—and discovered that Dao was as juicy and loose as a goose and I could slide right in along Max's cock. I think I could have gotten another cock in there if we had one handy. This Thai guy certainly was well prepared.

Max gave a gasp and another long moan as I slid in along his tool, and our faces met over Dao's tiny shoulder and we kissed as our cocks made love to each other at the same time as they made love to Dao's slack channel. Dao was there, but Max and I were making love to each other.

Later, as we were taking seconds, Max and I both standing in the center of the porch and sandwiching and working Dao's supple little body between us as he encircled my waist with his legs, Dao's sing-song voice broke into our harmony of sighs.

"Dao is good?" he asked, almost plaintively. "You keep Dao here and I go to school."

"Yes, Dao is *very* good," Max whispered after letting loose of my lips with his. "You can certainly stay. But the photographs—"

"Would you have invited Dao to come if I sent true pictures?" Dao's voice sounded dubious, and rightfully so.

"No, I suppose not," Max answered. And he started to laugh, but I felt his cock shudder alongside mine inside Dao's channel, and I knew he was ejaculating yet again. I had been holding myself back, but let it flow then—and all three of us moaned together.

"That was my friend Amphorn in pictures," Dao murmured in a low tone. "He would like to go to school in America too. Maybe—?"

"Uh, I don't know, Dao, we—"

"Amphorn takes two cocks one time too. Amphorn also gives extra-special-good blow job. Amphorn very, very good."

"We'll start the paperwork tomorrow," Max answered with a big grin.

The only regret we had that day was that I let dinner get charred to ash.

The Grotesques

Rosa and Johann had just finished their performance, and Rosa was cold, oh so cold. It seemed like she always was cold. These mountaintop castles were always so drafty, the late fall wind roaring down the Rhine and up into the mountain fasts along its channel. Rosa couldn't even cross her arms for some sense of warmth. The men gathered around the baron's throne were still looking at her, and they must be happy with what they saw or they wouldn't add anything to the fee. And Rosa and her reduced band couldn't live on the fees alone. So, she had to stand tall—or as tall as an under-four-foot dwarf could stand, arms at her side, both her breasts, oversized for her body, and her pelvis pushed out, giving them a really good view.

They were in the interlude period, while Dieter was putting away his juggling pins and stripping down from his green and yellow jester's costume. The baron and his men were watching and assessing Dieter and deciding what they wanted to see—Dieter topping one of the baron's serving wenches or one of the baron's men topping Dieter.

Rosa didn't care which they picked—she didn't much like it, but she didn't care as long as they paid well. They would have to pay well or The Grotesques—what little was left of the troupe—wouldn't be able to make it to Koblenz, a city large enough to give them some prospect of being able to survive through the winter, before they all starved. That was if

Koblenz wasn't under siege still by either war or pestilence. There was little hope that it wasn't besieged by famine. As had been the case for years, the war-torn Germanys were perpetually plagued with famine.

It was a miracle that Rosa and her reduced troupe had made it even this far. They had once been part of a large circus, traveling up one side of the Rhine in the spring and summer, performing their always-popular sex acts for the jaded and often bored German princes in their castles, and then wending their way back down the Rhine in the later summer and fall to winter in Cologne. Their merry parade of colorful gypsy wagons had always been welcome in the castle towns—the villagers always knowing far less of what their acts actually were than the barons deep inside their mountain castles did.

Internecine war, pestilence, famine, and the draining of resources and able men by the never-ending crusades to the Holy Land—the four scourges of medieval Europe—had been doing their damage to the Germanys for decades now, and this had taken its toll on the circus of The Grotesques even as the need for diversions among the impoverished nobility had increased. The key word was "impoverished." The forces of nature and of man had bled the barons of Germany to the point that, just when they needed the escape the most, they no longer had the means to pay for what Rosa and her troupe once gave them. Gone now were the muscular knife-thrower and his busty assistant who put on a sex show, she still bound to the wheel, as a finisher for their act; gone was the hermaphrodite; gone were the flexible Siamese twins; gone was the giant and his dwarf wife; gone was the bevy of garishly painted woman with sagging breasts and loose cunts, and the goatherd and his beasts. All that was left were Rosa and her husband, Johann, diminutive of stature but gifted in genital endowments, and the handsome dwarf juggler, Dieter, almost normal except for his small stature, and beautiful of face and figure. All else traveling in the two remaining gypsy wagons were just more mouths to feed—the very old and the very young—those who could claim familial rights.

Rosa now had to do the planning—and worrying—and had to make the hard decisions for them all.

The baron of Bingen's son, a tall, strapping muscle-bound lad, had claimed fucking rights to Dieter and had just wrapped a beefy forearm around the blond dwarf's waist and hoisted him up to his hips and impaled the dwarf's man-sized asshole in one swift thrust. The giant was waltzing around the drafty banquet room, strewn with soiled rushes and worn tapestries flapping ineffectually at the gaping windows in the moist and cold stone walls, moving Dieter up and down on his impaling rod with strong hands wrapped around the dwarf's waist and chatting with the circle of envious men of the court fanned around the performance circle, while Dieter flailed and cried out and whimpered at his undoing—as Dieter had been well-schooled to do on command.

With a sigh, moving into the other part of this performance, Rosa placed her hands on top of those of Johann, her husband, that were cupping her breasts, while he stood closely behind her and slid his man-sized dick back up into her woman's-sized slit and began to slowly pump her. Rosa sighed on cue as the baron hobbled down from his throne and waddled over to her and Johann and ran his hand up along her thigh and entered her with his fingers alongside Johann's moving cock to assure himself that what he saw happening was real and not an illusion.

The baron's fingers were trembling, and Rosa slitted her eyes and moaned for him. She was happy now—and wouldn't even look across the room at what was happening to Dieter—as the active involvement of the baron and his son promised enough of an extra fee to get the band within striking distance of Koblenz from Bingen.

That night, under the stars in a clearing on a hillside above the Rhine, while the old women were bedding down the children in the caravans and the old men were gathered around the fire and listening to old Klaus play the mandolin and sing songs of the little people of the forest, Rosa looked around for her husband, Johann, to discuss the rationing of meat for the next two days and his view of whether they needed to make a stop at the castle at Boppard en route to Koblenz.

The troupe avoided this stop whenever possible, because the Marquis von Boppard was a particularly cruel and demanding patron. After what they had received at Bingen, Rosa rather thought they could risk not stopping at Boppard this time. It was a chancy decision; otherwise she wouldn't even have asked Johann his view.

But Johann was nowhere to be seen within the light of the camp fire. And neither was Dieter. Rosa feared the worst, and moved silently toward the small copse of linden trees up the hillside and encircling the small spring that had determined where they settled for the night.

Rosa found them there. Dieter was lying on his back on a stone bench and Johann was crouched between his spread thighs. They were both naked. Johann had to stand on his tip toes to reach Dieter's channel with his man-sized cock. But he had managed and was plowing Dieter slowly and deeply. They were lost in their lovemaking. Dieter's hands were wrapped around Johann's neck and he was caressing his lover's hair and neck muscles, as Johann's mouth was working Dieter's and dipping down to the handsome blond dwarf's nipples momentarily and then back up to the lips for a tender kiss.

Rosa looked on with horror and anger for several minutes and then turned and silently returned to the caravans.

Later that evening, after Johann had returned and found the caravans unusually quiet this early in the night and Rosa was lying in their bed in the caravan and turned toward the wall, he climbed into bed and whispered.

"Are you still awake, Rosa?"

"No," she answered.

This was a common prelude to their intimate moments when Johann would start his foreplay and Rosa could pretend to be seduced. But he sensed a stiffness in her tonight—and she had been used so frequently and roughly earlier that day up at the castle in Bingen that Johann decided not to press her. Besides, he was pretty spent now too—quite happily spent. He had pursued Dieter for months and only now had Dieter given in to him. But Johann knew it wouldn't be the last time. They had made love so naturally. It surely was meant to be.

"Where to now, my love?" Johann whispered into the fuzzy hair at the nape of Rosa's neck. "Is it straight on to Koblenz?"

"No, I think not," Rosa answered in a thin, quiet tone. "I think we'd best stop at the castle in Boppard this year."

And stop they did. The gruff sentry at the gate of the castle keep challenged them loudly when they rolled up onto the drawbridge and, at first, declared that they could not bring their gypsy wagons into the castle keep, but then he was overridden by an even-meaner looking officer of the guard, who declared that the wagons were better inside than out, where the peasants would see them and become more restless than usual, seeing that the master of the castle could afford entertainment when he was squeezing the lands in his domain so hard.

When they rolled into the castle keep and pulled up over to one side, Rosa snorted in disgust at the filthy conditions of the castle. She would have made a remark about a pig sty, except that this was exactly what the courtyard was being used for—as a pig sty.

The men of the castle were already well drunk and screeching of conquest and debauchery when The Grotesques were brought into the shabby and drafty banquet hall to perform. And Rosa and the two men, accompanied by Klaus on the mandolin, barely started into the preliminary acrobatic, teasing introduction to what the noblemen who hired them ultimately wanted before the castle's master and his henchmen were clawing at them and screaming for cock play.

Rosa had been here before, and she knew they would be treated rough. But the Marquis paid well—and had to, lest no traveling sex troupes would stop here at all—and Rosa just gritted her teeth and took it.

Johann has working her cunt with his cock, showing how arousing for the onlookers the use of regular-sized genitalia on dwarfs could be, when the Marquis pointed at them and roared instructions. Rosa found herself lifted to where she was standing on a worn red-velvet upholstered footstool and Johann was lifted behind her. Johann thrust his cock up her bum channel upon command, as the Marquis ordered all of his henchmen present to drop their trousers and selected the one with the largest cock and sent him to stand in front of the stool and fuck Rosa from the front, while her husband took her from the rear.

Rosa put her senses on as low a key as she could, but her anger flared as she looked over to see that the old Marquis and his prime minister had a naked Dieter sandwiched between them now, standing in front of the throne, and were working Dieter's one hole with both of their cocks. Dieter was doing his usual flailing and wailing, but Rosa was not sure that it was all an act on this occasion. As old as the two noblemen were, they still owned mighty swords.

Rosa heard a cry from behind her and Johann was being pulled out of her and away and she looked over her shoulder in time to see his ass channel being lowered onto the vertical and hard phallus of one of the men of the court, who was lying on his back in the filth-matted straw on the floor next to a lounging and panting Great Dane hound. And as Johann was being lowered onto that pole and was crying out his shock, pain, and frustration, the man who had pulled him away from Rosa was undoing his codpiece and then crouching behind Johann and working his cock in on top of his henchmen's.

Rosa was not surprised. She had heard that this was a special fetish of the Boppard castle, and she had to admit that she half-way hoped, in deciding to stop here, that punishment such as this would be taken for what she'd seen several nights previously in the grove of trees on the hillside above the Rhine near Bingen. The man she loved was the reason she kept up with this life at all. Her jealousy at what she had seen in the grove had driven the last stake of despair into Rosa's heart.

She turned and looked back toward the throne, where the Marquis, spent and with a lopsided grin, was hunched again on the throne, holding his member in one hand and fondling that of his prime minister who was staunchly standing at his side with the other. And watching. They were both watching Dieter now as two of the Marquis's burly bodyguards were sharing Dieter's channel. Dieter was flopping around now like a rag doll. Rosa couldn't even tell if he was conscious anymore. Dieter was a consummate actor, but he had never been set upon this roughly before.

This was when Rosa decided what must be done, the only thing that could save the steadfastness of her connection with the love of her life now after what she had seen in the grove near Bingen—the rapture and love that had obviously radiated between Johann and Dieter when they fucked.

Late that evening, The Marquis and friends finally having let Rosa and her troupe go, the caravans were ready to roll out of the castle keep and down the winding road through Boppard to the highway paralleling the Rhine that would lead them to Koblenz.

Hearing her name being called plaintively, nearly taken away by the wind whipping cruelly around the castle's high tower, as if from miles away, Rosa looked up to a barred, high window of the tower. She saw his face—for the last time, she grimly thought. But then she jangled the black velvet bag of money hanging from her waist below her long skirt and smiled grimly. All rewards come at a cost, she thought. And this surely would be enough to see her family through the winter in Koblenz. Perhaps one more winter and the world would have righted itself again, and she could start to rebuild the troupe of The Grotesques. It was a small price to pay really.

He was pressing his face into the bars of the window and crying out to her. But then she saw the grinning, sneering even, faces of the two burly guards come up beside his in the window and beefy fingers went to the bars and pried other white-knuckled fingers away, and the three faces disappeared from the window. Rosa had no delusions what would be happening up in that room now.

"Aren't we waiting for him? Do you intend to leave without him?"

"Don't worry, Dieter, my love," Rosa said, turning to him on the driver's seat of the lead caravan and placing her hand lovingly, familiarly, possessively on the handsome young dwarf's thigh. "He wants to stay. He wants you and me to be happy. Johann was calling out just now to give us his blessing. On to Koblenz."

The Pizza Man Comes

(Excerpt from the novel *House on Park*)

I entered the living room of the house on Park to find that there had been an addition that was fully occupying Eric and Claude's attention.

"The pizza came, and maybe soon the pizza man will come as well," Eric said cheerfully to me, as I walked in. Eric was sitting in the middle of the sofa and had a young guy, certainly no more than nineteen, astride his lap, both facing the TV set. Both were naked.

I gave Eric a meaningful look.

"No problem," Eric said cheerfully, "He's just turned nineteen, and his name is Red."

Appropriate name, I thought. The guy was a natural flaming redhead, as attested by the big bush that surrounded his erect cock. The hair on his head was long and curly, but other than those two bushes, he was smooth as a baby and fair-skinned, but heavily freckled. He had a good build, although he wasn't heavy on the muscles. He probably was a basketball player. He gave me a bemused and disdainful look as if he was just trying out this man-to-man stuff for the first time, just to see how it might work out.

Eric was slouched forward on the sofa down under the guy so that his own cock jutted up from under that of Red's. Red's cock was a real attention getter. Long and slender, its astonishing attribute was that it took a pronounced curve back up toward his belly when erect. That would be an interesting feel in an ass, I thought. Eric had his arms loosely wrapped around him, and he was fondling Red's chest and belly. Claude was sitting to the right of Eric and the pizza man and turned a bit toward them. He still had his silk shorts on, but the front of these were tented up and Red was giving them an occasional apprehensive look. Claude's left arm was strung along the top of the sofa and under Eric's neck, and most of his attention was on the football game. All except for his right hand, which was cupping Eric's and Red's rods together and was gently stroking them as if they were one cock.

I walked over and sat down on the sofa on the other side of Eric and threw my right arm across the top of the sofa behind Claude's arm. Eric turned his face to me, and we went into a long kiss. The pizza guy tensed up, and I could tell he was getting a little worried about the size of the group and quite probably about the size of whatever Claude had there in his shorts. With my left hand, I joined Eric's roaming, rubbing, massaging, prodding, and tweaking of Red's chest and belly. Then I moved my hand down into his bush and traveled around in there a while. Eric and I came out of our kiss, and I started nibbling on Red's left nipple. He gave a little lurch as my left hand came out of his thatch at the root of his cock. As Claude had done, I encircled both cocks at their root and gave them a little shake. Claude's hand came back and encircled both cocks below where I had a purchase and we stroked in unison briefly. Eric relaxed, but the pizza guy remained pretty tense.

The TV went to commercial, and Claude stood up, stretched, and said he needed another beer. He padded off toward the kitchen.

When Claude had left, I felt Red relax under my hand and lips. I scooted off the edge of the sofa and went down on my knees in front of Eric and Red. I started at the young guy's nipples and slowly licked my way down his belly and into that fiery-red thatch. I lifted both Eric's and Red's cocks with my hand and went for the balls. I managed to get a ball of each of them into my mouth and sucked them into my cheeks. Red voiced objections, and his hands went to my head to pull me away, but Eric got his arms under Red's and pinned them up over his head.

"Relax, Guy," I growled after I'd plopped the balls out of my mouth. "If I lose my concentration down here, you could get hurt." I slapped him on the belly with the back of my hand, and he flung a dirty word at me.

"Watch your mouth," I said, as I took both of his balls in my hand and pulled them out sharply and gave them a little squeeze. He gasped.

"I said relax." And he did, collapsing like a deflated balloon.

I did some more gentle double work on their balls and then, bunching their dicks together again at the root with one hand, I got my mouth around both of their dick heads, having to force Red's cock into a straighter position to do so. I did some double dipping, running my tongue around both knobs and giving attention to the piss slits in succession. Red was doing some squirming and panting, but Eric was thoroughly enjoying himself and was keeping the pizza guy pinned with his arms. I was about to see how deeply I could throat this combined package, when Eric drew my attention to the tube of fuck lubricant on the table beside the sofa. Ignoring Red's questions of what that was, I reached over, opened the tube, took out an extra-large glob and started working it into both assholes that presented themselves under the cocks I was holding in my mouth.

The pizza guy was protesting and making definite "no" sounds until I nipped at one of his balls again and then he went silent, with just an occasional moan or whimper.

While I worked the ointment in with one hand, I continued holding the two cocks together with the other, and put my mouth into a churning, circular motion around the two rods, rubbing them together, and swirling down farther, farther toward their roots. I had most of both in when I felt Red tense as if he was ready to shoot off. I plopped the dicks out of my mouth and said, "No, don't you dare shoot off yet." We all held position, both Eric and the young guy now panting and twitching, until all had calmed down.

Then Eric gave a "Now" direction and lifted Red's chest up and out. In the same movement, I lifted the pizza guy by his buttocks, and positioned his asshole at the tip of Eric's hard-on. Red was giving little yip, yip sounds, not fully comprehending what was happening. As I spitted his asshole on Eric's cock a good two inches in the first push, though, Red understood enough to let out a big gasp and a little scream.

"Stop screaming, and put your mouth on mine and open your lips to me, or I'm going to jam you right down," I instructed. I hadn't liked that snotty look he'd given me when I'd first come in the room. The young guy gave me a wild-eyed look now, but when our lips joined and I pressured his open, he did open his lips to me. Then in one movement, I went ahead and jammed his buttocks down on Eric's rod, Eric thrust up to meet that movement, and I forced my tongue into Red's mouth. There was muffled screaming and a good bit of writhing on Red's part, which only helped Eric go in deeper and deeper. When I could feel Eric's pubic hair meet the pizza guy's buttocks, I brought my tongue out of his mouth and went into a more tender kiss. Our lips parted and he collapsed back onto Eric's chest. He had managed to take all of Eric's length and width, and the lubricant was increasingly loosening him up. He relaxed as he became more comfortable with his circumstances and he was reacting now like he could begin to feel the pleasure. My lips went to his nipples, which were now fully erect, and he moaned with pleasure. With my hands under his buttocks, I started rocking him back and forth, first side to side and then front to back on the buried cock, and he opened up more and could feel the pleasurable friction of Eric's rod. Then I started, ever so slowly an up and down, in and out movement.

Eric felt he was able to give Red back the use of his arms at this point. And that also gave him the opportunity to take control of the fuck. He brought his hands down between my hands and the young guy's buttocks and took over the motion of Red's pelvis. My legs tired from hovering over Red lapped by Eric, I crouched down and straddled the overlapping thighs of Red and Eric with my own thighs so that I was sitting in Eric's lap too, with Red sandwiched between us.

The pizza guy moaned at being held between Eric and me and he wrapped his arms around me. He was getting well into the lust bit himself now. He scratched his nails down each side of my spine, reaching as low as he could. He couldn't get anywhere interesting, though, so he snaked his left hand around to my nipple and mimicked the circular motion I was performing on his nipples. With his right hand, he dove for my cock, and was rewarded with success. I gasped as he cupped it, squeezed and then jerked it. I grabbed for his cock, in turn, and once again felt a ripple of pleasure at the way it curved up. I was fisting both our cocks together now and moving Red's pelvis back and forth on Eric's encased dick.

On impulse, I grabbed for the tub of fuck lubricant, lathered my own hole up, and disengaged from the pile. I jumped up on the sofa, went down on my calves, facing the TV, and, straddling Eric and the pizza guy, put my hand back and grabbed Red's cock and slowly descended my butt down to his cock head and slid back and down. We all gave a little jerk and shudder when Red entered me, but I sighed with pleasure as his long, slender rod slid right in. The bent cock was a whole new pleasure for me, and I could tell he got a thrill out of this too. It didn't go straight in; I could feel his dick head drag along the back of my ass chute as it entered. When he was all the way in, Eric and I set up a counter rhythm that had the pizza guy squeaking with pleasure. Eric would push Red's pelvis up, pulling Eric's cock out, on the same stroke that I thrust down in my squat, pushing Red's rod further in.

We hadn't been at this for very long when Claude reentered the room and, seeing the action, squatted in front of me, took my cock into his mouth, and started giving me vigorous head. After a while, he laughed, and stood up and raised me off Red's cock. Then he turned me and brought me down into Eric's lap again, facing Red. Claude reached over and put his hands under Eric's buttocks and pitched him up so that Red's pelvis arched up as well.

Red was beginning to understand what Claude had in mind, and he began to writhe and object and to pant hard. I'd never done this before, but the pizza guy had been snotty with me and deserved, I thought, to be brought down a couple of notches. So, understanding what Claude had in mind, I took my cock in my hand, slid my thighs closer in along the top of Eric's and Red's, and began working my cock in above Eric's in Red's hole.

Red screamed bloody murder and his eyes almost rolled back in his head, but I worked my cock inside him along with Eric's, and Claude was laughing and rocking our three linked bodies back and forth until Red's cries withered out to a gurgling whimper and Eric's and my moans rose to grunts of impending release.

Eric, Red, and I didn't come simultaneously, but it was a close race. We collapsed on the sofa and Claude just stood there, looking down at us, those silk shorts of his tented out.

The pizza guy clearly thought he was done here as Eric and I disengaged from him and left him on a pulsating heap on the carpet in front the sofa. We collapsed together on the sofa ourselves in exhausted wonder over what we had just done. Red, tears streaming down his face and no longer in the least bit cocky, got up gingerly and with a few moaning grunts of pain, made as if to gather his things and leave. But Claude was still standing there between him and the door, very close to him.

Red looked into Claude's eyes with an apprehensive look but couldn't keep his eyes from running down the huge chest of the giant and to those tented shorts.

"I know you're curious, guy," Claude said, with a grin, "So let's just satisfy that curiosity." Then he took both of Red's hands and stuffed them down the front of his shorts. Red gasped and his legs got a little rubbery by what his fingers encountered down there. He looked up into Claude's eyes with a look of both fear and admiration, and Claude, still holding the young man's hands in his shorts, brought his face down to his and gave him that same tender, full-tongued kiss that I had so enjoyed in my first encounter with Claude. Red's hands jerked, as he felt that the kiss had filled out Claude's desire even more than when the young man's hands had first touched that mighty oak.

Claude came out of the kiss, laughed, and, with a hearty, "And so, to the showers," picked Red up, threw him over his shoulder and headed for the stairs. Red lifted his head and gave Eric and me a pleading look. His long arms were dangling down, and he grabbed Claude's butt cheeks through the silk shorts to maintain his balance. If he thought this was going to cool Claude down, he was sorely mistaken.

Another Slice of Pizza

The pizza guy's hole was wide and loose, and he seemed to have taken the ultimate screw very well. But, was this really the ultimate screw, I thought. I looked at that hole pensively. Claude helped Red bring his legs down onto the bench press in the gym room, and he asked to have his arms untied.

"In a while, Red, Eric replied. I haven't had my dip in that hole yet."

The guy started to object, but Claude slapped him on the butt and told him to be quiet. Eric scooted the other bench press out from under the parallel bars and pulled it over into the center of the room. He laid down on it on his back, and I walked over, straddled him in the 69 position, and gave him head to pump him back up, while he licked my balls and rimmed my ass. When Claude could see Eric was erect again, he unstrapped Red's arms and manhandled him over to the bench. I got off of Eric, and Claude pushed Red down into a crouch above Eric, and I helped insert Eric's cock into his hole. Red was still so wide from Claude's drilling that Eric's rod just slurped on in. I told Red to stand perfectly still, while Claude walked around to the head of the bench and directed him to kiss his cock and give him some head. Eric could reach Claude's drooping balls and worked on them with his mouth and one hand, while he wrapped his other hand around Red's cock. I put my hands under Eric's butt cheeks and raised and lowered them and moved them back and forth so that his rod dipped around in Red's ass.

I kept on thinking about the concept of whether Claude's screw had been the ultimate fuck for this smart-assed guy, however, and decided that maybe we could do a little better. And thinking about what might be better stiffened my own cock right up. I dropped Eric's butt cheeks and his cock dropped down to the lower end of the hole without losing much of its depth. I then spread my hand over Red's left butt cheek in a steadying hold, took my hardened cock in my right hand, and inserted the head above Eric's cock in the pizza guy's ass, while I mouthed "another double fuck" across the bodies to Claude. The pizza guy had taken us together once; there was no reason not to give him a second helping.

Claude moved his hands down along Red's side to his waist and held him steady there in his grip. Red still tried to buck when I entered him, but we weren't giving him much room to maneuver. Eric figured out what was going on as well, and snaked his hands around Red's thighs to hold him in place there. Eric stopped reaching for Claude's balls with his mouth, and dug his heels into the carpet, ready to raise his hips when I was ready. I encased the root of both Eric's and my cocks around my fingers to hold the two rods together and slowly pushed the two cocks into Red's hole, with Eric rising up to the hole with his pelvis, as I pushed him. It was a much tighter fit now, and Red gasped and started to swear. Claude brutally took Red's mouth into his and used his tongue as a gag. Once in a good four inches, I released our cocks and let them work on their own. We pushed in, in unison until we were both in to the root.

I pushed down on Red's back with my chest until he was firmly sandwiched between us, and Eric's mouth replaced Claude's as an effective gag. I grabbed Red's upper arms and pinned them above his head, while Claude came around behind me and held his thighs forward and up. When Eric and I were well in, we both began a slow pumping action, but like the pistons of an engine. While Eric was pulling out, I was pushing in; this was more action than we'd given him the first time.

The friction of this on my cock was driving me wild, and I could tell Eric and Red were enjoying it to. I don't know when Claude had let go of the guy's legs, but I soon felt his big strong fingers playing with my ass, and, shortly after that, the feel of Claude's enormous dick head pressing on my back door, and I just widened my leg stance and let him in. A short time after that still, I could feel one of his hands coming up from under my balls and he inserted fingers alongside Eric's and my cocks as they were stuffed in Red's hole. The pizza guy did some more squirming, which just helped make us all come in quick succession, and we tumbled in different directions off the bench press and laid there panting, regaining our composure. Now, I thought, the pizza guy had finally felt his ultimate double fuck.

The Thunderstorm

I fully acknowledge my weakness, but I think Janine has a share in the shattering of my vows to her. I'd only had that one male-on-male fling back in college—with Phil. But Chet and Phil had had an affair after college, and now Chet was living in the next acreage to ours. Obviously Phil and Chet had talked about me, and Chet knew all about me before he moved here, because he had made quite clear to me that he wanted me and knew that I had an addiction to what he could provide. He was one hunk of a man, but I'd left that behind me—had convinced myself it was just youthful experimentation, and short-lived at that—and I was devoting my life to Janine.

I had done everything I could to avoid Chet, who had gotten quite direct in his approach, but it had been Janine herself who set up that fatal day. I had taken off from work to pull a couple of stumps out at the lower end of our yard. Janine was off that week for a visit to her mother and had pressured me not to work out there alone. I had resisted her suggestions, and, unbeknownst to me, she had asked Chet if he could come down to help me. He obviously was delighted to help.

So there we were, standing next to each other in the driveway in our work clothes, waving gaily to Janine as she drove off, doing all we could to act like there was no nervous tension just under the surface, ready to explode.

I would still see the tail lights of her car, and Chet was still waving when he said, in a husky voice, "Let's go into the house."

"God, no, Chet. We've been all over that. I'm going down to work on those stumps. You can go on home. I'll just tell Janine you were a great help."

"That's what I want, Rick. I want to be a great help to you."

"Help? God, Chet, how can you help? I've made a choice, and the only help you could be is just to stay the hell away from me."

"I've seen how you've looked at me," Chet replied. "I know you want it as much as I want you."

"I'm going in the house to get a couple of beers, Chet. It's a real hot day. When I come out, I'd like you to be walking back to your house. I have to get to those stumps."

"It looks like rain. And, you're right; it's hot as hell out here. Not really a day for this; a day to be relaxing in the house."

"Bye, Chet," I said, and I went back into the house and took four beers out of the fridge. Then I thought of the ax and being alone down there with the tree stumps, and I put one back. Chopping wood is no time to have a drunk on. I walked back out of the house, and Chet was gone. What a relief. He was right. No matter what I did to try to stay on the straight and narrow, I ached for him. I tried my best not to admit it, but there it was. I wished that Chet hadn't moved here at all. Everything was going fine until he showed up.

I walked down to the end of the yard, but I could hear the chopping noises before I even got to the garden shed down there. And I knew. Chet hadn't gone home.

He was stripped to the waist, down to his tight, low-slung jeans. He had a bandana covering his head and already was sweating. He was in great shape, bulging muscles of someone used to chopping all of his own wood, going down to a small waist and hips. He was darkly tanned and black hair curled around his forearms and down from his neck and across his chest and trailed down across his navel into his jeans.

He already had chopped one corner out of the biggest stump.

"This isn't really a one-man stump, Rick," he said as he stopped chopping and leaned on the ax handle. "Come on over here and let me show you what a tree stump can be used for. Or an ax handle, for that matter," he said as he winked at me.

"Give it up, Chet," I answered acidly. "I'll just work on this stump over here."

"It's hot as a devil's asshole," Chet said. "At least give me a beer. What, you've only brought three? Let's go up to the house and get some more."

"I don't think so, Chet."

"Well, maybe later."

I turned and started chopping at a smaller stump with my hatchet. Chet was right. This really was heavy work. I heard a roll of thunder from some miles in the distance but couldn't tell if it was just caused by the heat or was warning of a coming thunderstorm.

"Hey, it's too hot for that T-shirt, Buddy. I quickly found it's cooler without."

"I'll manage," I answered.

"Yeah, guess you're right," Chet answered and then chuckled. "I saw you in the gym—you know, before I told you about our mutual friend, Phil. I don't think I could control myself if you took off that T."

"I don't think you're controlling yourself very well now," I muttered under my breath.

"What's that? Couldn't hear you over the thunder."

"Oh, nothing, we'll have to work fast if we're going to beat the rain." But, of course, there was no way beating the rain. It started sprinkling then, but that didn't go long before it came more steadily. We both were immediately soaked to the skin.

"Holy Christ!" Chet yelled, as a lightning bolt hit a tree somewhere close in the forest. "We better get out of here right now; up to the house." And he dropped the ax and headed up the yard.

I just couldn't do it. Instead of following him, I headed for the garden shed, which was the size of a two-car garage, but which was stuffed with all sorts of gardening equipment and supplies. Dark clouds rolled in before I got to the shed, and it was pitch black inside when I got there. I knew we had lanterns around in there somewhere, and I was feeling around for one of them when I heard the shed door open and close, and I could hear Chet's heavy breathing.

"I'm over here, Chet," I said. "Looking for a lantern." I turned, and he was right there in front of me. I felt a hand on my crotch.

"That's me, Chet," I said. "I think the lantern's over there."

"I know that's you," Chet said heavily, and he pushed me up to the wall next to a window. His hand had found my cock through the fabric of my soaked jeans, and I involuntarily responded there, not having a prayer to control my response. "And that's a very nice you," Chet said.

"Chet, no," I said.

A flash of lightning brought light flooding into the shed through the window next to us. Chet was standing very close to me, rainwater flowing down his chest and into his wet jeans. The heaviness of the water in his jeans had pulled the waist down, and if he hadn't had a large, firm butt, they probably would have hit the floor. I could tell my own jeans were having about the same effect from the fast soaking they'd gotten. In that brief flash, I could see the urgency in Chet's eyes. And just before the shed went dark again, Chet leaned in and brought his lips to mine. His were searching, but I resisted him and turned my head.

"No, Chet, I've said no."

He leaned his crotch into mine, and I could feel the rising power of him there. He put his hands against the wall on either side of me, holding me there. I was so weak, however, that I don't think I could have moved if I'd wanted to. Having lost my lips and faced with the side of my head, he buried his face into my neck and kissed and nibbled me there. I moved my hands between us to push him away, but the feel of his

218

chest and nipples sent electricity through me that rivaled the storm expending its fury outside the shed. I couldn't will myself to take my hands away from him.

He was whispering at me. "I've had a hard on for you ever since Phil told me about you. He told me over and over again what a good lay you are. How you took nine thick inches. That you even took it double. What you could do with your ass ring."

"Chet," I moaned. "That's all in the past, and it was just a short fling, an experiment. I'm someone else now."

"Your dick tells me otherwise, Buddy," Chet said and then laughed. "I can feel it grow. It's growing for me. It wants me. It wants me to fuck you."

"No, Chet. No, you're wrong."

Chet's mouth moved down to my T-shirt collar, which he took in his teeth. He brought his hands up to the collar and literally ripped my shirt apart until it was off me. His lips immediately went to my chest and nipples, while his hands roughly undid my belt, unbuttoned my fly in a frenzied motion, pulled the pants and my briefs below my crotch, and wrapped themselves around my balls and engorging cock.

"Let me go, Chet," I whined weakly. "I'm not going to do this."

"Strip my jeans off," Chet commanded.

"No, no, Chet. This has already gone too far." So, he released his hands and stripped down himself. His lips came back up to find mine, and I turned away again.

"Touch me," he commanded. "Take my cock." I froze. He took my balls in one of his hands and squeezed. "Touch me, I said!"

I moved both hands down to his crotch and took his cock. He was big and thick—maybe bigger and thicker than Phil. I shuddered, and so did he. This time when he took my lips in his, I didn't turn, but I was as unresponsive as I could be. I felt so weak. I didn't for the life of me want to be doing this. But I couldn't stop doing it. I couldn't help myself. He could feel me relaxing, surrendering.

Once more his lips came down the side of my neck. He took my arms and raised them over my head and told me to leave them there. I did as he asked. He'd brought a bottle of the beer with him, and he popped the top and poured the cold liquid down my chest. His lips did another tour of my pecs and nipples and then up to both of my armpits, licking up the beer. His hands were on my sides and as his lips traveled slowly down my sternum and abs, his hands came down my sides as well. He tongued my navel and then traveled down my belly and into my pubic hair. He wrapped one hand around the base of my cock and cupped my balls with it, as the other hand went behind me and caressed my butt cheeks. Then he went down on me, tonguing the helmet first and then the rest of and my cock, swallowing and pumping, nibbling down one side and up another, flicking his tongue around the rim of the helmet and into my piss slit, and then going back to swallowing and pumping.

All the time I was moaning and sighing and admonishing him that this had to stop. I didn't even notice when his hand stopped caressing my butt cheeks and he had started fingering my asshole, but before I knew it, he had a finger past my sphincter and was rubbing my prostate and I jerked and lurched and came in three heavy spasms.

I collapsed against the wall. "That's enough, Chet. That's way more than enough. I've got to go. You've got to leave."

Another flash of lightning revealed the layout and contents of the shed. Chet took me by the hips and pulled me over to the side, where there was a compost drum we had recently bought but not put to use yet.

"On this; down on this with your chest," Chet directed with an urgency.

"Chet, no. Not . . ."

He pushed me down. "Spread those legs." I did as he asked and I felt his lips and teeth on my butt cheeks.

"God, you're beautiful," he said hoarsely. In short order, his lips were on my asshole, followed shortly by his tongue, and he was moistening me up real good.

"Oh, no. Never again," I croaked. But there he was. I could feel the head of his dick at my asshole. He tried pushing it right in, but I wasn't anywhere near ready yet. He took his dick and slapped it against my butt cheeks and inserted first one finger, and then two, and then three and then pushed them apart, opening me up. And then his fingers were replaced by the head of his dick again. I tried to rise up, but he pushed me down with a strong paw on the small of my back. He used his other hand to help gain purchase for his cock, and when he was a good three inches in, he rotated his cock with his hand inside me, opening me more. Another inch and my sphincter took the cock and drew it farther in. As the helmet of his cock dragged across my prostate, I flinched and moaned. He was sighing and moaning as well, clearly enjoying this. He pushed in farther, a good five inches now. He took me by the hips with his hands and rocked me back and forth, more than half in, fucking me in midstream.

"Oh, yes, God that's good. I've anticipated this for weeks. I could come right now." But he obviously decided not to, because he stopped the action and stood very still, holding my hips in place for maybe three or four minutes. And then he just glided right in, all the way, maybe almost eight inches, into me, up to the hilt. I could feel his curly pubic hairs tickling my ass. Memories of Phil flooded back. How could I have denied how this felt?

He pumped me for maybe five minutes, rhythmically, taking long strokes and then short strokes. Then I felt his hand buried in the hair at the back of my head and his other hand just above my belly, and he was pulling me up to a standing position. He just held us there for a few minutes, my back against his heaving hairy chest, as he once again gained control of himself, bringing his breath into a shallower rhythm.

He then turned me back to the wall.

"See that pipe up there? Grab for it. With both hands. Hang on." I did as he commanded, and he put his hands below my knees and lifted me off the floor. He was under me now, pumping his dick up my channel from below. This didn't last for long though, broken off by another flash of lightning and another look around the shed. Not far away, burlap bags of grass seed were strung out side by side. Chet turned me again and laid my back on the bags. He was standing over me now, and only my shoulders were on the bags. My legs were draped up his torso and my ass met his crotch. He held one of my legs against him with one arm and was supporting me by my hip with the other. He had not lost his position inside me, though, and now he pumped down into me for a few minutes. Once again, he had to stop to hold himself in check, and this caused him to cramp up.

He slid me down onto the bags on my back and came down with me, behind me, onto his knees. Now he took my legs behind the knees and wish-boned them out as far as possible, opening me to the maximum to him. He pumped me deep and he must have grown to almost nine inches now, because I felt split in two and did some yelping and moaning and maybe added some sound to the thunder that was still rolling outside. Once again he had to stop to rest and to check himself. He let my legs down, and with one hand he massaged my chest, abs, and belly, and, with the other hand, he slowly pumped my cock back up and caused me to sigh and start writhing under him.

"How's that, Sport? Feel good now? Do you remember how good it feels now?"

I closed my eyes tightly and didn't answer.

"Tell me it feels good. Tell me that you will want me to do this again."

I tried my best to ignore him. He pinched my nipples with one hand and squeezed my cock with the other simultaneously, and I involuntarily sent my hands to both locations. But, when I reached his hands, my body betrayed me, and I left them there, stroking his hands, rather than trying to get them off me.

Chet laughed. "You won't answer, but your body betrays you. I know you've enjoyed this. But I want to hear you admit to it. To tell me we'll do this again."

Silence.

"Okay," he said, taking his hands away from my body. "Here, over on your side." His cock drew out of me completely, and I felt an involuntary stab of regret. I hoped, though, that this hadn't been conveyed to him. We couldn't do this ever again. I couldn't let him through my defenses ever again.

I went over on my side, and he was kneeling there beside me. He tried to kiss me on the lips again, but I turned my head once more. He scooted back to below me, lifted my right leg with his left hand, and glided his cock right back into my ass. He then went back to pumping me slowly but deeply, while his right hand went to my cock and balls. He weighed and cuddled and pulled and rolled my balls until I started moaning again. Then he went back to my cock. He pulled the foreskin back as far as it would go. He pulled his cock out of me briefly and leaned over and kissed my cock head and tongued it until it was moist and I began to grind my hips. His dick entered me again then and went back to a slow, deep pump, while he wrapped his hand around my dick, with his thumb applying pressure to the piss slit and stroked me in rhythm with his own pumping action. I was writhing and grinding myself pretty well now, and had my torso up so that I could reach his pecs and nipples and shoulders with my wildly wandering hands. I could hear his breathing getting heavier again now and I sensed we were both coming to a climax. But once again, he stopped the action and held both of us very still, but only briefly.

He lay down behind me, his cock up me as far as it would go, and brought my right leg down, so that my ass canal closed in tightly around his cock. The muscles in my ass canal were contracting and releasing, caressing his cock. He wrapped his right arm around me with his hand coming back and massaging the nipple on my left breast. His other hand was giving my cock slow, deep strokes. We were both aware that I was about ready to shoot off again. I let my sphincter expand and contract, doing a job on his cock that was giving him a great deal of pleasure. I was remembering how Phil and I had experimented. He had his face in my neck, and he put his tongue in my ear and explored briefly.

Then he said, "Admit it, you have no defenses left. You were wanting me just now just as much as I ever wanted you. Let's have that kiss now."

He raised his head up and I turned and met him this time, opening fully to his lips and tongue, giving as well as I was giving. We were in that position, when I felt his cock jerk inside me and bathe my insides with his cum. Almost simultaneously I ejaculated again myself.

We lay there for a good fifteen minutes, listening to the thunderstorm move off in the distance and to the beating of each other's hearts. He pulled me over him, so that I lay stretched out above him, his cock still up my ass and my cock waving in the air.

"We didn't finish removing the stumps," he said softly, at great length.

A moment of silence.

"No," I then answered meekly.

"We must do that"

"Yes," softly.

"Tomorrow."

"Yes."

"But first I'd like to show what can be done with that big stump."

Momentary silence.

"Yes," almost a whisper.

"And maybe the ax handle."

Silence.

"Phil told me about the baseball bat. And I know about the night of the double."

Silence, but I shuddered.

"And maybe the ax handle," Chet repeated.

"Yes," weakly.

"And the day after that."

"Yes," no more than a whisper.

The door of the shed opened and a big, black dude was backlit in the door frame.

"Chet, that you? You told me to come over about now."

"Yep, Ned, it's me . . . and this is the lovely piece of ass I was telling you about."

"No," I moaned, trying to rise up off Chet, but he held me fast, with his arms wrapped around my chest above, with his legs wrapped around mine below, and skewered on his cock, which was on the rise again.

"Yes, I see," Ned said, coming over and looming above us. "Are you sure you were told he can do doubles?"

"No," I moaned.

"Yes," Chet mimicked my moan.

I lay there, bound and skewered, while big Ned peeled off his T-shirt and his shorts. He stood above us, so that both Chet and I could clearly see him working his tool. He was wiry and lean, but very well cut. But his most prominent feature was his long, thin cock, which sported a large mushroom cap.

Chet grabbed for my wrists and pulled my arms above my head and outwards, while Ned pushed our legs apart and crouched there between them.

"Very nice, very nice, indeed," he said and then gave a low whistle. He ran his hands over my thighs and my belly, abs, and chest. He gave me some licking there as well.

"Umm. Budweiser," he murmured.

Despite the predicament, my cock began to harden noticeably. He went down on me then, sucking noisily and twisting and turning my cock, getting it ever stiffer. At length, he crouched over my torso, his legs straddling my sides and slowly sank his ass down on my cock. I lost some of my tension then, thinking that this might not be so bad. I even let him bring his mouth, with his big, thick, sensual lips to my mouth and give me a deep, lingering kiss. His mouth tasted minty, not at all what I expected. While we kissed, he pumped my cock with his ass. I came again rather quickly.

This proved to be a mistake; because it became obvious that now it was big Ned's turn. While still in the kiss, he pulled his ass up off me, took both of my legs in his long slender hands and pushed them up and out. This rolled my ass up and dropped Chet's dick to the lower end of my ass canal. Then, horrors of horrors, I felt Ned's dick head at my asshole, above Chet's cock, He slowly entered me, stifling my screams with his lips and by forcing his tongue down my throat. Chet began to twitch and moan at the sensation of another cock up my ass with his, sliding along on top of his cock. I was panting and writhing, which only helped Ned's tool to move in and up and only excited Chet more. In all the way now, Ned slowly began to pump me, and Chet joined in the rhythm. And I passed out.

When I awoke, I was alone in the garden shed, the door flapping open, and a gentle breeze wafting in and caressing my body . . . and there was a good four inches of ax handle up my ass.

Tit for Tat

There hadn't been much of a firefight at all. The Hondurans hadn't really expected any of our Sandinistan bands to strike across the Rio Coco Segovia, the river marking the Nicaragua-Honduras border, so they hadn't really seriously established a defense of the Gringo mining engineer team at the project in Brus Laguna. The Hondurans apparently hadn't bothered to read our new manifesto for the year about expanding our operations outside of Nicaragua's borders. We really didn't care that much about disrupting the new strip mining operation on the coast of Honduras. But we wanted to make a statement.

We wanted to make the news with the Norte-Americanos. We were to capture a few and use them—not kill them—but use them to gain headlines. They hadn't been taking the Sandinistas seriously up North. A point was to be made, and my band was chosen precisely because of the point we could make.

It took a while to settle on the men we wanted. Most of the foreigners working in places we could access in Honduras were Europeans. But we wanted Americanos. And men of prominent, wealthy families.

We found what we wanted at the start-up strip mining project inland from Brus Laguna. Three Americano engineers, one the son of a federal congressman, and lightly guarded.

We had managed the trek across the Rico Coco Segovia from our base in Waspán in near silence and without encountering a single Honduran, civilian or military. The terrain was remote and a true jungle. And we were hardened soldiers now, experienced in the ways of stealth and steal.

At the first sign of an armed attack, the small band of Honduran soldiers guarding the Gringos melted into the jungle. We would rather have taken care of them there and then, though. They retreated in the direction of the army base at Brus Laguna on the coast. This would mean that the trek back to Nicaragua would have to be faster and more stealthy than our march to this point. The escaped soldiers would raise an alarm, and the army would soon be on our scent.

We caught the three Gringos trying to hide in one of the mining operation sheds. We'd attacked at night and they were all stripped down to boxers for comfort under the slow-moving paddle fans in their primitive quarters at the height of the Honduran hot season.

The youngest and most fit of the three, a blond Gringo of athletic build and more bravery than the other two, was crouched between the door and his two compatriots when we kicked our way in. He was shielding a middle-aged man who was starting to go to overindulged fat and a younger, dark-haired man of slight height and build. The blond Gringo was holding a knife, at an experienced "kill" angle. He could see that he was not armed to fight with the AK-47s of ten hardened Sandinistas, but he obviously was willing to go down trying.

I motioned to Hectoro to feint at him from the left, which drew the young Gringo's attention, and then I bore in from the right and caught him in the chin with the butt of my AK-47. He went down with a groan. He wasn't unconscious, but he had dropped the knife.

"David Winston," I barked. "Which one David Winston?" I wanted to know immediately which one was the son of the congressman. He would receive special treatment. And I was the only one in the band conversant in English. This was as planned. I didn't want there to be any chance of the

Gringos getting friendly with any of my men. It was impossible to tell, given our specific mission, whether that might become a problem.

The young blond's head lolled up at me. He was groggy from the hit on the chin, but he recognized the name when it was spoken. And he was quick witted. I could see that he understood in an instant that this hadn't been just a random raid.

"What—?"

"No questions," I commanded. "Get up and get those two up too. Where are your boots?"

Winston gestured in the direction of their sleeping hut, just a few steps from the door of the shed, as he whispered to the other two Gringos to stand up, that they were being directed to go back to their hut and dress. But he didn't stop there.

"He asked for David Winston," he was quickly adding. "This can't be an accident. They—"

"No talking," I barked, shoving the butt of the AK-47 into Winston's ribs. "No talking to each other from now on. If you talk, we will gag you. In the wet heat of Honduras, you may not survive that. Think about that. Now over to the hut and put socks and boots on. Now! Move!"

We hustled the three out of the shed and into the hut. Since their guards had escaped, there wasn't much time to get them on the move.

When they got to the hut, the blond started to take khaki trousers and a work shirt off a hook, but I nudged him with the butt of my AK-47 again.

"No, just the boots and the socks," I grunted. "And you won't need this either."

With that, I took the knife we had seized from the Gringo and I ran it under the waistband of his boxer shorts and cut the material to shreds. Winston gasped and tried to cover himself, but I knocked his hands away with my gun butt. He was magnificent. Not only was he built for power in his torso, arms, and legs, but he also had the longest, thickest cock I'd seen on a man, and heavy hanging balls.

229

This mission wasn't going to be hard at all.

I handed the knife over to Hectoro, and he quickly had the other two Gringos naked too. The pudgy middle-aged man was hung nicely too, and the dark younger man had a boyish body that would please a few of my men greatly.

Stripping the prisoners was prudent for more reason than one. It not only served the purpose of our mission, but it also helped make them docile and gave them the proper sense of helplessness and gave them something to worry about so that they could give less attention to scheming an escape. We needed to dominate and control them fully and as fast as possible.

Once they were booted, I made them group together, facing us, with their hands at their sides, and then it was Manuel's turn to ply his craft. Manuel had been the photographer for a newspaper in Managua before joining the Sandinistas.

I had Manuel take several photos of our Gringo prisoners, showing them being held by my men but careful not to show any of the faces of the Sandinistas. He had three cameras; One with good film in it to use later, a video camera, and a Polaroid camera, the latter of which gave us photos to leave for the inevitable Honduran search party to find—once the Honduran cowards had gathered their strength and resolve.

Time was short, though, and I quickly had the band on the move, prodding the prisoners along, their hands tied behind their backs with leather bindings. We melted, back into the jungle for a fast, hard march toward the Rio Coco Segovia River.

We marched the prisoners relentless and mercilessly through the jungle for hours. Twice the pudgy one collapsed and had to be prodded back to his feet. I wanted them to be utterly exhausted before we stopped for the first time. But I especially wanted the blond Gringo, the congressman's son, to be totally exhausted. And he was proving to be strong and up to the task of hiking.

Being naked and trussed, though, finally got to the blond one before any of my life- and battle-hardened

Sandinistas had lagged in energy. At the last, as we entered a fern-floored bowl at the base of a rocky hill, the blond collapsed in total exhaustion. The middle-aged Gringo had given out a long time ago. He was being nearly dragged along between two of my men, two who had gravitated to him. I had some idea what they liked, and I was content to let this order be.

The small dark one had also been chosen by natural selection. He was draped over the shoulder of the biggest, tallest of the band, like a sack of rice. The head and arms of the little one were just flopping back and forth between the Sandinista's broad, bulky shoulder blades; he appeared to be nearly unconscious, but I could tell he wasn't completely out, because of the expression on his face. He was in shock and his mouth was open in a look of pain and surprise. This most likely was because both of the big Sandinista's hands were busy. One was squeezing one of the small Gringo's pert butt cheeks, and the thumb of the other hand was buried inside the little one's asshole.

It was obvious that the band was ready to stop here.

I barked an order, and two of the band jumped forward and untied Winston's bounds, turned him over on the moist, fern-cushioned ground, and then retied his wrists over his head and around the trunk of a small tree. Then they both sprang down on either side of the blond Gringo, grabbed his knees, and spread his legs, each taking a well-muscled calf and lifting it up and out, which rolled his firm, rounded glutes up.

Before this, I'd had all of the Sandinistas pull on their black masks, and then I told Manuel to take out the video camera and to get everything from this phase of the mission on tape.

I opened my fly and pulled out my cock. I was proud of my cock. I stood between the Gringo's spread legs and made sure he got a good view of my cock. I had been mentally preparing for this for many kilometers, and now I saw that the blond Gringo was, at last, on the verge of exhaustion. So my fine cock was standing straight out from my body.

I opened the pack on my back and took out a jar of grease. I scooped out a glob and gave it over to one of my men who was holding the Gringo's legs, and he greased the Gringo's hole while I greased my pole, lovingly stroking myself up and down while standing above the panting Gringo.

The blond Gringo was panting as much now from the realization of what happened next as from his utter exhaustion. His exhaustion kept him from struggling much, but he whimpered some and bellowed his disapproval much, albeit in very weak, almost-spent tones.

I looked around, hearing other cries and moanings and gruntings and whimperings about me.

The two likeminded band members, we liked to call them the Siamese twins for their special proclivity—the ones who had taken to the pudgy middle-aged one and who had virtually carried him to this spot—were sitting on the ferns not far from me, facing each other close, the thighs of one over the thighs of the other. And with the naked pudgy Gringo sandwiched between them. He was floppy as a rag doll, his head lolling and his eyeballs rolling up in his head. Only his weak cries and whimpers told me he was conscious as, with two pair of hands on his waist and sides, the two Sandinistas were pumping him up and down and their ever-disappearing joined cocks in his single asshole.

The mountain man of a Sandinista band member was walking slowly around the perimeter of the open area, humming and laughing and singing lullabies, obviously pleased with himself. The small, dark Gringo was attached to him at the pelvis, his legs flopping back and forth over the hips of the Sandinista monster man. The Sandinista's big hands were encircling the waist of the small, boyish-figured man, and sliding the small man's ass up and down on his huge tool. The Gringo's body was arched away from that of his ravisher, and his head was lolled back and his arms were flopping down from his shoulders. In spite of his exhaustion, his weak screams were quite energetic and convincing.

I instructed Manuel to make sure he got good coverage of the big man's thick cock appearing and disappearing in the small man's hole.

With a thrill of excitement, I knelt down and placed one hand under the blond Gringo's tailbone and held the base of my cock steady with the other hand. I placed the ruby tip of my cock at Winston's hole, and he whimpered and gave his last argument for being spared, and then I reared my hips back and struck home, strong, fast, and deep.

The blond congressman's son cried out and his pelvis lifted up, trying to escape me as I drew back again. But he couldn't evade me. He was fully mine. Exhausted, trussed, dominated, fucked.

"Take that, Norte-Americano bastard," I cried out, as I thrust again, and again and again.

The video rolled, as loud cries and bleatings across the clearing turned to whimpers and moans, the heavy grunts to weak groans. The Gringo's ass opened to me. The two Sandinistas at his side worked his greased cock with their free fists, and as they sucked him off, his pelvis started to move with my rhythm. I certainly wouldn't be telling my leader that he seemed to be enjoying his fuck in the end, though.

Both of the other Gringos were unconscious when the video film played out.

The Sandinistas zipped up and took up what were now three burdens, and moved quickly off once more toward Nicaraguan territory.

At the banks of the Patuca River, about half way toward safe territory, we rested for several hours. When we woke, two of the prisoners seemed to be recovering themselves and were whispering stealthy. The pudgy one was still completely docile and doing no more than groaning and moaning, with his eyes tightly shut.

We bustled the prisoners into the three boats, separately, that we had hidden in the rushes upon our trek into Honduras. And when we got to the other side, I let the "twins" double fuck the congressman's son back into submission and I fucked the small one. His ass had tightened up again. I was covering him bent over a mossy boulder on his stomach, and taking him was like fucking a small woman, all gentle curves and slight frame on the outside and all sweet and creamy inside. He even cried softly like a girl as I took him roughly in long, deep strokes, one of my fists between his shoulder blades and the other buried in his hair and arching his head and torso back up toward me.

I had Manuel take still photos of both takings.

The small, dark one soon was completely cowed again and would not, I was sure, be doing any whispering against my command any time soon. I didn't complete my fuck, though, because we heard the sound of chopper blades in the distance, the sound coming from the direction of Brus Lagunda.

We hurriedly broke off our conditioning and propaganda photo op exercise, gathered up the three nearly comatose prisoners, and struggled back into the jungle, running now as hard as we could for the Rio Coco Segovia and the welcoming arms of our well-manned base at Waspán, across the border and in Nicaragua. The return trek was nowhere near as easy as the entry; we were hunted prey now, leaving spoor our trackers could follow—and carrying the dead weights of three fully used Gringos.

They caught up with and cornered us not more than fifty kilometers beyond the Patuca. I sent Manuel and the spent film off on another track toward Waspán. At least the mission we were sent on could be accomplished.

* * * *

I'm not sure what happened to any of the others in my band. I was knocked unconscious early in the hand-to-hand fighting. And I woke up here in a cell—I assume at the army base outside Brus Lagunda. At least I assume I was brought back to where it started. That was two nights ago. Since then I've had two, body-crunching sessions with the Honduran soldiers.

I am hunched on a narrow, hard bed against the back wall of the cell. The wall is clammy, rough, badly stacked bricks, but cool against my cut, aching, naked body. They must have tortured me for hours. They beat and whipped and punched every part of my body, careful not to break anything—yet—although I'm not at all sure about two of my ribs. They ache so badly. I am totally exhausted—physically, but not mentally. I am a Sandinista. And I have accomplished my mission—as long as Manuel has made it back. This will be a propaganda statement for the world as has never been made before. The Norte-Americanos can be fucked—can be screwed—by the Central Americans. They cannot lift their heads down here in pride ever again now. As long as Manuel and the film made it to safety.

My body aches badly and I want more than anything else to curl up on the hard wooden bed here and die. But I'm held in this sitting position, my back to the wall, by the shackles at my wrists chained close to the walls and holding my torso up.

I close my eyes, wanting to make it all go away. Listening to every part of my body separately, checking out my wounds, trying to determine whether anything is seriously broken or violated.

But I hear the noise of metal screeching on metal. The door of my cell opening. So, I look up, expecting to see the sneering Honduran captain again.

But there *he* is. The blond Gringo. The one we'd taken prisoner and fucked for all the world to see. The American congressman's son. He is walking into the cell unsteadily and with a grimace at each step, bowlegged, his ass stretched and worried hard. But he is moving with the resources of determination I had seen from the beginning that he possessed in full measure.

"Winston. David Winston," I croak.

"No, dumbass," he retorts, his voice full of venom and anger. "You stupid insurgents attacked the wrong camp. David Winston's camp is several miles to the east of ours. We are with a Canadian archeological dig."

I want to say something, I'm trying to say something, but he is shouting, "Just shut the fuck up," and then he strikes me hard across the face with an open palm. Nothing compared with what the Honduran captain does.

But then I gasp and watch in horror as he unzips his pants and rolls out that huge, thick cock of his. He is taking a tube of cream from his pants pocket and giving me the most cruel expression. And he is greasing up his monster cock.

My eyes look wildly around the cell, searching for escape, but I know there is none. I hear a noise in the corridor beyond the open door, and I call out for help. But I know there will be no help from that sector.

There, beyond the doorway, crossing the open space, from one side of the yawning opening to the other, being dragged between two burly Honduran soldiers, his feet dragging the ground. Manuel. His head lolling down. Spent. Beaten. His photography certainly unsent.

Two more huge soldiers appear at the doorway, cocks of a horse thrusting from the flies of both of them, being worked with their hands. They are looking hard at me.

The Norte-Americano turns to them and says, "Me first. Then you both—together. As hard as you want."

My legs are being roughly parted and spread and lifted, and my bare butt rolls up and the cuts in my back are opened anew as they scrape along the undressed bricks. And, Yiyiyi! Excruciating pain. The violation of my last protected body part. A telephone pole jamming up into me, running far and deep, swiftly, stretching and splitting soft tissue as it fills me and expands and thrusts deeper. Yiyiyi!

Tuesday at Three

All of his friends told Peter Townsend that he was crazy to buy the apartment in Cartagena, Colombia, in the luxury medium-rise building overlooking the ancient harbor, now yacht basin, as his retreat. But it was so convenient for him to sail his boat right up to the building's dock and whisk himself up to his retreat, with its heavy security, and Cartagena catered to some of the special interests he didn't want to own up to back in Chicago. When they said, "But Colombia, with all the drug warfare and the kidnappings of executives?" he'd just laugh and think to himself, "Hiding in plain sight."

He certainly didn't want to tell them that he made far more money from the drug running between Cartagena and Naples, Florida, on his yacht each year than his position as CEO of the major pharmaceuticals manufacturing corporation had made him in the last twenty years. What was a little balancing of Colombian drug cartels in the face of an early retirement without a financial care in the world—and with some added benefits in the meantime?

The sun was high over the harbor, beating down on the bulletproof glass covering his terrace as he swam lap after lap in the pool that took up most of the terrace he'd had covered and that jutted out toward the old castle walls guarding—not always successfully—the approach into the harbor for centuries. He was reviewing the distribution plans for this week's take across the States via his network of Florida bush pilots. He had to review the particulars every day; he had to keep it all in his memory; nothing was consigned to paper or computer file. He was careful and discreet in all of the activities he wanted to hide from his other world back in Chicago.

After he finished his laps and rested in the lounge on the small square of terrazzo between the edge of the pool and the sliding glass doors into his living room, he planned to go to the closet in his guest room and cut the stash he'd just acquired into marketing-share portions and pack it into sample drug kits he carried around with him on corporation business. Hiding in plain sight was a favorite ploy of his. No one had ever supposed that selected packets of the dietary fiber powder his company was peddling to the world actually held heroin.

Laps and delivery network review finished, Townsend rose out of the pool and padded over to the lounge. He was in great shape for his forty-five years. His muscles were toned, his face was as square-jawed and handsome as his plastic surgeon could sculpt, and he'd managed to keep his own hair, although he'd stopped dying the hair at his temples when he was told that gray there looked distinguished on him. He was barrel chested and thickish in the waist, but he was just a solidly built man, with excellent musculature, a Neptune or Zeus rather than an Apollo or David.

Townsend lay back in the lounge and closed his eyes briefly. But after a few moments, he sighed and reached for the sex magazine on the table next to the lounge bed. He was keyed up and wanted to let off a little steam. He flipped the magazine over and started to peruse the photos. As he turned the pages, his hand slowly glided down his torso and under the waistband of his Speedo. As he became more engrossed in the photographs, he pushed the Speedo down and off his legs and started up a slow, but steady, rhythm of stroking his engorged cock.

He was lost, safe in his world of security, in his fifth-floor apartment, with the bars over the windows, solid bulletproof canopy covering the terrace, the latest in security alarm systems, and his small armory of personal protection assault rifles, most of them back in the closet of the guest bedroom with the drug stash.

He'd have every reason to feel very safe if the security alarm system actually had been armed that afternoon and if all of the double locks on the service door into the laundry room from the service elevator shaft had been bolted. If. But they weren't, just as the times that lax security at the Castillo de San Felipe de Barajas at the harbor entrance had nullified the protection of Cartagena at the wrong time when it was sacked by pirate navies more than a century earlier.

It took the two men practically no time at all to pick the locks of the service door and to steal silently into the apartment's laundry room on moccasined feet. They were dressed all in black, from nylon trousers, to Ts, to the silk hoods they pulled down over their heads before they carefully moved across the kitchen and dining room and into the living room and positioned themselves behind the draperies on either side of the open sliding glass door out onto the terrace.

When they spied Townsend masturbating on the lounge bed by the pool, they smiled at each other and began to strip down to only the hoods covering their heads and knives in sheaths strapped to their thighs. The taller of the two, the dark Colombian, was also the younger of the two, strongly built, an obvious devotee of the gym. The cock he began to stroke while watching Townsend was long and thin. The shorter one, the darker Colombian, was of stouter, more solid build, probably the more heavily muscled of the two. His cock was barely noticeable when he first freed it, but it was impressively thick and was lengthening out nicely as he enjoyed the view of Townsend masturbating in supposed solitary splendor.

At a signal from the darker Colombian, the two moved silently out on the terrace, keeping to the late afternoon shadows for as long as possible.

Almost before Townsend knew they were there, the taller, younger one was straddling his chest and pushing his arms above his head. Townsend began to struggle, but then he felt the cold steel of a knife at the base of his ball sac. He saw that someone else was down there, but he couldn't make him out around the looming torso of the dark man straddling his chest. In any event, Townsend's immediate attention was focused on that long, thin cock slapping him in the face.

"Suck his cock and do it nicely or you lose your balls," a gruff voice rose from behind the young man hovering over his chest. "You can feel the knife, can't you?"

Townsend certainly could feel what thus far was the flat side of a hunting knife up under his balls. He also felt a large hand gripping his upper thigh.

The head of the younger man's cock was pressing at his lips, and, with the knife at his balls, there was little else to do but open his mouth to several minutes of sucking and gagging on a cock exploring his inner cheeks and the back of his throat.

The knife was withdrawn, and he could see out of the corner of his eye a beefy arm swing over to the table. His bottle of lotion was taken up.

He felt cold cream being roughly fingered into his ass entrance, and Townsend began to squirm. But he stopped again as he felt the steel move up under his balls. Thick, moistened fingers were probing his ass, loosening him and widening him, searching deep inside him and pumping him slowly. He groaned and moaned in arousal despite his predicament. He swallowed hard and whimpered as something harder probed a few inches inside him—the handle of the knife—but it soon was replaced by the fingers

The dark one pulled his dick out of Townsend's mouth and turned to say something to the darker one, who went back into the living room. He came back with a handful of condom packets. Still standing over Townsend's chest, the dark one made Townsend open a packet and roll the condom on his dick, while the darker one apparently was crowning himself. Townsend certainly couldn't feel a knife at his balls in that moment.

With a surge of strength that took the two by surprise, Townsend pushed up, rolled off the lounge bed, and lurched through the open glass doors into the living room.

He stumbled toward the back of the apartment, toward the guestroom. The two caught up with him there. Leaning in the guestroom doorway, his back to the frame, the tall, dark one wrapped his arms around Townsend's belly and pulled the older man to his chest. The stouter, darker one faced Townsend and pulled his legs off the floor with strong hands under his hips.

Townsend moaned and threw his head back against the shoulder of the younger Colombian, as the dark one lifted his hips and forced his hole down on the younger one's upward-curved, engorged cock. Townsend writhed and struggled as he was being set down on the long, throbbing cock, but his efforts only served to ensure he was skewered to the deep.

He really cried out and began to grunt and groan as the darker one spread his legs with his own beefy thighs and crouched under his pelvis and started to enter his hole with a thick cock running up on top of the younger Colombian's thinner cock. The darker Colombian kept a firm grip on Townsend's thighs as the two double fucked the American executive, the older Colombian doing most of the stroking. The younger Colombian reached down between Townsend's and the other Colombian's bellies and fisted Townsend's cock and began stroking it in rhythm with the counterpistoning of the two cocks inside Townsend.

All three, otherwise silent with intense strain, were huffing and puffing and moaning and groaning at the exertion of the taking. Townsend came first, and the two Colombians came a short time later.

The American executive collapsed in a fully taken heap between the two hooded men as they pulled out of his channel and released their hold on him.

After a brief pause of regaining their breath, the two took him up again as if by prearranged agreement of a plan, the stouter man carrying his legs and leading and the younger man holding him by the armpits. The two hooded Colombians carried Townsend through the living room and into a narrow, terrazzo-floored room forming an L on the terrace with the living room. This room, probably originally part of the terrace, had a full glass wall looking out on the terrace and the side of the swimming pool and was furnished with expensive workout equipment, a tribute to Townsend's good shape.

Moving Townsend over to a massage table, they pushed him down on the edge of the table's end, his feet on the floor and his chest on the surface of the table. The younger of the two held a totally exhausted and sore Townsend down on the table with one fist in the small of his back and the other hand gripping the back of his neck, while the darker Colombian roamed around the room and found lengths of nylon roping.

Minutes later, Townsend's legs were spread and tied to legs of the table at his ankles and hips, and his wrists were tied to where the middle legs of the massage table frame met the top of the table.

Leaving Townsend there to moan and contemplate his possible fate, the two Colombians retreated to the kitchen and raided the refrigerator for beer and whatever they could find to eat to replenish the rough work they'd done—and to prepare for the rough work still ahead of them.

After they'd eaten and taken a piss and drank off another beer, they reentered the exercise room. They stood in full view of Townsend, and he trembled as they both rolled on condoms once more.

The younger one with the long, thin cock fucked him first. He just walked up behind Townsend and between his legs and thrust his cock deep inside Townsend's now-gaping hole and stroked hard and deep and fast. He reached up and buried a fist in Townsend's hair and arched the American's back toward him as far as the stretched arms and tied wrist would permit. He used his other hand to slap Townsend on the butt cheeks and flanks while he fucked him in a virile, relentless, long- and fast-stroked taking.

Townsend cried out at the taking, and the young Colombian seemed to enjoy that and responded to every moan with a harder thrust, which produced a louder groan.

When the younger Colombian finished with Townsend, he slapped him hard on the rump and untied the American's bonds.

Townsend started to straighten up, but there was no time. The two Colombians were forcing him up on the massage table on his knees, and his chest and cheek were being forced down on the surface of the table. The stouter, darker Colombian was hopping up on the table, crouching over Townsend, his thighs encasing the American's hips, and he was working his thick cock inside Townsend and fucking him doggy style. The Colombian had his arms encircling Townsend's chest, covering him close, and he was gnawing on Townsend's ear as he fucked him.

This one was a whole new trial for Townsend. The second Colombian's dick was stubbier, but it was very, very thick, and he had a rotating motion he set it too that made Townsend feel all the more stuffed. After several minutes in this position, the Colombian went down on his knees behind Townsend and pulled the American up and back onto his chest and lap. He was able to gain greater depth this way.

Townsend was utterly exhausted, wondering what came next. As he felt the darker Colombian reaching his climax, Townsend looked over and saw the younger one pulled on another condom. Townsend shuddered in recognition of what came next. Then he knew. They were going to do it again. The older Colombian had grabbed his legs and spread and lifted them and the younger Colombian was coming into a crouch and pushing his knees under the older Colombian's buttocks. Townsend panted and moaned as the second cock entered him again above that of the older Colombian's and it was the younger man's turn to stroke in a double fuck.

After the two had doubled him for a short while, Townsend was turned on his back on the massage table, his legs spread up and out, and the younger Colombian stroking hard and deep inside him again for the last fucking.

After younger, fast-rising Colombian was done, Townsend was dragged between the two still-hooded men down the hallway and toward the back of the apartment. Inside the guestroom door, they pushed him to the floor and stood over him, fingering the handles of the knives strapped to their thighs and looking intently at him, ready for what came next.

Townsend looked up at them and spoke, in a hoarse whisper for the first time since the two had invaded his apartment.

"Next Tuesday, same time? Three?"

"Could we make it five?" the stouter of the two Colombians asked. "I'm getting my truck detailed that day."

"Sure, five is fine," Townsend said in a hoarse whisper. "You'll find envelopes with your fee in it on the credenza in the front foyer. Please leave by the service entrance."

Western Tail

It had been a hot and dusty ride from Kansas into Colorado en route to my new posting as the postal agent and sutler at Fort Hayden. I'd ridden all day with the Rocky Mountains tantalizingly near without having reached the river they told me was still more than a day's ride out from the fort. I now saw the river ahead, cool and inviting, but I knew I wasn't going to make Fort Hayden today. So, I rode down the side of the river for a couple of hours, thinking about one more night on the trail and about how hot, dusty, and smelly I'd gotten.

The river beckoned to me—clean and clear and shallow enough to be safe. At last I gave in, deciding to camp out for the night at a place where the land gently slanted down to a quiet section of the river well away from the central current. There was a small grove of cottonwood trees to one side and smooth rock outcroppings to another side, where I could lay my clothes out to dry.

I tied my horse to a tree in the cottonwood grove and laid out some food and water for him. I set up camp at the edge of the grove and laid my rifle up against a tree there. My saddle had gotten pretty smelly, so I scrubbed that down good and dropped it in the sun between the rocks and the grove to dry. Next I stripped off all my clothes, scrubbed them real well, and stretched them out on the rock outcropping to dry. After that, it was my turn. I dove into the river and luxuriated in the cool, clean water rolling over my body. I splashed around a good bit and did some hoopin' and hollarin' out here in the world all by myself. Eventually, regretting my time in the water had to come to a close, I stood and walked up out of the river until the flowing water just reached my knees. It was time to get serious. I took up the bar of lye soap I'd used on the clothes and then soaped myself up real well. I felt so good when I got to my cock and balls that I did some extra soaping there and pulled on my rod for a few minutes, enjoying the moment of freedom after weeks in the saddle as well as surfacing fond memories of my romp in the sack with that cowboy in Abilene that night not long ago.

Not long ago in terms of time, but a long time since in terms of the need I felt for the arms and cock of another man.

I heard an unfamiliar horse whinnying, and I froze solid. There, fanned out before me between the rocks and the cottonwood grove was a small band of Indians riding fine-looking horses bareback. I have no idea how long they'd been watching me, but they'd had the drop on me for some time.

There were five of them, all young bucks—any one of them with enough muscle to easily handle me. Besides that, the one who evidently was the leader, a particularly impressive-looking bronzed specimen, was holding a bead on me with a rifle. The other four strapping bucks had bows and arrows at various stages of readiness.

They weren't wearing paint, so at least they didn't appear to be on the warpath about anything. In fact, they weren't wearing much of anything beyond loincloths, moccasins, and thin beaded bands with leather fringe at the top of their bulging biceps and calves. The apparent leader, though, was also wearing a breastplate made of feathers and turquoise beads held together with silver wire. My immediate assessment was that they were a hunting party that had been attracted by my foolish cavorting in the river. That didn't mean that they weren't hunting for me—not me specifically but me in "he'll do for the point we want to make." I'd been told to be on the lookout for small bands of renegade Indians in these parts ready to pick off the lone white man. And there couldn't be a

246

more lone and naked white man around than me at this moment.

I held my arms out wide in supplication (which may have been a mistake, considering what happened soon thereafter) and slowly walked up the shore, sidling a bit toward the cottonwood grove and my rifle.

The leader of the tribe raised his rifle a bit and gave me a look that told me in no uncertain terms that it wouldn't be a good idea to go for my gun. I was a little surprised that he was grinning at me, but then so were the other four. I soon found out why they were doing that.

The leader slipped off his horse and halved the distance between him and me in long, deliberate strides. One of the others in the band rode up close to him, and the leader handed off his rifle. Then he pulled strings at the hips of his loin cloth and the scanty covering fell to the ground. Oh God, was my first thought. It had just been my luck to have run across a band of Indians that swung in my direction. My second thought was that this Indian, at least, swung real well. He had a cock and set of balls that equaled or surpassed his other collection of well-tone muscles. And my third thought was that he must have really enjoyed my unintentioned performance with the soap, because his horse-hung cock was standing straight out.

Unfortunately for me, he was such a fine specimen of manflesh that my cock reacted in similar fashion to the situation.

Before I could have a fourth thought, the tribe leader was at me like a pouncing cat. While he moved, the other four Indians came off their horses and gathered around fairly close to us in a semicircle. The Indian leader wrapped a hand around my neck and brought my face to his in a liplock that showed me he did a lot of this. The other hand went to vice-like grip around my balls and the base of my cock that brought tears to my eyes and me to my knees in front of him just as soon as his lips and tongue released mine. This put me at a convenient level for him to stuff his hard cock between my lips, which he proceeded to do.

247

He was face-fucking me real well, when I managed to look around and notice that the four others had paired off and were fingering each other in shared excitement. This meant no one had the drop on me with anything but a hard and pumping penis at the moment, and I realized I might have reached the closest point to escape and survival that I ever was going to get. I knew I couldn't get to my own rifle or horse in time, but the Indian leader's horse, a gorgeous big golden palomino stallion, was standing unattended within striking distance.

So, I seized the moment and made a break for the stallion. Miraculously, I was on the horse's back and getting him to start into a trot before the Indians recovered. But then my luck ended. The Indian leader merely whistled, and the horse stopped in its tracks. I thought I was dead now, that they'd just pull me off the horse and rip me to shreds. But the Indian leader did something completely unexpected. He leaped up on the horse behind me, yelled something the horse understood, and we were off, two naked men on the back of a quivering horse, thundering across the plain beside the river. The Indian was wedged behind me. He grabbed my wrists, pushed me forward on the neck of the stallion, and forced my hands into the flowing mane of the horse, where I wrapped my fingers in the white mane and held on for dear life. The Indian's beaded breastplate was digging into my shoulder blades, and his raging hard was rubbing up and down the small of my back as we were tossed and turned in the charge across the rolling countryside.

I was scared, but that rubbing dick of his and the whole wildness of the situation was turning me on, too. We hadn't ridden far before he made his move. His thighs had been just behind mine, with both of us hanging on to the horse as best we could with them. But in one swift, dexterous move, he took those powerful thighs of his and lifted them around and in front of mine and flipped me even more forward onto the neck of the horse. This tilted my pelvis up as well, and I screamed in fear and then in surprise and pain as I felt his cock head slide down the small of my back. It held briefly at my asshole as a much too-large a peg came into a much too small a hole. And then the rough rolling of the horse's gait solved the Indian's problem, and with one excruciatingly painful lunge—painful to me—he had breached my asshole and split me in two with his ramrod, which just kept on screwing up into me as the motion of the horse's gallop naturally stroked his cock and my ass canal together.

I screamed into the wind and struggled against the powerful embrace of the Indian chieftain as we thundered on. With the aid of the motion, he was pumping me deep with the natural interaction of our bodies and gait of the horse's forward motion.

I realized not only that I was aiding the wild fuck myself with my struggling but also, after the shock of being taken started to wear off, that I now was enjoying this incredible invasion of my body. In addition, I realized and that, once stuffed with his cock, there wasn't much else for me to do but make the best of the situation. The trembling of my body started to decrease, I slowly stopped struggling against what was happening to me, and I started going with the motion of the horse's gallop and the rhythm of fuck it created.

This submission to the inevitable—and suddenly quite pleasurable—must have been what the bronze hunk had been waiting for, because as I quieted down and my body started to go with the rhythm, the horse slowed down, until we finally were standing still, beside the river, not that far from where we'd started. The Indian's body was covering mine closely from behind, and the pattern and depth of my breathing was beginning to come into synch with his. His cock was still buried deep inside me, but he slowly decreased the thrusting of his hips so that he wasn't pumping me anymore. He still held my wrists in his steeling grasp, and I still had my fingers wrapped in the white hair of the golden palomino stallion's mane. The horse was breathing hard from the wildness of the gallop, but it responded instantaneously to the Indian's indecipherable verbal commands. It now stood very still, it's strong legs rigid, and it remained so until the bronze stud commanded it to move again.

It dawned on me then and this was what this ride had been all about. The Indian chieftain was training me the same way he had trained his horse. He rode me until I got tired and acknowledged that he was in command. I wondered what was next, still afraid for my life, but I decided that my only chance was to calm down and go with his wishes and wants. I had to pretend that I enjoyed being fucked by him. I had to admit to myself, though, that I did enjoy being fucked by him, so it wasn't a case really of pretending. Not only did he have a fat, long cock, but he had a strong, virile thrust to his stroking, and there was nothing more exotic than being fucked by a hunky bronze savage. It was more a case of showing and convincing him that I had been successfully broken to his will.

His lips were in the hollow of my neck, and I turned my head and sought them out with my own lips. He smiled and looked very satisfied as he pushed my lips open with his and put his tongue to work. I responded fully.

I heard him give a sigh and then a grunt of approval, and he released my wrists and, quick as a cat, with the horse holding still and solid, he had changed his position on the horse in relationship to me. He now was in front of me, between me and the horse's neck, and had pushed my shoulders down onto the withers of the horse. We were pelvis to pelvis and dick to dick now. He took my hands and had me wrap them around both dicks and stroke them together. I complied, fully cooperating with him. He massaged my chest and pinched and gently twisted my nipples into full erection as I stroked us both. He was thicker and longer than I was, but we were both engorging further in response to my stroking.

When he was satisfied I was fully broken to his will, he pushed my hands away and started stroking me vigorously himself with one hand, while he fingered my asshole with his other one. When I shot my load, he cupped his hand over the head of my cock, capturing my amazingly prodigious production of cum, and I watched as he rubbed the cum over his cock and down into my hole. I found this an unbelievable turn-on, and when he then cupped his strong hands under my butt cheeks, lifted my hips off the horse, and looked at me expectedly, I correctly interpreted his unspoken command and took his cock in my hands and guided it into my asshole.

The ultimate surrender, and with a yell of joy that reverberated in the red-rock cliffs in the near distance, he crushed my hips into my pelvis, sending his cock deep inside me, and vigorously pumped my hips against him with his strong hands, fucking me deep and wildly. The horse held perfectly still, trembling ever so slightly under us, as I lifted my legs to the Indian hunk's shoulders and lowered my arms to the horse's side, holding them close against the warm silky hair of the horse's hindquarters, holding myself as still and steady as possible.

The Indian's heavy spouting at the center of me was accompanied by another one of his healthy-lungs yells, which no doubt told the rest of his tribe nearby both that he had had his way with me and that we'd soon return to them.

And, indeed, soon thereafter, we were riding back into my impromptu camp, the bronze stud once again riding close behind me, his dong well up into my ass canal, making sure I wasn't planning yet another escape attempt.

He needn't have worried, because his vigorous fuck had worn me out, psychologically as well as physically. I still feared what the Indians were ultimately going to do with me, but I was so broken now that, whatever it was, I hoped they'd do it soon and get it over with.

The four remaining tribesmen had been entertaining themselves with themselves while we were gone and they were in quite a fucking frenzy. If I'd entertained any thought that I was going to be reserved goods for chieftain, I was quickly disabused of that notion. When we reached the encampment, I simply was pushed off the horse into the waiting arms of the tribesman who seemed to be the second in command. He was older than the youthful tribal chief, and thinner and more sinewy. But his cock was longer than that of the chief, which meant it was quite long indeed. He simply grabbed me by my upper arms and pushed me back against the slow-rising rock formation where my now-dry clothes were stretched out to dry. He grabbed me by the neck and banged my head down on the rock, the blow being cushioned by my dried shirt, but taking any fight I might have give out of me just the same. His other hand folded one of my legs up against my body between my chest and his. He then positioned his cock, which he just slid up into me to the end, and fucked me vigorously to his ejaculation.

I was then handed off to the youngest and bulkiest of the tribesmen, who had the thickest cock of all. He pulled me off the rock and twirled me around to the area between the rocks and the grove. He pushed me down into the sand right beside and across my saddle. My pelvis was elevated on the saddle, with my cock rubbing into the leather. My butt was pointed at the sky. The young hulk then crouched down behind and above me, forced his thick dick into my hole, and fucked me in fast, hard downward strokes. I screamed for him, although I was feeling strangely quite fine to be stretched and pumped in this way, and the Indian chieftain put a stop to the noise by working his knees under my chest and pushing his cock back between my lips and making me deep throat him.

The young Indian was quite virile, because he loaded right up again after his first round of coming inside me and fucked me a second time, this time rotating his rod inside me with his hand to stretch me even wider the second time around.

The remaining two of the tribe were allowed to take me together. One laid flat on the ground and the second pushed my asshole down onto his rod, which, thankfully, was a normal size. Then the Indian chief stood and watched with a big grin on his face, while two braves got on each side of me, each with a grip on one of my wrists and ankles and spread-eagled me. The remaining tribesman, who also thankfully didn't have a monster cock, then rolled my hips up and entered me, his cock running in along the top of the rod of the brave spiking me from below. The two of them didn't even bother to coordinate their rhythm of the double fucking they were giving me, but they both were so excited about the exoticness of the scenario that they both came rather quickly.

As they double fucked me, I watched the brutal one who seemed second in command and the youngest warrior settle down in what I initially thought was some sort of ritual. Both of them were sitting on the ground. They were facing each other closely, the younger warrior's thighs on top of the older Indian's thighs. The older Indian fisted their cocks together and was stroking. I was watching them and they were watching me being taken by the other two warriors together. The Indians were babbling together and it was only when the chief of the group was pulling me out from between the two originally double fucking me and carrying me over to force my buttocks down between the other two that I realized I would be having two rounds of double fuck. I panted and cried out as my channel was being pushed down on the bundled cocks the second in command was fisting. I had gone from one meaty cock to two normal-sized ones to two, when bundled, supersized ones. What else—what bigger—could they force up inside me.

There didn't need to be anything else. With the Indian chief helping to raise me and then jam me back down on the two cocks, I was thoroughly fucked. Exhausted, spent, totally taken. When they were done, they pushed me over on my side, where I remained, babbling quietly to myself—as satisfied as I was bruised—and still panting.

When the tribe was finished with me, the Indian chief sat close to me astride his magnificent stallion and pointed his rifle at my bruised and collapsed body, as the rest of the tribe members milled around my meager goods, looking, quite unsuccessfully for any souvenir of their adventure that might interest them.

Very quickly, though, the chieftain issued a stern command and the braves donned their loincloths and jumped onto their horses.

I knew we were at the moment of decision. The rifle lowered, looking to my eyes, to be centering more on me. I closed my eyes and something hit me in the chest. But, when I opened my eyes, the tribe was galloping into the distance and I didn't think I had any bullet holes in me. I looked down and saw that the Indian leader had gifted me with his feather- and turquoise-beaded breastplate, which I'm sure was about the only thing he owned in the world other than his horse. I had been gang banged—including doubled fucked twice—but I couldn't say I hadn't enjoyed it. And the bronze hunk had obviously enjoyed me too. I had to admit that this was a welcome to the West that I hadn't exactly anticipated.

White Beards

If what happened to Bernard could be traced back to anyone, it probably would be his grandfather, Heinrich. He was just too good to Bernie. When Bernie's parents died in an automobile accident, Bernard's grandfather took him in and raised him without hesitation and without denying the boy anything he needed or much of what he wanted. Thus, from an early life, Bernie trusted elderly men with white beards and gravitated to them for comfort. Klaus Keller, who owned a clock shop near the square in Bamberg down near where the Regnitz flowed by, had been a good friend of Grandfather Heinrich's—and was of much the same age. When Heinrich died, Klaus took the nineteen-year-old Bernie in as an apprentice in clock repair. And Bernie trusted Klaus and was comforted by his white beard.

Bernie was a fair and finely formed young man. And Klaus comforted him. In time Klaus took Bernie into his bed on cold nights in the cold drafty flat above the ancient clock shop near the square in Bamberg, where, eventually, Klaus came to comfort Bernie closely and deeply. And Bernie, who had no one else but Klaus to care for him, was grateful and comforted and felt needed when Klaus embraced him close and filled him with his love.

When Klaus died, Bernie was barely twenty-four. He had learned enough about clock repair in his apprenticeship that he managed, if only barely, to keep body and soul together in the shop that he inherited from Klaus. It was a very lonely profession, though—and not one where a young men would meet many more young people.

There was a hole in Bernie's life. Since he had been a child, there had always been a gray-bearded man to comfort and protect him. Bernie missed that—and, in particular, he missed the way in which Klaus had shown how much he valued the young orphan, Bernie.

Not long before he died, Klaus had bought Bernie a computer and had helped him learn how to use it. Bernie found the Internet. And in those dark months after Klaus died, Bernie spent his lonely evenings exploring the Internet.

He found a Web site named Whitebeard.com, where, when Bernie had paid a fee to discover what lay behind the intriguing name that made him feel so comforted and mellow, he found, to his delight, that there were stories of young men seeking connection with something called "daddies" and nice-looking white-bearded men saying they wanted to be daddies to young men.

Bernie was a young man who felt the loss of several men who had been good daddies to him. He looked at the stories of all of these white-bearded men who were looking to provide just what his grandfather—and later, in a more intimate fashion, his mentor, Klaus—had given to him—back when he felt protected and comforted and needed.

Bernie decided he would put his story on this Web site too, and maybe he would find someone as comforting as his grandfather and Klaus once again. He looked at the stories— which they called profiles—of the young men who seemed to have the most notes from white-bearded men, and he used many of the same words in his profile so that he might find someone to talk to as well. He had no trouble describing his body—which was some of what was required in the profile— because he did indeed have a very nice body. He didn't want to mislead anyone, though, so he did admit that, although very well proportioned, he was quite small for his age—almost boyish—and he felt it only right to acknowledge that his penis was really quite small—more the size of a boy's than of a man's. Klaus had said he shouldn't be ashamed of that, though, that it was one of the reasons that Klaus loved him all the more—that he looked almost exactly like a statue by a Renaissance sculptor.

When it came to what Bernie would write that would tell anyone else the void he was seeking to fill from the loss of his kind and attentive grandfather and then of his mentor, Bernie was at a loss for words. In the end he just said he was interested in someone who would love him and hold him close—and, having seen how well it worked for other young men in encouraging older men to contact them on the Web site, at the last minute, Bernie added "group and 2-on-1," whatever those meant. Bernie figured out how to add to his profile a picture that Klaus had taken of him in the park one day when he was very happy. Some of Klaus's other friends, gray beards too, had been in the park that day, and the photograph showed Bernie sitting close between two of Klaus's friends on a park bench, big smiles all around. After Bernie inserted the image in the message, he pressed the submit button and went off to open his clock repair shop for the day.

Johan and Hans were gray beards, and very nice looking ones, as well. They were not all that old—Johan was fifty-five and Hans was sixty—but they certainly would seem like the grandfather type to Bernie. And they were just the type Bernie would find comforting. They were both tall and well filled out, but not fat really. And they were prosperous looking—and both had benign smiles—in the photos they put on a shared profile on the Whitebeard.com Web site. They posted a shared profile because they were very good friends indeed and they wanted any young man interested in exchanging messages with them to know they liked to share. They put it right there in their combined profile—they liked to share—"group and 2-in-1," and another two letters Bernie couldn't understand and therefore didn't worry about—DP. Bernie thought that was very nice and unselfish of them. It was good to share, he thought.

Johan and Hans lived in Nürnberg, where Johan was a banker and Hans was a lawyer. They saw Bernie's profile on Whitebeard.com, and they were excited, because he was just the sort of young man they were interested in and Bamberg was not all that far away from Nürnberg. And because he had signaled that he was interested in double penetration sex.

They messaged Bernie to his Whitebeard.com account.

And Bernie, when he came upstairs into the flat after a day of repairing clocks and talking to almost no one, was delighted to see that he had a message in his Whitebeard.com account on the very first day—and from not one, but two, men who were much like his grandfather and Klaus. For the first time since Klaus had died, Bernie felt that someone else might exist who could comfort him and make him feel special. And two men. That surely would be double the comfort.

In no time, Johan and Hans had convinced Bernie that he deserved a day off from repairing clocks and could think of nothing better to do with that day off than to come to Nürnberg and have lunch with his new friends at a little café they told him they were sure he would enjoy.

"It's a very nice café," Bernie said after he met his new friends Johan and Hans in a downstairs room on Jacobsstrasse in Nürnberg. "But I'm not sure I see anything special about it. Except maybe that there are no women here. Just a few young men—mostly sitting with older men."

In what he didn't say, he had arrived early and looked in the window of the café for some time before the two gray beards arrived. In watching, he had noticed that, a little strangely, it seemed that all of the tables were first occupied by either two older men or one younger man, but when one younger man showed up at a table with two older men, they all left after a brief time. The same thing happened when two older men entered and sat down with a younger man. Always that three-man combination; two older men, one younger. Bernie couldn't figure out why that pattern was working out— each time. But when he couldn't get his mind around such things, he just smiled and let them be.

He smiled at the beaming Johan and Hans and said, "A strange sort of café. But it's a very nice café. It has a comfortable feel to it."

"Come, let us find a nice booth and have a nice drink and become better acquainted," Johan said.

"Yes, let's," chimed in Hans.

And Johan slid into a booth and beckoned Bernie to slide in beside him, which Bernie did. But then Bernie was surprised that Hans slid in beside him—leaving the other bench free. The three of them were wedged together like sardines in a tin. And although Bernie found this strange, he also found it very comforting. And Johan and Hans seemed to find it very pleasant too. They had their arms around Bernie and were hugging him and saying very comforting things to him.

They brought up that term Bernie hadn't understood in the Internet profile—DP—but Bernie was too self-conscious about his own naïveté about life that he didn't ask about it. He just smiled and nodded his head.

Bernie had not had anyone pay attention to him—focus on him—since Klaus had died. And he found himself opening up to these two very nice white-bearded gentlemen and talking of things he'd never talked to anyone before. This included the nature of his relationship with Klaus.

Johan and Hans were very interested to hear of this—and they were smiling and Bernie could almost feel them trembling in pleasure of how good Klaus had been to him.

"We can be very nice, too," Johan said in a low, hoarse voice. "I think we could be as nice and comforting to you as your good friend Klaus was."

"Yes, I quite agree," Hans agreed. "Would you like that, Bernard?" Hans squeezed Bernie close to him in assurance and affection.

Bernie didn't quite fully comprehend what his two new friends were proposing, as he was noticing for the first time that where some of the groups of three men were going to was through a door at the back of the café.

"Yes, that would be nice," Bernie said absentmindedly. And then, "I wonder where those men are going? I wonder if there is another room back through that door."

"Yes, I think there are several rooms back behind that door, Bernard," Hans said almost in a whisper.

"Would you like to see the rooms back there, Bernard?" Johan added in that low, hoarse voice he had acquired while Bernie was talking of the comfort Klaus had given him.

"Is that where this DP you talk about can be found?"

"Yes it is," Hans said, the excitement in his voice obvious.

"Yes, that would be nice then," Bernie said—again absentmindedly—wanting to return all of the good feelings these two nice white-bearded men were bestowing on him with their hugs and friendly smiles and happy that he was going to find out what this DP business was all about.

Within minutes of finding a room of their own beyond the door at the rear of the café, Johan and Hans proved they were not that old at all. First, they managed to undress Bernie quickly even though his enthusiasm for their friendship was waning a bit in the process and, although he didn't fight them, he didn't exactly help them either.

And then they showed that they each had a very nice long, although not all that thick, cock that could still get quite hard.

And then, Johan embracing Bernie from the front and Hans embracing him from the rear, his legs lifted off the ground and straddling Johan's hips, the two white beards showed just how well they shared, as they both managed to get their cocks into Bernie's channel together and fucked him until he was exhausted in perfectly choreographed counterthrusts, all the while making love to each other over his shoulder with their lips.

To show him how comforting they could be, they each fucked him separately as well on the cot in the small room behind the Nürnberg café on Jacobsstrasse.

Although Bernie did enjoy the first close attention—and sexual arousal and release—he had gotten since Klaus died, he wasn't sure he wanted the comforting that was going on to be more between two others rather than toward him—when he left the Nürnberg café, Johan and Hans were fucking each other and didn't seem to notice him leaving at all. Thus, when he got back to Bamberg, he opened his profile on Whitebeard.com and made a few adjustments. In his description of what he was seeking, he changed the "make love to him" part he said he was looking for to merely "seeking a daddy"—he'd seen how this had seemed to have gotten a good response for other young men on the Web site, and he certainly would like to correspond with someone like his grandfather, Heinrich. And he struck out the "group" reference—as he seriously suspected that Johan and Hans had rather misinterpreted his interest on that one—and he changed the "2-on-1" to "1long-on-1" because that looked like an interesting term, if he had just marked "2-in-1" out, there would not have been much of anything else in that space. He made sure he didn't key in "DP" at all, though. He still wasn't real sure what that meant, but the two white beards had seemed much too interested in that term.

Almost immediately, he received a message from a very nice looking white-bearded man named Bigdaddy10inch who said he lived in Heidelberg and had some toys he thought Bernie might like to see. Perhaps, he said, Bernie could come to Heidelberg on his next vacation day—Bamberg wasn't that far away from Heidelberg. Bernie thought he just might do that. Grandfather had played with him with toys—and he'd found that very comforting.

About the Author

Habu is one of the pen names of a former supersonic spy jet pilot, intelligence agent, male model, movie actor, and diplomat. A wild youth in South East Asia was spent enjoying whatever sexual opportunities came his way, and much of his gay male writing is about recalling incidents from those days and inventing ones he'd perhaps have liked to experience. He now leads a very quiet and ordinary happily married family life.

An American, he is a published mainstream novelist and short story writer under another name and in another dimension of his life. He has written or cowritten (with Sabb) approaching 1,000 published short stories and over 100 published erotica e-books, primarily of gay fiction but also memoir, straight fiction and ménage fiction. His hand and creative writing can be seen in stories and books by habu, sr71plt, Dirk Hessian, Shabbu, and Stephen Kessel—among unrevealed others that might surprise readers. The fictionalized GM memoir *Flying High, Diving Deep* is loosely based on his life experiences. He can be found at the adults only gay male site www.BarbarianSpy.com, which he shares with Sabb and Dirk Hessian.

You can send feedback about this e-book directly to habu, or send general feedback on this e-book to BarbarianSpy.

Our authors always like to receive feedback, and appreciate it when readers post reviews at Goodreads, and other sites.

BarbarianSpy

FOR LITERARY HEAT

Not all books listed below may currently be on release.
BOOKS BY DIRK HESSIAN
Xtreme Erotica
The King's Men
Shores of Tripoli
Prophecy of Noto
Pretender's Fate
General Erotica/Romance
Fire Down the Valley
Constantinople
The Beautiful Way
Blue and Gray
Colonel's Treasure
Beginning of Time
Labyrinth
BOOKS BY HABU
Gay Erotica
Memoir Faction
Flying High, Diving Deep*
Xtreme Erotica
Second Coming: Emile La Cour Unleashed
Vortex: Sacrificed by Curiosity*
Dark Angel Sounding *(in e-book & included in
Sounding:Ultimate Control Paperback)**
Sounding: Ultimate Control (*Print Only*)*
Sounding Five *(in e-book & included in
Sounding:Ultimate Control Paperback)*
General Erotica
Romance
Four Coins

Lower Than the Heart
Brambleton
Gotta Keep Trying
Finding Amnad
Platres Conclave
Other Novels/Novellas
Prepared in Cape Verdi
Gilded Cage
House on Park
Anything for Ambition
Dance of the Ravishers
Hard Knocks U*
My Neighbor's Spa*
Man's Man: Tales of a High Priced Gay Hooker*
Trip Money
Clint Folsom Mysteries Compendium Volume 1*
Death to Blonds - Stolen Judgment (Clint Folsom Mystery)
Clint Folsom Mysteries Compendium Volume 2*
The Indian Doctor
Sailorboy
Home to Fire Island
Choke Hold
Gay Erotica Anthologies
Doubled*
Doubled Again*
Tails in the Tropics*
Tails in the Med*
Rough Riders*
Grab Bag 1*
Grab Bag 2*
Grab Bag 3*
Grab Bag 4*
Grab Bag 5*
Beyond the Beaded Curtain*
Habu's Christmas Balls
The Sporting Life*

Fetish Galore!*
Literary Gay Erotica
Cairo Surrender*
The Handyman*
Homeward Bound
Journey to Mirage*
Menage Erotica
13 Ways for Halloween
Luther*
The Indian Prince
BOOKS BY SHABBU
Finding Jason
Dirty Pool
Operation Black Jade
Cigars!*
Angel in the Barn
Gayly Complicated
Despoiling David
The Tree of Idleness
I Met a Man
The Interview
Rough Road to Happiness
BOOKS BY SABB
Hiring in Hollywood
The Legend of Holleystone Grange
Surprise Encounters
She is He
Wrong Man
Loyal to his King
Barbarian Tales - Book One - Traveler's Tales*
Barbarian Tales - Book Two - Journeys Begin*
Barbarian Tales - Book Three - The Inheritance*
Barbarian Tales - Book Four - Road to Persepolis*
~
* indicates the book is available in paperback and e-book.